GOING South

HOT TREE PUBLISHING

Going South Anthology
Dared © 2017 by Elena Eames
Playing for Keeps © 2017 by Gen Ryan
Crazy © 2017 by Kolleen Fraser
Upside Down and Back to Front © 2017 by Megan Lowe
Pineapple Dreams © 2017 by Aria Peyton
Finding Love Down Under © 2017 by S. Hart

All rights reserved. No part of this book may be used or reproduced in any written, electronic, recorded, or photocopied format without the express permission from the author or publisher as allowed under the terms and conditions with which it was purchased or as strictly permitted by applicable copyright law. Any unauthorized distribution, circulation or use of this text may be a direct infringement of the author's rights, and those responsible may be liable in law accordingly. Thank you for respecting the work of this author.

Going South is a work of fiction. All names, characters, events and places found therein are either from the author's imagination or used fictitiously. Any similarity to persons alive or dead, actual events, locations, or organizations is entirely coincidental and not intended by the author.

For information, contact the publisher, Hot Tree Publishing.
www.hottreepublishing.com
Editing: Hot Tree Editing
Cover & Interior Design: RMGraphX
ISBN-10: 1-925448-73-8
ISBN-13: 978-1-925448-73-3
10 9 8 7 6 5 4 3 2 1

Contents

DARED BY ELENA EAMES
PLAYING FOR KEEPS BY GEN RYAN
UPSIDE DOWN, BACK TO FRONT BY MEGAN LOWE
PINEAPPLE DREAMS BY ARIA PFYTON
CRAZY BY KOLLEEN FRASER
FINDING LOVE DOWN UNDER BY S. HART

Dared

BY ELENA EAMES

Dedication

This one's for Liv.

LEESA OLSEN LOOKED AT THE LAST DREGS OF COFFEE IN HER CUP.

She couldn't delay any longer. She'd said she'd do it when she finished her coffee. Those dregs were stone cold and had been sitting there for over fifteen minutes. She really had no more time to delay.

She picked up the coffee cup and swallowed the last mouthful. It sat like a ball of steel in her stomach—cold and impenetrable. Or perhaps that was just the fear.

With fingers that only trembled slightly—okay, furiously—she gathered her notebook and stowed it away in her bag, then clutched her stopwatch, her finger hovering over the start button. She'd timed the lift and now knew how long it would take to get from ground level to basement level. Twenty seconds. That seemed to be the average. So she'd rounded up to thirty seconds. Thirty seconds in a metal box that was two metres by two metres. And a closed door. She could do thirty seconds.

She left the coffee shop that was directly opposite the

lifts, where she'd sat drinking her coffee and panicking for an hour. She could do this. She could get in a metal box for thirty seconds and *survive.* Paul was *not* going to win this one.

Her brother had dared her that she couldn't do it. And nothing was worse than being dared by your sibling. Being dared had gotten her in all sorts of trouble. Being dared had gotten her naked in deserted oceans, sick from eating disgusting concoctions, and once meant she'd spent three days in Sydney by herself. That one had turned out to be a fun dare. Paul had dared her to walk into Perth's domestic airport and take the first flight out, no matter where it was going. She'd told him she would if he would.

She'd ended up in Sydney and had climbed the Sydney Harbour Bridge. Paul had walked into the airport just two hours later and ended up in Karratha. In the middle of summer. And no one, not even kangaroos, went to Karratha in the summer. It was basically hot, dry, and full of flies. And there's nothing to do because every intelligent being on Earth has nicked off. Or at least that was what Paul's peeved texts had told her.

Now he'd dared her to get into the lift at the local shopping centre. Just one floor down from shopping level to basement level. Easy, right?

Easy if you didn't suffer from extreme claustrophobia. But Leesa wasn't going to let Paul win. She could do this. Thirty seconds. She just needed to walk up to the metal box, press a button, wait for the doors to open, walk in, press another button, bite her lip to stop from screaming for thirty seconds, and then walk out when the doors opened again.

Her knees shook. Her tummy threatened to rebel and bring

up coffee. Her head spun and her vision tunnelled. She vowed to think up a torturous dare for Paul. He deserved it.

She straightened her spine with difficulty. She was a twenty-six-year-old woman. She could handle payroll every week for two hundred-plus workers. She could handle working in an industry where she was one of the only women on site and called names such as "honey" and "li'l darlin'" by men twice her size. She'd been swimming with whale sharks at Ningaloo, climbed the Sydney Harbour Bridge, hiked Cradle Mountain in Tasmania, survived the Daintree Forest in Queensland, and even camped out at Uluru without being taken by a dingo. She could do a lift.

Adjusting her oversized black glasses on her face, she slung her oversized red-and-brown carryall over her shoulder and marched towards her doom on oversized chunky heels. She fixed her sights on that small silver button she needed to press to open the doors to her coffin, and beelined to it… only to stop short when another finger pressed the button instead.

She blinked. That finger wasn't supposed to be there. It wasn't supposed to be attached to an arm either. That arm wasn't supposed to be encased in crisp blue and looking ever so muscular. She drew back. This was not going to plan.

Leesa threw her head back to try to make sense of an unexpected situation and found herself staring… at beauty. The man was gorgeous. Like "OMG, my ovaries are weeping to have his babies" gorgeous. Black hair, shaven but shadowed jaw, blue eyes, luscious lips, and a begging-to-be-crumpled-during-lunch-sex navy blue suit. She put her hand up and adjusted her glasses again—nervous habit more than anything. He was giving her a questioning look.

Oh, my God. Was he astounded at her beauty and poise? Was he attracted to her as much as she was to him? Did he feel the connection? She wiped her hands nervously on her knee-length denim skirt and tried to suck her stomach in a little bit more without seeming obvious. The skirt was a bit tight, and she had to shuffle more than stride while she was walking in it, but it looked good on her curvy figure. Being born with more hips than grace was her burden to bear in life. Trousers just didn't do a thing for her, and she hoped Mr Blue Suit could see that.

Then his hand was reaching for her, and her heart stuttered in her chest. Was he going to touch her? Would the sparks of electricity fly? She sucked in a breath… only for it to whoosh out loudly when he reached to hold the lift door open. It had begun to close because she'd been hesitating at the altar of his gorgeousness.

"After you," he said in a deep voice that just made her uterus start dancing the cha-cha. He inclined his head and she tottered forward, an obedient puppet to his every command. She felt him move in after her and her breasts became heavy, as if swelling in the confines of their thou-shalt-not-jiggle stretch elastic material. She breathed slowly. This could not be happening. They couldn't meet like this in a lift and….

Lift?

With a gasp of fear she spun around in time to see the metal doors press together. She was in a *lift*. Her heart stopped. Her knees weakened. Her fingers clenched convulsively, and she heard the familiar *beep* as the stopwatch started.

Time slowed around her. Hundreds of thoughts crashed through her mind all at once. *I'm going to die. Thirty seconds. Paul is sadistic. Mr Blue Suit is in my coffin with me. Thirty seconds. I never got to have his babies. I'm going to die. Basement level. Paul deserves to die. Metal box. Not enough air in here. Thirty seconds. I never even kissed him. I'm going to die. In thirty seconds.*

She stared down at the numbers of the stopwatch as the digital display to the far right changed too fast for her eyes to read and her brain to comprehend. She felt the floor under her give way and she was falling into the abyss. She focused on the seconds, counting up on the screen. Eight seconds. Nine. Ten.

Then there was a large jolt that had her staggering for balance, and the lights went out.

***

Alastair "Dare" McCarthy heaved the access panel on top of the lift to the side and stuck his head in to assess the situation. Two passengers in the darkened car—one male looking somewhat harried and anxious, one female curled in a ball on the floor in the corner. Contact from the outside had been made with the male, who'd given his name as Keith Johnstone, and when the firemen had arrived, they were told the two passengers were unhurt. Keith had apparently told the building manager that the woman with him had "freaked out" and hadn't said a word since the lift had malfunctioned, stopping halfway between the two lower levels. The building manager had made the decision to call in the fire brigade since he couldn't be sure the woman hadn't suffered some sort of medical episode. So Dare and the rest of the team were playing saviour.

"Thank goodness you're here," Keith breathed in relief. "Can you get me out? She's psycho."

Dare looked over at the woman, who hadn't even lifted her head. It was more likely that she was scared out of her wits. He pulled back and looked up at Rich, who was peering over the ledge and down the lift shaft from the open doors at the ground floor.

"I'll go in," he said. The lift had blown some sort of fuse and the car was stuck, but only by about a metre off the ground. If it fell, it didn't have far to go. Rich's head disappeared for a moment, and then his legs slithered over the side. He lowered himself down, careful not to jolt the car and make it fall.

Dare stuck his head back through the roof and said to Keith, "Stand to the side. I'm coming in."

Using his upper body strength, Dare lowered himself gently and then dropped to the floor. The ventilation system had stopped and the air was hot and muggy inside the car.

"Are you okay?" he asked Keith. His visual check of the man said there was nothing wrong with him, but the way Keith answered the question would tell him a lot about the man's physical and mental state.

"I'm fine," Keith said, pulling up the cuff of his suit to consult his watch. "I'm going to be late for my meeting, but I guess being stuck in a lift is a good excuse."

Dare assessed that the man was more anxious about his

missed meeting than he was about his companion. "Okay. We'll have you out of here soon," he promised and then bent to check the woman on the floor.

He lightly touched her shoulder and she recoiled violently. Her eyes were open but had a vacant stare to them. She didn't respond to any of his questions about her well-being or even what her name was.

"She's psycho," Keith repeated impatiently from the other side of the car. "Screamed for a while until I managed to turn a light on. She's been no help whatsoever."

The panel on the lift display was lit up, giving off a faint glow, but most of the light in the room was from the iPhone in Keith's hand. Dare reached for the torch in his pocket and flicked it on. It illuminated the woman more, and Dare took in her trembling fingers, the protective curl of her body, and her rapid breathing. She was in shock.

Dare turned to Rich, who was leaning through the access door. "Let's get some oxygen down here."

Rich's face disappeared and Dare heard him call out for the required items.

"Can you get me out of here?" Keith puffed impatiently.

Dare wanted to snap at him that his needs were far less than the woman's, but it wouldn't help the situation and Dare needed Keith calm and rational. Not everyone dealt easily with confined spaces, and he had a feeling the woman with the big glasses and curly black hair was one of them.

"We're doing everything we can," he told Keith as he checked the woman's pulse on her wrist. It was far too rapid, but understandable. She was also cold and clammy despite the heat in the car. "Did she fall? Hit her head?" he asked Keith.

"I don't know," Keith said tetchily. "It was dark."

Dare made the decision that for his own calmness and rationality he needed Keith out of there. Rich handed down the oxygen cylinder and mask, so Dare said, "Get a rope down here and we'll get Keith out."

Rich's gaze said that it wasn't normal procedure, but he didn't argue. "And the woman?"

"She's nonresponsive to verbal stimuli. I can stay here with her for a bit while they see if the fuse can be fixed."

Within ten minutes Keith was attached to a safety harness, and Dare boosted him up and out of the car. Rich helped him climb the ladder to the ground floor, and there was the brief sound of applause from the curious crowd as he emerged. Dare promptly forgot about Mr Late-For-A-Meeting and concentrated on the woman. He'd placed the mask over her face and turned on the oxygen, but she hadn't reacted to his touch at all. She seemed to be staring at something in her hands, so Dare peeled them apart and stared with amusement at the red stopwatch that was counting up seconds and minutes. It was something like a track coach would use.

But when he tried to take it off her, she pulled away. "No."

The word was muffled through the mask but clear in both intent and sound. Dare wondered if she was autistic or similar. He'd met enough people who were unable to function when routines were thrown out of whack that he could recognise the signs. Focusing on a single object for safety was often a good marker of someone not coping.

The woman had one of those ginormous handbag thingies

that women often felt the need to lug around in case they forgot something they really needed. Like a newspaper from three years ago. It was squished between her knees and the wall, so he tugged it out and had a peek. Notepads, make-up, a cardigan, a scarf, breath mints, tissues, painkillers.... Dare shoved them all aside until he found something that resembled a wallet. He unzipped it and had a look inside. There were no medical alert-type cards, so he dug for her driver's licence.

"Well, Ms Leesa Olsen. Very nice to meet you."

At her name, Leesa jerked and her gaze met his for a moment. He smiled, trying to look reassuring, but at her wide-eyed alarm he realised he still had on all his safety gear. He probably looked like a mad scientist coming to inspect the possible contagion. He pushed off his helmet, then wrenched open his jacket and took it off. It was warm in the lift and the possibility of a fire was small.

"Are you okay?" he asked in a soothing voice as he settled on his rump beside her. It looked like they would be sitting there for a while, so he might as well make himself comfy. To his relief Leesa nodded jerkily, but her eyes were still fixed on the stopwatch in her hand. She whispered something, but he didn't catch it. "What was that?"

He leaned closer to her, lifted the mask off her and turned the cylinder off so he could hear.

"Thirty seconds," she said again.

It was one of those "follow the white rabbit" moments that didn't make sense, but he nodded anyway. He looked around her cupped hands and glanced at the stopwatch.

"Twenty-two minutes and sixteen seconds," he observed.

"Did you have somewhere to go?"

"The basement. Thirty seconds." Her words were whispered still, and Dare leaned in to hear clearly. He understood from the building manager's quick summary of the situation that Keith and Leesa had entered the lift on the ground floor, pressed the button for the basement level, and then got stuck.

"You were heading for the basement?" he asked soothingly.

She nodded, tearing her eyes from the stopwatch and managing to keep his gaze that time. Dare could see that she was slowly coming out of her panic and beginning to respond to the world around her. Which was good because she was too cute to be panicking on the floor of a lift. Dare smiled at her and mentally noted her frizzy, crazy hair and her large brown eyes behind the lenses of her black-framed glasses. She had on a white shirt that had some sort of frilly, lacy bit down the front. Her denim skirt was plain and currently hiked to about midthigh, which he had the feeling she wasn't aware of. Her slip-on heels were still on her feet and he found humour in the huge black leather flower with the centre jewel that adorned each shoe. They were zany and just perfect. He had a feeling this woman was fussy and complicated, but trying to pretend otherwise.

"Thirty seconds," she repeated. "It was supposed to take thirty seconds."

A light bulb dinged in his head. Ahh. He glanced at the stopwatch again. "And instead it's now taken twenty-three minutes?"

She nodded rapidly, relief crossing her face. "Did I press the wrong button?"

Dare didn't know about wrong buttons, because this woman was pressing all the right ones for him. He wanted to gather her up in his arms and whisk her away from this situation. Be her hero. Kiss the princess. Banish the dangers.

The whisking would have to wait, but he could do the gathering bit. He moved until he was leaning back against the wall next to her and put his arm around her shoulders. He could feel her trembling, but she leaned into his warmth.

"No. You didn't press a wrong button. It was just a small malfunction. But it means I got to meet you. So a good thing, right?"

Okay, so he was fishing. He'd been told by more than one woman that his face was handsome enough. His light brown hair, angular cheekbones, and green eyes apparently appealed to a lot of the females of his species. He was also in good shape because he didn't want anything to jeopardise his job or the people he was trying to help—and being unfit could be a risk to that. Add that to the fact that he was a *fireman*…. Women were usually pretty receptive to that. He could use it when he wanted.

But Leesa didn't respond. She glanced up in panic and her gaze skittered around the small area, finally focusing on the open access door in the ceiling.

"Oh. He's gone." Her tone was definitely disappointed.

Dare frowned. "Who? Keith?"

Leesa gave a big sigh and slumped back against his chest. "I was going to have his babies."

When trying to flirt with a woman, said woman mentioning another man *and* babies in the same sentence was usually a desire killer. Not this time. Dare let a flicker of amusement cross his face because he knew she was facing away from him. "No. You didn't want him as your baby daddy."

She twisted in his embrace to give him a glare. "And why not? Who are you to argue with my ovaries and uterus? Didn't you see how pretty he was?"

Dare decided that in twenty-four hours' time, when Ms Leesa Olsen realised she'd been sitting on the floor of a lift, her skirt hiked high, with a fireman's arm around her, arguing about her uterus, she was going to be embarrassed. In the meantime, he'd enjoy his view of those legs, his arm around her shoulders, and the argument about the desires of her uterus.

"I really didn't stop to consider how pretty he was," Dare confessed. "But I did hear him call you psycho. You don't want a baby daddy who thinks you're psycho, do you?"

Leesa wrinkled her nose and gave a you've-twisted-my-arm-type shrug of agreement. "Fine, then. But just so you know, we would've made beautiful babies."

"You win some, you lose some," Dare sympathised.

To his surprise her eyes narrowed. "I'm going to win this one. Paul cannot win."

He was about to open his mouth to ask who Paul was when Rich stuck his head through the access door again. "You okay here?"

"Yes," he said, giving a thumbs up.

"Okay. They're going to try resetting the fuses again. I have to clear out of the shaft. Radio in if there's a problem."

Dare nodded and squeezed Leesa's shoulders. "We'll have

you out of here in a jiffy."

"A jiffy is thirty-three-point-three-five picoseconds," she responded, and Dare decided that yes, his attraction to his rescue was complete. Any woman who knew that fact was the one for him.

The lights flared on and the lift gave a jerk. Leesa squealed and dove for his chest. With a crunch of metal on metal, the lights flickered out again. Against all regulations and orders, Dare pulled her onto his lap. Her hair stuck up in crazy directions and tickled his nose, threatening to make him sneeze. He flattened it down so it was out of his face as she burrowed under his chin.

The lift jerked again, rising up before dropping. It was only a few centimetres, but it jolted. Dare wrapped both arms around his charge and enjoyed her weight on him. "Shh," he soothed. "It's going to be okay, Leesa."

"Thirty seconds," she cried softly.

"I know, I know. What a horrid trick they played on you."

"I'm going to die." Her voice cracked that time.

He gave in to the impulse and dropped a kiss on her head. "No, you're not. Not on my watch."

"I'm going to kill Paul."

"Who's Paul?"

"My brother. He dared me to get in this lift. Now I have to think up a callous dare for him. Because his dare chased away my chance with Mr Blue Suit."

Dare bit his lip. "But you got to meet me."

"He was so pretty," she sobbed.

He chuckled. "Better off without him."

Dared

The lift cranked upwards slowly, then changed its mind and moved gently down.

"I was going to have his babies," she whispered.

"You'll just have to have mine instead," he murmured.

She sniffed pathetically. "Okay."

There was a thump as the lift hit the basement level. The lights died again.

"I don't even know your name," she said, still using a hushed tone as if talking too loud would break the walls.

"Alastair," he told her. "Alastair McCarthy."

"Yes," she said more firmly. "Stair. Always take the stairs."

He chuckled again, this time more loudly. "I'm a fireman. We *always* take the stairs."

His radio hissed to life, and he picked it up. "You okay still, Dare?" came the crackling voice.

"All good," he reported back. "What's happening?"

"We should be about five minutes," the voice said again, and that time Dare recognised it as Mike. "It's still not working, so we're headed down to open the doors manually."

There was a nearby echo which sounded like a dozen boots clattering down the adjacent fire stairs. But Dare was distracted. Leesa had burrowed one hand under the dark blue T-shirt he wore underneath his fire suit and was stroking the sparse hair on his stomach while humming.

It was one thing to be attracted to a person he was supposed to be rescuing. It was another thing entirely to allow her to touch him intimately in the dark shadows while the rescue was happening. And it *was* intimate. That was his lower stomach. And in case she needed him to draw her a picture, it was the place his erection touched when he was naked and aroused. Aroused as he was becoming right then.

He frowned and was trying to mentally will it down when the familiar tune she was humming pinged on his consciousness. He stopped and hummed along in his head until the words of the song began coming to him.

"Uh, Leesa? Are you singing 'Soft Kitty' to me while we're trapped in a lift?"

Her nails dug in, scratching his stomach as she hissed "Shh!" at him and resumed her stroking. There was a bang at the doors, a male voice, a scrape of metal, and the lift finally opened.

Dare choked back laughter as Leesa crawled on hands and knees into the light. The rest of his team stood back and allowed her to escape, where she scrambled to the nearby wall, sat again, and consulted the stopwatch.

Dare heard a faint electronic beep and then her voice. "Thirty minutes. Dammit. My average is thrown all to pieces. Paul is going to die."

***

Over the next five days, Leesa died a thousand deaths of mortification.

She couldn't have had a meltdown in a broken lift.

She couldn't have cuddled up to a fireman, told him about wanting Mr Blue Suit's babies, and sung him "Soft Kitty."

She couldn't have crawled—literally—out of the bad situation, her hair flying everywhere, her skirt raised so high that she might as well have been without it.

Could she?

But then she found the picture on social media. Damn people with their bloody camera phones and access to the Internet. Some teenager had snapped a picture of the rescue with the caption, "Come and save my life. Please?" The camera had been focusing on a hot fireman guy, but there in the background was her. She was sitting in the foyer, knees up, skirt up, hair up, and dignity nowhere in sight.

She'd. Sung. Him. Soft. Kitty.

That one she couldn't get over.

She'd go to bed and the tune would play through her head. She'd smooth down her top and the brush of material against her fingers would bring back the memory of her fingers touching his bare stomach. She'd straighten her skirt at work and she'd remember when her skirt wasn't as straight as it should've been.

She needed to make amends. She needed to show Alastair that she wasn't usually like that. So she screwed up her courage, made choc chip muffins and sampled them, then had to remake them all over again because her sampling turned into nervous eating and there wasn't enough left for him. Once baked and painstakingly resisted, she would take them to the nearest fire station at the same time as her incident five days prior. She hoped he'd be on the same shift.

She loaded up her car with the muffins and headed out. Then she drove straight past the fire station, turned a few corners, and sat hyperventilating in her car until she talked herself into going back. It was lucky she had the day off because this was turning into an all-day journey. There were a couple of bays off to the side where she could park and not be in the way of a racing fire truck, so she pulled in there. She'd worn her favourite power dress, just so she'd look like an intelligent woman. It was dark blue and buttoned all her bulges in nicely. Of course, she couldn't bend or sit properly in it, but shortcomings could be accounted for. It just meant that when she slithered out of the car and dropped those last couple of inches to the ground from its high seat, she had to spend thirty seconds straightening up the material again so that the white buttons down the front of the dress were straight and the skirt was pulled into place.

She looked down at her feet and wondered whether the shoes were too much. The white buttons on the navy dress just called out to have white shoes on as well. Her wedges were a beautiful white lace with straps that criss-crossed over her ankles. The straps were merely decorative and didn't hold the shoe on at all. The bamboo three-inch wedge heel made sure those puppies weren't coming off. They didn't suit the power image, but sacrifices could be made.

Leesa shuffled around to the passenger side of the car—her skirt didn't allow for a stride—and opened the door to retrieve the muffins. As she did she caught sight of her reflection in the window. She'd dithered on whether she should spend an hour with the hair straightener before she came, but in the end decided that she was trying to change Mr Alastair McCarthy's impression of her as a flake, not impress him with her beauty. Intelligent women could have hair that was dead straight or impossibly curly. Hair did not make the brains. Hair did, however, require decoration, so she'd pulled it back, forced it into a ponytail, and popped in a clip with a row of white daisies on it to hide the hair lackey.

Grabbing the Tupperware container, Leesa headed to the side that appeared to be an office and pushed open the glass doors. There was an attractive young woman sitting behind the reception desk and a very attractive man leaning over it. It was immediately obvious that he was flirting or trying to sweet-talk the woman into something. He turned to the door and Leesa saw it was Mr Hot Fireman from the social media photo. She had a feeling her ovaries would've been jumping up and down and waving had it not been for the knowledge that Mr Hot Fireman had seen Leesa *crawl*. Instead, her ovaries were curled up in the corner, sobbing and rocking back and forth in mortification.

He flashed her a smile that was designed to give women hot flushes, but Leesa was wearing her armour of humiliation. Nothing was penetrating that puppy.

Mr Hot Fireman surveyed her from head to toe and then back again, and gave a low whistle. His voice was husky and flirtatious as he murmured. "Someone call the fire brigade because something smokin' hot just entered the building."

Leesa flushed red. Okay, so her armour of humiliation leaked like a sieve when it came to compliments. But she was on a mission and her head would not be turned. She squeezed her hands around the container she held and found her tongue.

"Hi. I'm looking for Alastair."

Did a flicker of disappointment cross Mr Hot Fireman's face? Leesa told herself she must've been imagining it when the man flashed another grin and said, "I'll be your messenger boy. You write down your message, with your name and phone number, and I'll see he gets it. The message, that is."

The receptionist stood and tsked, leaning over to whack the man on the shoulder as she said, "Just go and get Dare, Brady. Make yourself useful for once and stop cluttering up my office."

Brady heaved a sigh, affected a ginormous eye-roll, and peeled himself away from the counter, walking off in the direction Leesa hoped Alastair was.

"Thank you," she said to the receptionist.

"No problem," the woman replied. "Was there anything else I could do for you?"

Leesa shook her head. "No. I just wanted to thank Alastair for helping me the other day. I'm afraid I didn't exactly put my best foot forward, so I'm hoping to redeem myself with my baking." She hoisted the container up proudly.

"Dare," said the receptionist, whose name tag proclaimed she was Jennie. "He doesn't like Alastair. So if you're trying to impress him, go with Dare. It will make your life so much simpler."

Dare? It figured that the man's nickname was the same word that caused her greatest joys—and greatest disasters.

"My life is littered with dares, and it's what got me into trouble the other day," Leesa said, then briefly told Jennie about the lift rescue.

They chatted for a minute until the door through which Brady disappeared once again opened. That time it was the hot fireman Leesa had been waiting for.

"Leesa," he said in a surprised but happy tone. "What brings you here?"

She girded her loins, took a deep breath to calm her trembling hands, and lifted the container.

"Muffins," she said.

"Muffins," he repeated flatly. Why was he disappointed? Was there something else she was supposed to bring?

"I like her muffins," Brady said from behind Dare. He had wandered back in, parked himself against the reception desk, and seemed to be settled down for the duration.

"It appears her muffins are just for me," Dare growled to the side, sending a withering glare in Brady's direction. Brady shrugged it off as if it happened frequently. Leesa had an idea it did.

Dare turned from the unruffled Brady and smiled at Leesa. Her armour melted like the liquid Terminator guy. Dare said, "Thank you for bringing them by—"

"Yes, thanks for bringing your muffins by, Leesa." Brady received a quick kick for his interruption, hissing in pain before he moved farther down to be out of range.

"—and are you feeling better now?"

Leesa gave Dare a big toothy smile. Just like she'd practiced in the mirror. "Yes. Now that I'm no longer trapped in a metal coffin that's doing a good impression of a malfunctioning lift, I'm fine. Thank you. So I wanted to bring you some muffins to say I appreciated your concern and assistance."

Dare went to reply but once again Brady got in first. "I was concerned. Can I have some muffin now?"

Dare's face froze. He blinked very deliberately and held

up one finger. "Excuse me a moment, Leesa. I need to take care of this."

He whirled abruptly. Brady jumped, skittered away, and ran for the door. Dare chased him out, slammed the door after him, and had started walking back to Leesa when the door opened and Brady stuck his head in, singing something about milkshakes and boys and yards. Then he skedaddled, shutting the door firmly before Dare could reach him.

Leesa tried hard to keep a straight face. She had a feeling she wasn't succeeding when Dare gave her a chagrined look and said, "I'd apologise for him, but an apology implies it won't happen again. And I can't guarantee that."

Wiping a sweaty hand over her hip, Leesa giggled. "Yes. Well. The muffins were more of an apology to you that you had to deal with me, rather than a pickup device."

Dare's face rearranged into a sorrowful expression. "You mean you're not here to finagle a date from me? I'm heartbroken."

Leesa pursed her lips. Was he serious?

"No. I'm here to show you that I'm a calm, rational woman who can usually take control of her emotions. The woman in that lift wasn't the usual me. I'm not really like that."

Dare clutched a fist to his chest like a Shakespearean character overacting on stage. "Now I'm really heartbroken. You mean you usually don't curl up in corners and have big handsome firemen come and rescue you?"

Leesa tried hard not to laugh. "No. Sorry."

"And you don't usually threaten to kill your brother on a daily basis?"

She bit her lip. "That usually only happens on a weekly basis. The veracity of the threat last week was in direct proportion to the danger I felt I was in."

Dare still kept the expression of disappointment and sorrow on his face. "Oh. And the 'Soft Kitty' song? You mean you don't usually sing that to men who rescue you?"

Leesa was about to open her mouth to reply when Jennie's head popped up from behind the reception desk.

"You sang him 'Soft Kitty'?" Her eyes were wide open with admiration, but then her glance flicked to Dare's and she put her hands up in defence. "I'm going. I'm going. Sorry for the interruption. Carry on." She sank back down, hiding behind the counter but still obviously listening.

It was obvious she was listening, because when Dare then said, "And the baby thing? Promising to have my babies? You didn't mean it?" Jennie's head popped up so fast Leesa wondered whether there was some sort of jack-in-the-box spring back there.

"You're going to have his babies?" Jennie asked with excitement.

Leesa frowned. "I didn't say that. Did I?" She shot a look at Dare, who crossed his arms over his chest.

"I distinctly recall you agreeing to it," he said with a smug smile and nod.

"It's definitely true love, then," Jennie agreed with finality.

"And so now you have to go out on a date with me," Dare proclaimed.

"I—" Leesa stopped. How did she get herself into these situations? Oh, that's right. Dared.

"After all, you brought me muffins," Dare said encouragingly.

"In a Tupperware container," inserted Jennie knowledgeably. "No one brings muffins in a Tupperware container unless they plan to return to pick up that container."

Leesa stopped. Her eyes flicked from Jennie to Dare and then to the Tupperware container. No. Her subconscious couldn't have done that to her.

"And are you going to tell our kids that their mummy and daddy never went on a date?" Dare asked with fake horror.

Leesa gave him a considering look from the corner of her eye. "Are you telling me that you were called out to rescue a hysterical woman with paralysing claustrophobia from a lift, had her curl up in your lap and sing you 'Soft Kitty,' had her tell you that she was going to have your babies, then watched her *crawl* out of the doorway like a demented person rather than stride out with confidence… and you want to date her?"

"The lap curling did it for me," Jennie interjected.

Dare gave Leesa a huge smile. "Yep."

"You're crazy. I know I'm stupid for getting into that lift, but my brother dared me to do it and I can never turn down a good dare. But going on a date with you is just insane. You don't know anything about me other than if you expect me to talk to you in rational sentences, don't take me to that revolving restaurant on the top floor of that tower in the city. I could be a serial killer. I could be your cousin. I could be an illegal immigrant who causes problems regularly, just hoping for cute firemen to come and rescue me and hopefully fall in love and marry me so I can live in Australia. There's no possible way you're going to get me to go on a date with you."

She finished with a "so there" tone. He wouldn't get her to go on a date with him.

"I dare you to," Dare said on a whisper.

Leesa froze. He couldn't have just dared her to….

And then a siren began to sound in the office. Leesa was in a fire station. A siren could only mean one thing.

Dare strode forward, grabbed her startled shoulders, and pulled her in to his firm body. Then he lowered his head and dropped a kiss… on her cheek. Her lips cried in disappointment.

"Gotta go. Daddy needs to work. Leave your phone number with Jennie and I'll call you after my shift. Bye."

He raced through the door into the station house. Leesa heard the rattle of the large roller doors as they creaked up slowly. There were shouts, the sound of running boots, door slams, and an engine starting. The fire engine and accompanying smaller truck were out of the building and along the street before Leesa gathered her far-flung wits. She turned to Jennie, who was speaking into a headset. Leesa placed the Tupperware container she still clutched on the counter and took the pen Jennie handed her. With fingers that only trembled slightly—okay, furiously, and she really had to stop lying to herself about that—she printed her name and phone number carefully. She didn't want any possible misreads.

***

Dare picked her up, took her to a beautiful restaurant overlooking the Fremantle Harbour, and made sure they were seated in front of the floor-to-ceiling windows.

"See," he said softly. "No metal box."

She was touched that he'd remembered and gone out of his way to make her feel comfortable.

She was feeling very comfortable, in fact. Her outfit was a success, and only she knew exactly what was under it. Leesa was a big fan of *Grease* and adored the long skirts the girls wore in it. The length of the skirts made her look like an extra out of *The Hobbit*, so she had to compromise and make them knee-length to suit her shorter body. She'd bought the royal blue skirt online, then placed a red petticoat beneath it, rockabilly style. The plain white shirt just emphasised the red. Then she accessorised it with a wide red belt, chunky red earrings, a red bandana headband, and of course, open-toe red heels.

She felt beautiful and in charge. And of course, no one knew that she'd put on her frilly knickers. There was just something about the outfit that called for her to have those frilly white knickers on. So she'd stepped into them and held the secret close to her heart.

After all, this was just the first date. Dare's chances of seeing her frilly knickers were close to zero.

***

Dare stared at Leesa and wondered what the hell she had on under her skirt. He'd been bowled over when she answered the door. She looked like she'd stepped right out of the 50s, complete with ruby-red lips that begged for his kisses. From her hair that had been allowed to poof all around her face, held back only by a scrap of red fabric, to those red-painted toenails that peeked at him through the toe hole in her shoes, she was perfection.

Every time she pushed those black glasses back up her nose he wanted to kiss her. Every time her lacy skirt brushed his trousers he wanted to kiss her. Every time she took a sip from her wine glass he wanted to kiss her. Every time she dithered over something—the menu, whether she'd been polite enough to the waiter, whether pelicans felt the cold—he wanted to kiss her.

So basically he spent the whole night fighting the urge to lay her on the nearest flat surface—the table—and kiss her until he was satisfied.

Or until the cops came.

Because he had a feeling that if he shoved all the plates and cutlery to the floor and started to kiss her, the only thing that would stop him would be the cops pulling him off her.

Or her saying no, of course. Because wow. She didn't know it, but he was her slave for life. If she wanted him to walk through fire for her, he would. And not just because it was his day job. He'd knit all the pelicans in the harbour a bloody cardigan if she demanded. He'd take her to this restaurant twenty times, just so she could sample everything on the menu if she couldn't decide what would be most delicious. He'd sit at her feet, an adoring fan, and never touch her if she decreed it.

He'd probably peek up her skirt while he was down there, but heck, he was only human.

With dessert over and every piece of whipped cream scooped from her bowl—which both his brain and his rock-hard dick were ever so thankful for—he suggested a stroll along the boardwalk. She agreed with a pleased smile and grabbed his hand.

Moving lights caught his eye and he turned to her eagerly. "How about a ride on the Ferris wheel?"

Fremantle hosted a tourist attraction of a large Ferris wheel with fully enclosed cars. The wind off the ocean could be icy, therefore the gondolas were weatherproof and made of glass so that the entire view could be appreciated.

Leesa looked up at the highest gondola with apprehension. "A closed-in box?"

"Made of glass so you can see out," he told her. "Can your claustrophobia handle that?"

They wandered over and Leesa checked it out. The gondolas allowed three-sixty degree uninterrupted views.

"You're not afraid of heights, are you?" he teased.

She giggled. "No. Heights don't bother me. Just something that's enclosed. If I can't see the outside, my brain thinks I'm buried underground." She gave him a playful glance from under long black lashes. "What about you? What's your phobia?"

He debated briefly and then ended up telling the truth. "Big spiders. If they're bigger than my hand, I go screaming from the room like a—" He stopped, just in time. But obviously not soon enough that Leesa didn't guess what he was about to say.

Dared

She gave him a narrow-eyed glare. "Like a girl?" she asked with contempt. "Let me make something clear to you, Mr Fireman. Girls can be tough. Girls can be brave. Girls can be tougher and braver than men. By saying you scream 'like a girl' or that some guy catches a ball 'like a girl' you are implying something is wrong with being a girl. Are you unhappy that I'm a girl?"

His heart was threatening to pound out of his chest. His lips were begging to kiss her. His legs wanted to jerk to a kneeling position and beg her to marry him. She was everything he wanted—beauty, intelligence, and sass.

"Leesa, I'm the opposite of unhappy about you being a girl," he told her sincerely.

She tilted her head and gave a small smile. "Great. Now buy me a ticket and let's see what the view is like from the top."

Dare assumed that a Ferris wheel ride would be the perfect end to the perfect date.

Boy, was he wrong.

It went splendidly for the first ten minutes. They were placed in a gondola by themselves due to the lack of other customers. The wheel moved smoothly on for a section before stopping so that the subsequent gondola could expel its passengers and pick up the next lot. Dare had settled next to his future wife with his arm around her shoulders and had begun talking about favourite movies as they slowly climbed the rotation. They were two sections away from being at the top of the wheel and enthusiastically debating their favourite Australian movies—*Red Dog* versus *The Castle*—when a familiar smell hit Dare.

There's one thing a firefighter knows, and that's the smell of smoke. He abruptly cut off midsentence and jumped to his feet. The cart swayed as he rushed to the side and looked down.

"Dare?"

He gritted his teeth. "Nothing to worry about," he said on an upbeat note. "Just a small fire in the mechanical housing of the wheel. It's not a problem. Look, the flames are only waist-high."

***

Dare wondered if their children would ever ask them about their first date. They would be able to tell them about the hour they were stuck in a gondola and had discussed everything from Australian politics to the plight of the endangered Carnaby's cockatoo. He told Leesa all about how being a firefighter had been his life's dream, and she told him all about the time Paul had dared her to go to a sex club with him.

"I swear, the amount of people who mistook us for a couple and wanted a threesome was ridiculous. But the amount of people who shrugged and said they didn't care when we said we were siblings…. I mean, I love my brother and love hanging out with him, but there are things called boundaries."

Dare had to think about the amount of work it would take to knit a pelican a cardigan in order to stop thinking about Leesa at a sex club and embarrassing himself.

The question that kept running through Dare's head was

how many other people were in professions where their work colleagues had to rescue them. He supposed doctors needed consultations from other doctors, and lawyers probably needed to hire other lawyers from time to time, but how many accountants didn't do their own taxes? How many mechanics got someone else to fix their car?

That's how stupid he felt when Adam's head appeared at their window, lifted high by the ladder.

"Oh, hey there, Dare."

"G'day, Adam."

"What have you been up to?"

"Oh, nothing. Just hanging around waiting for a lift."

They grinned at each other and Adam swiftly made arrangements for them to get back to the ground. That was until Dare said to Leesa, "Come on. Let's blow this joint."

Leesa took one look at the ladder and then gave Dare a stare that made him realise he'd missed a vital piece of information. But what?

"Dare. I can't climb down a ladder," she said flatly.

He frowned. "Sure you can. You'll be safe. I guarantee it."

"Dare. I'm wearing a skirt."

This was not a complication he needed at that moment. "Sweetheart. I know you're wearing a skirt. I love that skirt. Had I known we would be climbing ladders at the end of the date, I'd have made sure you wore something else. But I guess that's what you get in life. Now buck up. Let's get out of here."

But Leesa wouldn't budge.

"I cannot climb down a ladder in a skirt. Everyone will see up it."

Dare held in a sigh. "We won't look. Right, Adam?"

Adam nodded. Leesa wasn't convinced. "You don't know what it's like to wear a skirt."

"Leesa? If you promise to climb down this ladder right now as well as have a second date with me, I'll promise I'll wear a skirt on the date."

Her eyes narrowed and she pushed her glasses back up her nose again. He could see her assessing the risks and looking for the shortfalls.

"Your other option is to stay in here until the ride is fixed, which will probably be a few days," Adam put in helpfully. "And I haven't spotted a bathroom up here."

"I can dare you if you need it," Dare added. She gave in with an unhappy moan.

"Just so you know?" Leesa said reproachfully. "This is a crappy end to the date. You go first." She nodded to the ladder.

There was a slight delay as safety gear was employed, but then Dare coaxed Leesa out onto the ladder. He helped her find her footing, encouraged her to keep going, and praised her as she made it down.

Finally they were on solid ground and Dare thanked the crew before handing over his details to the extremely worried wheel operator. Then he took Leesa's hand and walked her back to the car. After the excitement of the rescue, her adrenaline was sure to be running high. She'd probably be better at home when the adrenaline crash happened.

He saw her into her seat and then jogged around to his side of the car. They were pulling out onto the main road when she said, "You're really going to wear a skirt to our second date?"

"You bet your frilly white knickers I am," he replied.

Then he laughed as she huffed and refused to talk to him for the rest of the journey.

***

Sunday promised to be fine and Leesa was looking forward to her second date. He said he'd pick her up midmorning and take her for coffee down by the river. In a skirt. There had to be some sort of trickery afoot.

There was. But Leesa couldn't be angry at him. Not when there was a sexy fireman standing on her doorstep wearing a red-and-green tartan kilt.

"Where did you get that?" she laughed delightedly.

Dare grinned. "Never ask an Irish lad where he got his kilt from, lassie."

"You're Irish?" she asked in surprise.

"McCarthy? Of course it's Irish."

"But I thought it was the Scottish who had kilts?"

"'Had' being the operative word. What's a wee bit of thievin' between neighbours?"

She gave up on the mystery of Dare McCarthy and locked her front door, promising herself just to enjoy the day ahead—and the view. There was only one thing…. "And what does an *Irishman* wear under his kilt?"

He affected a bad Irish accent. "Ah, lassie. You're ne'er to ask that question."

He took her to a café as promised, where Leesa received an avalanche of jealous looks from each female she encountered.

She grinned her pleasure and enjoyed herself immensely.

"Shall we walk?" Dare asked her once they'd finished coffee and cake.

She was wearing another dress. This one was not her power dress. This one was feminine and girly and she loved it. The dress was black with tiny white polka dots all over, interspersed with bold and eye-catching red cherries. Cinched in at the waist with her wide red belt, it flared out from below her hips but was form-fitting above, shaping her bust and revealing a dark shadow between her breasts with the sweetheart neckline. She'd worn her red tennis shoes, so a stroll along the river path was very doable.

"Last time we did that, we got caught on a Ferris wheel," she said with a twinkle in her eye.

"No rides this time," he protested. "This time we'll stay on the ground."

So they walked, wandering the mostly deserted path along the river and chatting contentedly. An occasional jogger passed them, and a couple of cyclists. They smiled at the baby in the pram as the mother approached from the opposite direction, and they watched the scullers smoothly row by on the gleaming water. Leesa felt happy and content and comfortable all at once. There was no awkwardness between the two of them. In fact, it felt like they had been dating for years. She was very attracted to him, that was for sure, and he seemed to be attracted back. They shared humour and got along.

Was he a keeper?

He had to have some sort of flaw, she decided. No one

could be that handsome, that nice, that funny, and that smart without a flaw. He was the perfect specimen otherwise.

Maybe he'd be a flop in bed.

According to the magazines she read, you could never tell. Size apparently didn't matter for much, and neither did athleticism. She'd once read an article where the reporter swore that the key to a good lover was how unselfish they were. The theory went that the cuter the guy, the more he expected the woman to work for it and give *him* pleasure. The article claimed that the less handsome species of men worked harder to please their women.

Leesa gazed at his handsome profile and gave a sigh of disappointment. Dammit. That *had* to be his flaw.

"What's wrong?" he asked curiously.

She couldn't say *I was just wondering if you were a flop in bed*, so she quickly said, "We've walked for ages. We should probably turn back now."

They had walked a long way and now were in a high-end suburb with little traffic. They'd stopped and prepared to turn around when a faint honking up ahead made them both look up. It came again, and that time Leesa realised it was quacking, not honking. It was a duck and it was distressed.

She quickly moved towards the sound, which was coming from some reeds and weeds off the path. Dare was right behind her. She went around a tree and spotted the noisy duck immediately. Then came the answering sound of ducklings… from below the ground. Mumma duck was calling her babies and they were stuck somewhere.

"Oh no. Dare, the babies are lost."

Dare pressed past her and approached the distressed bird. The babies' cries could be clearly heard, so he pushed aside some branches and found the problem. A grill had been placed over a drain, and the babies were inside.

"How the heck did they get down there?" Dare asked in exasperation. Mumma duck was still honking but had moved off a little, wary of the humans but unwilling to give up on her offspring.

Leesa manoeuvred in and looked down the hole. She could see some fluffy yellow balls in the dim light, about two metres down. "Oh, Dare. We have to get them out." Her heart was breaking. Mumma wanted her babies, and they wanted their mumma. You could tell from the desperation in their mutual cries.

Dare pushed on the grill to try and move it, but it was screwed in tight. "This isn't coming off without some serious tools, Leesa."

"We can't just leave them there," she wailed, close to tears at the thought.

"I'm sure they'll be fine," he said. "Nature will find a way."

"Or a cat will," Leesa said, her voice trembling. "We can't leave them."

"Fine. We'll go back to my place and look up a number of an animal rescue or something."

"And meanwhile Sylvester has come in and eaten them all," Leesa replied stubbornly.

Dare gave her a look that said she was being ridiculous, but Leesa just grabbed the grill and tugged, hoping to move it.

"It won't move," Dare said, exasperated.

"I have to try."

"I'll ring someone," Dare offered.

But Leesa shook her head. "It will be too late by then. I bet mumma will give up and disappear when people start all coming down. She'll be devastated and traumatised for the rest of her life. And those poor babies will be orphans."

Then the tears began to flow.

Dare looked at the tears coursing down her cheeks and his resolve melted like ice cream in the summer sun. He looked again into the drain and saw that what the grill was covering was actually an access to a large storm water pipe. That pipe had to lead somewhere.

He tracked the pipe back to the road where it disappeared under the footpath. Frustrated, he turned the other way and tracked it to the river. The peeps from the ducklings and the answering call from their mother continued on unabated. On the other side of the bushes, the silver pipe emerged out of the sand and fed its contents to the river. The end was half submerged in the water. A grown male could probably squeeze inside the pipe if he had to. But there were so many things that could be down there. Including large spiders.

Deadly tiger snakes and small-but-deadly redback spiders he could deal with, no sweat. But those large wolf spiders….

He strode back to Leesa, who was still crying and watching the ducklings down the hole.

"The pipe goes into the river. If we can get the mother to call the babies from the river end…?"

But it proved impossible. The mother wouldn't leave the

area where she could hear the babies, and they couldn't catch her. Frustrated, Dare watched the mother move even farther away from these humans hunting her. The last thing he needed was for her to abandon the babies.

"Please?" Leesa begged him, her face still stained with tears.

How could he refuse when the mother of his future children said please so prettily?

In one smooth action he pulled the white T-shirt he was wearing over his head. Her reaction was satisfying. There was surprise, and then The Look. The Look was Dare's favourite. It was the oh-wow-check-out-this-hot-guy action. He saw her take in the years of hard work he'd spent on his chest muscles, the pain endured for the tattoos he loved, and the endless sit-ups he did for that flat stomach. She looked. She blushed. She liked.

"You wanted to know what an Irishman has on under his kilt? Well, if you're feeling maidenly, you should look away now."

Seriously? He was putting on an impromptu strip show for her and he thought she may want to look away?

The chest was more than she could ever dare hope—wish, pray, dance naked under the new moon chanting—for, muscular and decorated with a variety of ink. There was the triangular figure on his pectoral muscle, some cursive words written across his ribs to the side, and a tribal design on his shoulder.

Her body forgot how to blink when his fingers went for the buckles on the side of his kilt. Then the material was opening to show… a pair of black aussieBum briefs.

"Leesa? Can you hold this?"

She came out of her trance to see Dare holding out his kilt and shirt to her. She had the impression from the grin on his face that it wasn't the first time he'd called her name. She grabbed them.

"What are you going to do?"

Mumma duck was still quacking away, but keeping her distance. Dare was now dressed in a pair of sneakers and briefs.

"The pipe entrance is in the water, I'm going to wade out and see if there's access from there."

He turned and walked through the tall grass towards the river. Like a homing beacon had been placed on his bum, Leesa followed. At the river's edge he stopped and took off his footwear, then charged into the water. Leesa couldn't look away. Nuh-uh. Not for the police. Not for a hurricane. Not for a nearby plane crash.

Her eyes were in missile lock mode, and she was not taking her gaze off that missile, baby.

The bank was shallow, so the water was only halfway up his calves at the end of the pipe. Leesa watched him bend over—oh, yeah baby—and look into the tunnel. Then he looked back at her and seemed to sigh as if he were being tortured to do something.

"Go back to the grill," he called. "You'll be able to hear me if I yell."

Mumma duck had returned to the open drain and eyed Leesa off warily. Leesa put Dare's clothes over a nearby branch to keep them out of the dirt and waited. There were a couple of scrapes, a moan, and then what Leesa thought were a string of curse words. But she waited patiently because she had faith in Dare. He could fix the problem.

Even when she heard him muttering about never forgetting the moment, she decided that it was a good thing. Even when he cursed about slithering on his belly, half-naked and getting sand in his underwear, she decided it had to be worth it. And it was. When Dare finally made it to where Leesa could see him and stood up in the light, she knew he was the one for her.

"Can I say that I love you?" she called softly down to him, not wanting to startle the babies.

"Yes," he growled. "But I'm not really appreciating it at this time."

"Okay," she agreed. "I'll just have to tell you again later when you're not muddy from head to toe and stuck down a drain."

She ignored the grunt in reply and reached out to take the little fluffy yellow duckling Dare passed through the grill to her. It peeped and cheeped frantically, so she snagged Dare's white T-shirt off the branch, folded it in half, and shoved the frightened baby into the middle. Then she grabbed the next duckling and shoved him in with his brother. There were seven of them. When the last one was passed up, Dare said he was going back through the pipe, so Leesa gathered the babies and walked them away from the drain. The last thing she wanted was for them to fall in again.

As she hoped, mumma duck followed at a distance. The babies wriggled and cheeped within their ad hoc enclosure. She took a few steps, waited for mumma to follow, then walked on a little again. By the time she made it to the water's edge, Dare was emerging from the pipe. He looked up and saw her.

"Did the mother follow?" he called.

Leesa squatted on the narrow bank, lowered the shirt to the ground and opened it up. The babies skittered away from her and mumma came charging out of the grass, calling her offspring to her. Then she plunged into the water, seven little fluff balls following her eagerly.

"Huh. Not even a thank you," Leesa huffed as she watched the family paddle off.

"Not everyone brings their muffins around for you," Dare chuckled. He was completely covered in mud. He looked down at himself, grimaced, and turned to throw himself into the water deeper out. Leesa watched as he scrubbed at the mud all over him. Even though he was standing in water up to his chest, Leesa followed the movement of his hands, her imagination making up for what her eyes couldn't see. From the placement of his arms she knew exactly when he pulled down the front of his briefs and swished around a bit to try and get rid of the dirt and sand.

Finally he waded out—her sleek, wet, handsome, gorgeous, dirty fireman. Wearing nothing but black briefs.

"Do you have my clothes?"

With a grimace of her own, Leesa held out the white T-shirt that was now smeared with baby duck poo.

"I'll wash it for you," she promised. She looked at his muddy briefs. "And those. I'm really sorry, but really grateful."

"And where's my kilt?"

Leesa's eyes flew wide. "Shit. Up a tree. I hope no one stole it." And then she charged back into the grass.

***

Dare's mood was content despite his bare chest, slightly wet and sandy feet in his socks, his damp and muddy jocks, and his river-water-smelling body. Leesa was happy and that's all that mattered. They walked back along the path, getting plenty of odd looks from other pedestrians, as if they didn't often see a man wearing only a kilt going for a walk with his favourite woman.

Back at the car, he looked at Leesa. "Would you mind if we stopped by my place first? It's closer and on the way to your house. I can grab a quick shower and a change of clothes."

She agreed. He drove to his house and waved her towards the kitchen. "Grab a coffee or anything you want to eat. Ignore any mess. I wasn't expecting guests."

He jumped in the shower and washed, half listening for noises in his house. Leesa was there with him, and he was surprised at how satisfied he felt. Yes, he'd joked that she'd be his wife and the mother of his children, but he hadn't really thought beyond that. It would mean sharing every aspect of his life. There would be the good bits—companionship, happiness, and sex—but there would also be the bad bits. There would be adjustments to be made—like living space. He was twenty-eight and had been living mostly on his own for four years. Could he rewire his brain to put the toilet seat down, not throw his dirty clothes in the corner of the bedroom, and share the bathroom with 643 different cosmetic products? Could he be happy to sit through chick flicks and put up with flowers in vases on the tables?

He heard the kettle come to a boil and switch off. It made him smile. For Leesa, he'd put up with a lot more. He happily soaped his hair, thinking of having her smile at him on a daily basis and wondering if he'd have to rescue ducklings often for her.

Then there was the sound of his bedroom door opening, and he turned around in the shower stall with surprise. His bedroom had an open en suite—you could see everything from the bed. Not that he was modest, but he didn't know if she was ready for that bit.

"Leesa?" he asked hesitantly. "Did you find the coffee? Was there something you needed?"

Her voice floated back to him from around the wall separating the en suite from the bedroom entrance.

"I decided I didn't want coffee."

"There are teabags in the green tin," he suggested. "If you wanted tea."

"Nope. Not tea either."

Was her voice getting closer?

"What do you want, then?" he asked, staring at the corner where it sounded like she would appear any second. And then, there she was. Her brown eyes were cautious, as if she wasn't sure. Was she not sure about doing this? Or was she not sure he was okay with doing this?

"You. I want you," she whispered, and her stare dropped from holding his gaze to running down his body.

Dare froze. Shock warred with excitement. Desire warred with the need to go slow and not scare her off. Exhilaration warred with anticipation.

She stood in front of the bed where he could see all of her through the glass wall of the shower, then shrugged the dress straps off her shoulders, and Dare realised the zip at the back was already undone.

"If you want?" she asked softly, and Dare realised he hadn't moved. Hadn't responded. The water beat down over his shoulders and disappeared down the drain, but most of his body was frozen. Only *most* of his body. One part of him was responding. One part of him was rising rapidly. Did she *really* think he would say no?

The dress inched a little lower, revealing the pale slopes of her breasts but stopping before it fell completely. He was in the fiery pits of hell. Did he want to stay in the shower and enjoy the show, or did he want to join in? It was a hard decision. And at that moment, Dare's body was all about hard.

"Yes," he murmured. "Yes, I want."

She hesitated. He went supernova hard. Did she need a last push over that edge?

"I dare you," he said, and watched raptly as the black, white, and red material fell to the ground. She wasn't wearing a bra, and he didn't know if it was a good thing or bad thing that he hadn't known that sooner. On one hand, they'd have never made it through coffee if he'd known. On the other, there was a type of deliciousness to being out with a woman and knowing what she had on—or conversely didn't have on—under her clothes.

Without taking his eyes off her, he fumbled with the taps, turned them off, opened the shower door, stepped out onto the bath mat, and groped for his towel on the rail. Leesa stood there in the puddle of her dress with a saucy little smile on her face, clad only in red knickers—no frills that time, to his disappointment—and oversized black glasses.

He dried off quickly but approached slowly, leaving the wet towel discarded and forgotten on the floor. Once he touched her, the excruciating pain of anticipation would be over, and the ache was so sweet he drew it out. He watched her gaze take him all in and stopped in front of her, his toes nudging the material of her dress on the ground.

"I'm naked. You're not," he challenged her.

She reached up and pushed her glasses back up her nose, which had the effect of making her breasts move slightly. "We'd better rectify that immediately," she said merrily, then hooked her red-painted nails under the elastic of her knickers and pushed them down. They were kicked away, but neither of them bothered to look where.

Dare found his tongue in the back of his throat and said, "Boy, am I ever so glad I subjected myself to 'Soft Kitty.'"

Leesa gave him a coy look. "If you work hard enough at it, 'Soft Kitty' becomes 'Soft Pussy.'"

He decided it was because the blood in his body was trapped in areas far from his brain that it took him two seconds to process the pun. He froze, shocked to stillness from the deliciously naughty joke.

"I like 'Soft Pussy' much better."

She lifted her hands to cup her not insubstantial breasts. "Anything else you like?"

"I also like 'Round and Round the Garden,'" he growled low. When she gave him a questioning look, he narrowed his eyes predatorily and began to circle her body where it stood in the pool of her dress. "Round and round the garden, like a teddy bear."

***

Leesa grinned with delight and anticipation. Why did she think that sex with Dare would be anything but fun? He was gorgeous. He was fully aroused. He was focused just on her. It had taken a lot for her to strip off without shame. She was acutely aware of her not-so-flat tummy and yeah-they're-wobbly thighs. But it was her, and if Dare had the nerve to make an issue out of any of it, he wasn't the man for her.

Instead he was giving her everything she wanted. Arousal without rushing. Fun without mocking. Sexiness without shame.

"One step, two step…," he chanted as he deliberately placed his feet on the floor in exaggerated movements, and she tensed. What would he do?

She squeezed her thighs together to try to stop the pulsing between them.

"Tickle under there!"

With a war whoop he charged at her, easily swinging her off her feet and bearing her backwards onto the bed. She shrieked and hung on to his shoulders. The bed took the impact of their two bodies without a problem and they fell in a delicious tangle of limbs. There was a bit of wiggling until

Dared

they were comfortable, but then they lay together, panting as the laughter left them, experiencing the first touch of skin on skin.

Dare stared down at her, their faces just inches apart, then reached out and gently lifted her glasses off her face and stowed them safely on the bedside table.

"Do you know that I haven't kissed you?" he whispered.

The laughter bubbled up in her again. "I dare you to."

His eyes dropped to her mouth and each square inch of her skin became sensitised as it waited. Then his head lowered, and she moaned with the first contact. He kissed her gently, butterfly kisses that were soft and almost ticklish, then harder as desire began to take over. Leesa groaned louder and opened to him, asking him to take what he wanted. Her arms entwined behind his neck, her thighs moved and invited him to settle between them, and her spine arched as she welcomed his weight. He thrust his hips and drove his erection closer to her softness, touching the sensitive skin between her legs with the tip of his penis while he moved his hand down her side, tracing her ribs.

He pulled back and panted slightly. "Leesa? Do you know when you asked me if it was a good time to tell me that you loved me? And I said that it probably should wait until I wasn't covered from head to toe in mud?"

She felt herself blushing, but responded prettily. "I recall it was me who said I would wait until you weren't covered in mud before I told you that I love you. You just told me you wouldn't appreciate it at that particular moment."

He sighed and rolled his eyes in a teasing manner. "Always

needing to be 100 percent right. Fine. You were the one who said it, but I'm assuming you recall that situation?"

"Of course."

He thrust his hips again and Leesa nearly screamed with desire. She really needed him inside her. Soon. Or her hysterics in the lift would look like a preamble to the main event. Then he reached up and cupped both of her breasts, moulding them and running his rough fingers over the responsive nipples.

"So," he said on a whisper, "I really want to tell you that I love you too. But I just thought you would be more appreciative of it, and probably believe me more, if I said it for the first time when my hands weren't on your naked breasts and my cock wasn't sitting restlessly in your wetness, almost begging for entrance."

Heat flooded her. "I'm not sure if you're right," she panted. "But I'm kinda busy thinking about something else at the moment. So if you could hold that thought, find us a damn condom, and get on with that something else, we can come back later to the subject of our mutual love for each other?"

He kissed her again. "I knew in that lift that you were the one for me." And he reached for the bedside table drawer.

***

Two hours later, Leesa swam from sleep and stretched lazily. She felt lethargic, energised, beautiful, rumpled, sore, well-loved, and excited, all at the same time. Any fears she'd had about them not being sexually compatible had been very firmly put to rest, and in fact, she was wondering if it were too soon to suggest doing it all over again.

Her gorgeous fireman would surely be up to the task, right?

Dare's bedroom was very monochrome, with off-white walls and carpet, pale grey quilt covers, and only a couple of black-framed photos on the wall. Reaching out, she retrieved her glasses so she could see more clearly. She inspected a nearby black-and-white photo of some city, then turned in Dare's arms so she could see the opposite wall.

Dare muttered something unintelligible and moved his hand from her naked hip to her naked breast. She grinned while she decided that her gorgeous fireman appeared to be up to the task after all, but didn't take her stare off the far wall.

"Uh, Dare?"

"Shh," he said and burrowed his head into her shoulder. She didn't really think he was trying to go back to sleep. Not with his hand moving like it was.

"Are you, um, awake?"

"No."

"But I have something very, very important to ask you."

"Of course I meant it when I said I loved you," he muttered. Then his hand slid over her stomach and began inching farther down.

"That wasn't the question," she said, fighting amusement and desire. "It's a question about if you really meant something you said, but not about your love. I think I'm pretty sure about that one now that you've told me a dozen times, and very nicely and thoroughly proved it to me too."

He cracked an eyelid. "Oh? What other thing did I say that you want me to prove?"

Leesa fought bravely. She really did. But the smile came out. She gently kissed the tip of his nose, then let her gaze slide to the wall to check again before colliding back with his. "Did you really mean it when you said you had a phobia about spiders bigger than your hand?"

He froze. For three long seconds his eyes bored into hers. Then he yelped loudly. The covers went flying off their naked bodies and Dare scrambled over her in his flight to get to the far side of the room, which happened to be the opposite of the bedroom door. He hugged the wall and then turned around in terror, his eyes searching for the danger and alighting on the huge huntsman spider Leesa had spotted.

He yelled a wordless scream again. "What the fuck is that doing in my house? In my room? Was it watching us while we slept?"

"Probably," Leesa agreed.

"Fuck. I need my flamethrower. Where is it?"

He began looking around on the floor, so Leesa sat up and surveyed him with amusement. "What? You actually *have* a flamethrower?"

"No. But in the games you just need to spot the treasure chest nearby or something to defeat the beast. Fuck. Is it looking at me like it's about to go for my throat? I'm going to die naked. What if I come back as a naked ghost? I could never haunt children then."

Leesa realised then that Dare wasn't going to be rational about this. "Would you like *me* to take him outside?" she asked, overly solicitously.

"No," shouted Dare. "That thing needs to die. And don't

get out of bed. Don't try and distract me with your lovely, gorgeous, delightful, sexy, naked body. No. I'll climb through the window instead and call the police."

She ignored him and pulled her dress back on. The spider hadn't moved, so she presented her back to Dare. "Can you please zip me up?"

"What?" he cried.

"Zip me up," she said clearly. "Unless you want me to battle the eight-legged beast naked?"

The zip went up smartly. Leesa skirted the bed and disappeared into Dare's walk-in closet. There she found underwear, shorts, and a T-shirt, and threw them over to her terrified lover. "Clothes on. If you need to climb through the window, you may need something covering you."

Then unconcernedly—okay, so she watched carefully— she strolled past the spider to gather what she required. The laundry room yielded her a mop, and the only other thing she needed to do was open the front door in anticipation.

Upon entering the bedroom again, she found Dare had pressed himself farther into the corner. He was now dressed— although she had a suspicion his shirt was on back to front— and was unlocking the window closest to him. "Dare," she said with exasperation.

"It moved," he defended himself, pointing at the huntsman.

Remembering how he'd rescued her from the lift, helped her from the Ferris wheel, and then saved seven ducklings because she'd *cried*, Leesa bit back her irritation at his irrationality and lifted the mop up to the spider on the wall. Like he'd just been waiting for the ride, the spider nimbly scurried onto the grey rope strands and perched expectantly. With hands that trembled slightly—okay, furiously—she quickly strode outside with her unwanted passenger. Dare lived opposite a park, so she gingerly walked across the street in her bare feet and stuck the mop head into the nearest tree branch. She swore Mr Spider waved to her as he dismounted happily.

Returning to Dare's house, she found him watching from the doorstep.

"Did I tell you I love you?" he said with appreciation.

"Yes," she said, and pushed her glasses up her nose again.

"So when are you going to have my babies?" he asked.

Leesa chuckled. "We've known each other less than two weeks, had exactly two dates, and had sex once. You can't be serious about the babies."

He stared at her. Seriously.

She frowned. "Dare. You can't be serious, right?"

His expression didn't change. She was standing barefoot on his doorstep, with a mop in one hand and no knickers on. It was rather surreal.

"Dare."

He reached out and ran the backs of his fingers down her cheek. "Leesa. I love you. Will you have my babies? I dare you to."

The End

Playing for Keeps

BY GEN RYAN

Dedication

For my Hot Tree ladies, you all rock.

Chapter One

MASON

"Holy Fuck." I looked down as the woman's head came up for air. She smiled before diving back in. Pushing her head farther against my raging cock, she gagged. I grinned as she looked up at me, laughter dancing in her eyes. To her, I was just another famous person she got to blow. To me, she was a means to an end. A release I needed to survive. I groaned as she flicked her tongue on the tip of my dick, licking the precum that had made its way out.

"You like that, baby?" she mumbled in between sucking me off.

"Less talking, more blowing." I clenched my jaw when she cupped my balls in response. I loved a good blow job. No mess and no worry about pregnancy scares.

As the star player for the Sydney Roosters, my face was plastered all over every billboard and on every channel. Women chanted my name, showed me their boobs, and screwed me whenever I wanted. The problem was, women would also do anything to keep me around, so I had to be extra careful with protection. Despite that, though, I was living the life. A different girl every night. I had an endless buffet of pussy and arse.

"What the fuck, Mason?" Oliver, my manager, stood in the doorway to the locker room where I was currently getting serviced. I ignored him as I clenched my teeth, my release close. Putting up a finger to stall him, I grabbed the woman's hair as I released inside her mouth. My muscles tightened, my entire body going rigid, then like butter I melted into her touch. She giggled, rocking back on her heels as she swallowed.

"That was amazing." She bounced up and went to place a kiss to my lips.

"No kissing." I flashed her my dazzling smile.

"Time to go," Oliver said, moving closer to her as I shoved my dick back into my pants.

"What? He said he'd take me to brekkie." She stuck out her lower lip in an effort to pout. I was immune to it all. Feelings, pouty lips, all of it. I crossed my arms and leaned against the lockers.

"Sorry, babe. Duty calls."

She scoffed, grabbing her handbag and muttering profanities.

"You don't even know her name, do you?" Oliver asked as he sat down on the bench and glared at me.

"Don't need to know her name for her to suck me off." I shrugged.

"Mason, this is getting out of hand. You're always humping like a goddamn koala! It's messing with your game. The drinking and excessive sex."

I laughed at his reply. He brought this up a lot lately. How I was a liability and giving the rugby organisation a bad name. So, what if I was a bit off lately? I was always a good player and they knew it.

He shoved his mobile in my face, and I looked at a picture of me from the other night, my face bruised and bloodied from fighting with some fool who called me a wanker.

"That was a fun night," I said with a smile. Opening my locker, I took out my stuff to change into.

"This can't happen anymore. The club is threatening to let you go."

I slammed my locker door. "Bullshit. They've never said that before."

"Now people are talking. You're fighting everyone who looks at you wrong, and you've been off at the last three games, which you never do. You need to straighten up your act or you're out." Oliver straightened his tie as he stood up.

Grinding my teeth, I let out a staggered breath. "You're supposed to be my mate, have my back."

"I am your mate, but I can't keep pretending that you aren't spiralling out of control. That's why I hired you a PR rep. Someone who can keep an eye on you and help you revamp your image."

"I don't need a babysitter." I took off my T-shirt and

replaced my jeans with workout shorts. Our game didn't start until later but I wanted to run first, let out some of this pent-up energy. Even though I fucked a lot, it wasn't enough. I had an itch that needed scratching, and that was only met on the field. League was my life.

I started sleeping around and drinking when Rachel, my girlfriend since high school, dumped me. I drank too much which led to fighting. Rumours soon flew that I was losing control. If they were going to spew these accusations my way, why not live up to the image? And that's exactly what I did. Every single night.

"Don't think of it as a babysitter." He paused and placed his hand on my shoulder. "Think of it as the only way you can keep doing what you love."

I shrugged him off and hightailed it out of the locker room as Oliver's voice travelled. "She'll be here tomorrow. From New York City. This is your last chance. Don't fuck it up."

A Yank? It was bad enough that Oliver was pushing someone on me, but a Yank? Oliver was a fucker. Too bad I loved him like a brother.

I didn't respond, my feet finding a rhythm as they hit the grass. The stadium was empty, calm, a contrast to what it'd be in just a few hours. Fans would be screaming, every seat filled with people who loved rugby just as I did. I lived for their chants, their cries that egged me on.

Glancing up at the seats, I noticed a woman looking down at me. Even from afar I could tell she was attractive, with a lean body and dark hair. She stood there, her arms crossed over her chest. I shaded my eyes to get a better look. Seeing a scowl on her face I smiled, giving her a wave and blowing her a kiss. My fans loved that. Especially my female fans. I ran faster to try to impress her, thinking about how I needed someone to keep my bed warm that night. My lungs burned as air pumped into them. I loved the thrill of a run. The way my body pushed hard to propel me forward even when it wanted to collapse. My legs ached, my breathing became staggered, but that was only the beginning of what my body could do. After a few laps around the stadium, I glanced back up again at the spot where the woman was standing. It was empty.

"There goes my good time," I mumbled. I headed back into the locker room, where the rumble of my teammates greeted me. Girls surrounded the entry and I grinned, the woman in the stadium a distant memory. Good time officially reinstated.

Chapter Two

DELANEY

Yup. He was a man whore. I hadn't even been standing there five minutes before he blew me a kiss. I'd dealt with men far worse than Mason James St Patrick. Men who thought they were God's greatest gift to the world and deserved their dick sucked by anything with tits. I didn't play that game. I didn't play any games, for that matter.

I was known for my crude humour but kick-arse PR skills that improved the images of politicians, athletes, and celebrities who'd screwed themselves over due to pure stupidity. I could run with the big boys and I usually did, grabbing each man by the balls when he tried to seduce me. I was immune to their advances. I was immune to all male advances, which was why my firm usually stuck me with the male clients. At twenty-seven years old, I had my V card firmly intact. Not knowing what I was missing out on made it easier to decline opportunities when they arose. And they did, quite frequently. I let the advances roll off me and put the men who hit on me in their place. No one was getting in Delaney Matthews's pants. I liked men, don't get me wrong, but they were unpredictable, like many things that had to do with relationships and love. I lived by my regimented schedule and liked knowing what could happen at all times. That was what made me good at my job. I knew what could happen often before anyone else.

I watched Mason run for a while and couldn't fight back my scowl at how gorgeous he was. I'd watched all of his PR nightmares when Oliver asked me to take this job. I'd been looking for a way to come back home for a while, having left Australia to boost my career options. I dreamed of living in New York City and working for some big firm. I loved the high skylines and hustle and bustle of a big city. But truth was, I missed Australia and when Oliver mentioned needing help with Mason, it was my chance to come home.

All of Mason's time on the TV lately focused on him drinking too much alcohol and screwing too many women. Normally that wouldn't be an issue; he was single and was a damn good footy player. But now, it was impacting his career. He was showing up late to games, screwing up, and fighting anyone who looked at him wrong. I must admit, though, that my favourite was from the other night when he went out drinking with his friends. He grabbed a woman and started making out with her. When the woman's boyfriend showed up, he punched him. Of course, the paparazzi were there to capture the loving moment and plaster it all over the TV and Internet. There was no denying the fact that Mason was all over the media for his violent behaviour lately, and although some would say there was no such thing as bad publicity, I knew better. The fucked up thing was, as I stared at him running and his obvious attempt at flirting, I couldn't help but think he was even hotter in person.

Problem was, he knew it. In each video I watched, he teased the camera and put on a show that said he liked the attention. Even if the paparazzi were harassing him, which they often did, he'd flip off the camera, or my absolute favourite, moon the reporters. *Side note, he has a fantastic arse.* Despite his crude behaviour, I knew his issues were deeper than just partying. I could always tell by my client's eyes. He didn't have a fire in them, a desire to party and let loose. There was sadness there. A void that made me feel sorry for him for a minute. I had to figure out what the issue was to get him to stop before he lost everything. And from what I read, he was worth a fortune.

The sun danced off his skin, highlighting his toned abs and strong legs. Of course he ran shirtless, because who wouldn't when you looked like an underwear model? When I found myself checking out his arse again as he slowed down, I turned on my heels and walked away, frustrated with my hormones for betraying me. The damn bitches.

I noticed a familiar figure and relief filled me. I could focus on business.

"Oliver?" I called.

"Delaney!" he exclaimed, jogging towards me before

bringing me in for a hug. "It's so good to see you again. I wasn't expecting you until tomorrow." I'd met Oliver a few years back when travelling back to Sydney for a conference and to visit family, and we'd kept in touch off and on ever since. His phone buzzed and he glanced at the screen and frowned. "This goddamn wanker is going to be the death of me."

"What's going on?"

He showed me his phone. The five o'clock news top story was a picture of Mason with the headline that he'd punched another guy who said he was washed-up.

"This guy is a clusterfuck," I commented, quickly reading the rest of the article.

Oliver sighed. "He's my best mate. We've been friends since uni. This isn't him."

I gave him a weary smile. I didn't know what relationships like that were like. I had no friends, other than those I talked to at work. I travelled a lot and it was hard to keep friendships with a schedule like mine. We had similar lifestyles, so our friendship was easy. I guess you could say he was my only friend.

"I know if anyone can straighten up his act, it's you." He grinned, nudging me with his elbow. If I were looking to date, Oliver would be my type, with his tailored suits and strong work ethic. Easy on the eyes, a few inches taller than my five five. He was average. I liked average, not flashy or—

"You holding out on me, Oliver?" Mason rounded the corner and looked me up and down. He wasn't trying to hide that he was checking me out, and that infuriated me. Heat pooled in my stomach at the intensity of his dark eyes. I didn't fidget because that wasn't how I rolled; I never shied away from anything or anyone, and Mason would be no different. *Lord, take me now. His chest is actually glistening.* Didn't normal people sweat? I looked like a drowned rat when I ran. Of course, Mason didn't. He looked like he bathed in the nectar of the gods. It made me hate him even more, along with my vagina, which currently had its own heartbeat.

"Mason, this is Delaney."

I held out my hand, which he took and brushed his lips against. *Soft lips. Perfect for kissing.* I took my hand and wiped off his kiss on my slacks.

"Ouch." He laughed. "No woman has ever wiped off my kiss before."

I snickered. "Well, I'm not just any ordinary woman."

"She's going to be your lifesaver. She's your PR rep." Oliver grinned.

Ah yes. PR rep. That was why I was there. Not to flirt. *Get your head in the game!* I needed a pep talk. A huddle and a smack on the arse that told me to knock 'em dead. Because right then, Mason was making me feel like putty in his hands.

"Delaney. You're the fucking Yank?" He grinned. "And the chick who was checking me out while I ran." He whispered to Oliver, "She likes me."

Oliver shook his head. "She's not a Yank, per se. She's lived in New York for the past few years, but she's an Aussie," he explained. Mason looked me up and down as if trying to decipher whether I was worthy to work with him.

I inhaled, remembering how many zeroes were at the end

of my pay cheque for this job. *Stay professional. Don't let him break you.* I glanced up as Mason licked his lips.

"Oh, for fuck's sake," I mumbled. "I wasn't checking you out. I was looking at the field. I've never seen one before." I pulled down my shirt and glared at him, willing my eyes to stay on his. They wanted to look at his chest. I mean, come on, he was shirtless and in phenomenal shape. But I didn't crack. *Delaney 1/ Mason 0.*

"You've never seen a footy field?" Mason's mouth hung open before he turned to Oliver. "You hired me a PR rep who knows nothing about footy?" Oliver shrugged.

"I don't have to know anything about the game to represent you. I'm not the one playing." I pointed at him. "You are."

"Wrong," Mason interrupted. Oliver went to interject and Mason put his finger to his mouth to shush him. "You want to represent me, then you have to know about the game. Or no deal."

My body reacted to the demand in his voice. I didn't like being bossed around. While normally I'd put the person in their place immediately, I was too focused on clenching my thighs together, fighting the urge to stick my fingers down my pants and flick my clit. Mason's voice was like silk, his accent like a fine wine, and hot damn, I wanted a tall glass. Annoyed that this arsehat was turning me into a hormonal mess, I moved closer to him, my eyes never leaving his.

"The contract has been signed. I'm all yours." I immediately regretted my words when Mason flexed his chest muscles and tapped my nose with his finger. I glanced down at his pecs. *Fucking traitorous eyes. Delaney 1/ Mason 1.* Holy mother of all things manly. His chest was even better up close. Broad and chiselled, smooth, with not a single hair in sight. I wanted to lick him. I'd bet he tasted delicious. Maybe like peaches, because that's what he smelled like. Peaches mixed with man sweat. I was allergic to peaches. Figures. Fuck my life. Even his sweat was unnatural!

I shook my head, alarmed that my thoughts were more focused on this hunk of man in front of me and what he looked like shirtless instead of cleaning up his image.

"You're not all mine, but you will be," Mason said with a grin.

I inhaled. *Here, have my virginity.*

"Listen here!" I wiggled my finger in his face as he laughed.

"Enough, Mason. She's employed by you, so show her some respect." Oliver turned to me. "I can take you to your hotel if you'd like?"

Thank you, Oliver, for giving me a way out and bringing me back to reality.

"That'd be nice." I stepped back and tried to focus on Oliver.

"You're not staying for the game?" Mason asked, a slight pout forming on his lips. "I'm pretty good." His smile returned as he stretched. Muscles tugged and reached across his arms. My fingers twitched and I had to shove my hands in my pockets to avoid reaching out and running them across him. I was losing my shit.

"I'm totally jet-lagged. I need to sleep it off." I yawned, the trip finally catching up with me.

"Totally." Mason mimicked my voice and snapped his

fingers like he was some valley girl. My time in the States was definitely showing. I shook my head and allowed a small smile to creep on my lips. I hated that he was somewhat funny.

"Training tomorrow at 8:00 a.m. at the field by the stadium." Mason crossed his arms over his chest.

"She isn't here to be your toy, Mason. She's here to help you," Oliver said with a sigh. "Don't play games. You could lose everything."

Mason furrowed his eyebrows before nodding. "Agreed. Now come on, mate. It will help me focus, and then she can talk image and all that after I show her what I do." He pleaded with Oliver to see logic in teaching me the game. They stared at each other, a creepy stare-off that lasted much longer than any grown man should allow.

I rolled my eyes before interrupting their nonsense. "Whatever gets you to focus," I said.

Oliver shook his head and looked away from Mason. He led the way, and I followed him. Glancing back, I caught Mason checking me out as I walked away.

"Damn, I hate to see you go, but I love to watch you leave!" he yelled after me.

Staring straight ahead, I focused on the clicking sound of my heels against the ground.

"Don't let him get to you. He's like that with all the women," Oliver said, looking at me from the corner of his eye.

"I saw in the videos. Don't worry, I'm immune to idiot advances." I repeated it in my head a few times because right then something was off.

"No one's immune to Mason's ways." He quickly looked away. There was a change in his voice, almost a sadness. It must have been difficult being in the shadow of Mason St Patrick, a man who stood at six four and looked more like an underwear model than a footy player. His hair swooped in his eyes just a bit, and I wondered if it got in the way when he played. Everything about him screamed perfection, and Oliver, while handsome in his own way, looked average in comparison. Oliver sighed, bringing me back to reality.

"Hey. You okay?" I asked.

"Fine. Just be careful around him, okay?" Oliver warned.

"No worries. Like I said—"

"You're immune. Got it." Oliver's tone sliced at me.

I hadn't even been in Sydney a day and already Mason was becoming one of the most challenging clients I'd ever faced, mostly because my vagina had decided that it wanted to have feelings of its own. I'd always been able to hold it at bay and let my mind rule the situation, but now a man whore who played a sport I knew nothing about complimented me on my arse and I wanted to jump his bones. I shook my head, blaming my temporary horniness on jet lag, because I knew damn well that Mason wouldn't and couldn't be anything more than a client, even if my lady parts had other plans.

Chapter Three

MASON

The water cascaded down my body. Pressing my head against the cool tile, I stared down at my rock-hard dick. It'd been hours since I'd seen Delaney. I played my heart out in the game and we won by a landslide. Normally, that'd be all I needed to sleep like a baby, but as the blood pooled to my dick yet again, I knew sleep wasn't coming without release.

I could call many of the women I had on speed dial for a quickie. There was Rhonda, who'd come and be whatever I wanted her to be. A naughty schoolgirl, a dominatrix, a submissive; she was up for whatever. Then there was Jessica, my professional screw. She was a lawyer, actually she was *my* lawyer, and gave the best head this side of Sydney. That's all she'd do, claiming to want to keep it professional, but the way she sucked my dick was anything but professional. The only problem was, none of them interested me right then because of her. *Delaney*.

There'd been many women that I wanted over the years. I'd kiss them, woo them with slick words, and fuck them senseless. Delaney seemed immune to my charms. The damn woman brushed off my kiss to her hand. I knew she found me attractive. I'd watched her fight to keep her eyes off me, but she'd let them slip and that was enough to make me want her even more.

Reaching down I pumped my cock, groaning as I kept my body upright. I hadn't touched myself like this in forever, preferring someone else to get me off. But my thoughts were consumed with the dark-haired beauty I'd met earlier and I couldn't shake her. My balls tightened as I stroked myself fast and hard. I thought about her perfect mouth, turned into a scowl as I deliberately hit on her. The slight blush on her cheeks as I checked her out. Then her arse, the tight round cheeks bouncing against her pants as she stormed away. I licked my lips at the thought of ploughing into her, and my balls tightened as I came. It wasn't a relief; it just further fuelled my frustration. Even as I emptied myself into the shower it wasn't enough. Fuck me, I had to have that woman.

I towelled myself off and went to bed, not bothering to check my mobile for dirty messages from any of my girls. I wanted to get to sleep so I could see her the next day. Show her what my world was like. I grunted and turned on my side, flicking off the light. I'd never done anything with any woman besides Rachel that resembled dating. I wondered if I even remembered how. Delaney wasn't just any ordinary woman, and somehow that was okay with me. Maybe that was exactly what I needed.

***

I slung my gym bag over my shoulder as I made my way to the field. It was 7:30 a.m. and Delany wouldn't be here for half an hour, which was plenty of time for me to get a run in. I walked out on the field as I did many times to train by myself or just be alone. That time, though, she was there.

Delaney was bent over, her arse on display as she did some weird pose. Seeing her like that made my dick twitch and I thanked the gods that she was flexible. *What I could do with that....*

"Mason." She straightened and tilted her chin at me. "You're early."

"So are you." I grinned as I walked towards her.

"I like to do yoga in the morning. Figured I'd get some in before you showed me what you do." She smiled. It was a genuine smile, not like the terse ones she'd flung at me the day before. She looked different, her hair in a ponytail at the base of her head and her suit replaced with yoga pants and a tight tank top. I could tell she was slender when I was running after my eyes first landed on her, but now that I really saw her body, I could see she was toned. Muscles in all the right places and two perky breasts that were begging to be sucked.

"Are you checking me out again?" She sighed, crossing her arms over her chest.

I put my bag down and opened it up, pulling out the ball. "I can't help it, love. You're wearing all that spandex goodness." I put my fist in my mouth as I tried to fight back the urge to take a bite out of her arse. "Remind me to thank the man who made yoga pants, by the way."

"How do you know it was a man?" Delaney said with a smile.

"Only a man would think of something as ingenious as pants like that."

She shifted, a blush creeping across her cheeks.

"All right. It's my night-time and I'm super jet-lagged, so let's get this going," she responded as she walked away a bit and stood with her feet farther apart. I didn't have the heart to tell her we were playing footy and not sumo wrestling, because she was damned cute looking like she was going to charge at me. She brushed a piece of hair behind her ear that had fallen into her face. "We need to talk about revamping your image, so lay it on me."

Clutching the ball in my hand, I raised my eyebrow. She certainly had a way with words.

"Oh, you damn perv. I meant footy. What's it about? What's the purpose?" she asked.

"Please tell me you at least watched American football when you were over in New York?" I asked. I walked towards her as she straightened. She opened her mouth to speak but abruptly shut it.

"Hell, woman. You're not even a Yank. Don't all Yanks watch football and eat chicken wings?"

"I'm not a Yank! I was born and raised right here in the

North Shore, thank you very much. And no, I never watched football. No time for silly games." She shrugged.

Lunging closer, I stood in front of her and placed the ball in her hands. "Footy is not just a silly game. It's my life," I stated.

Her eyes grew wide at my proximity. Refocusing, she reached down and took the ball from my hands. "What do I do with this?" She held it far away from her body like it was breakable.

"I'm going to run away a bit and you throw it at me."

"I think I like this game already," she said with a smile.

Taking her hand in mine, I positioned her fingers at the end of the ball. "Hold it like this," I said, just as a shock radiated through our bodies, causing us to both drop the ball.

"Static," she said as she bent over to pick it up. I nodded as I shifted my semihard dick in my pants.

The tension swirled around us and for the first time in forever, I didn't have something smart to say.

"You better run, Casanova, before I pelt this at your head," she promised.

I smiled, thankful she'd broken the awkwardness. I didn't do awkward, which was probably why I settled for fucking more than using my words.

Running away, I watched her throw the ball and smile wide when I caught it. The throw was wobbly but watching her jump up and down, her boobs joining in on the excitement, well, footy became even more of my favourite sport.

"Good job. Now let me throw it to you."

She smiled and started running away.

I threw a bullet, certain that no way in hell she'd catch it. Opening her arms, she eyed the ball with a fierceness I'd seen in many of my competitors. She stopped, keeping her eye on the ball, her hands wide. It was like slow motion, the ball spinning, me holding my breath as she closed her eyes. Not sure how she planned on catching the ball when she couldn't see where the hell it was coming from. Then she slowly opened her eyes just as the ball made its way into her hands.

"Yes!" she screamed. I fist-pumped the air as she did a little victory dance. Jogging towards her, I gave her a high five. "Did you really just give me a high five?" she asked through a laugh.

"Yeah?" I was confused. What else was I supposed to do? Pretty sure if I hugged her, she'd punch me in my dick. And truth be told, I was fond of the thing.

"You give your teammates high fives when they do an awesome play like that?" She questioned.

"No. I slap their arses," I taunted.

She stopped dancing as her mouth formed a perfect O shape at my response. With a grin, I raised my hand to tease her. Normally the women I was around would run around squealing and giggling, but not Delaney. Her shoulders squared off, her lips pursing into a little scowl.

"You had your fun. Now we talk." She stormed away, heading back towards the parking building. "I'm showering and changing. Meet me outside my hotel in forty-five minutes."

After telling me which hotel that was, I watched her walk away for a minute, letting myself admire the view. Well, that was fun until she went all Dr Jekyll and Mr Hyde on me.

I picked up the ball, ran to my bag, and shoved it in. Everything had been going so well. What had I done to flip the switch? There was more to Delaney than met the eye. She could try to hide behind her professionalism but there was no fooling me. She wanted me just like I wanted her, and I was going to love making her admit that.

Chapter Four

DELANEY

It had been weeks since I stepped into the life of Mason St Patrick. It felt more like months, years even. Not because he was horrible to be around, but because I've been enjoying his company. Shocker, right, but the guy was growing on me and we just meshed well together.

"Mason!" I banged on the door to his house as I checked my phone yet again. We were supposed to have a meeting at 8:00 a.m. It was currently eight twenty, and no Mason. "Wake up!" I banged harder as I finally heard feet coming down the stairs.

I heard the door unlock and shoved my phone in my bag.

"Morning, love." Mason's voice enveloped me. Glancing up, I tried to not let my mouth hang open. Other than his skintight and dangerously short boxer briefs, he was completely naked.

"Cat got your tongue?" he asked as he tilted his head to the side. It was adorable and pissed me off.

I glared at him and pushed him aside, walking into his house. Over the past few weeks, this had become our routine. We came up with a plan for him to stop drinking which would hopefully eliminate the fighting. I watched him closely and made sure he didn't say or do something to screw up again. He spewed sexual innuendos in my direction and I tried to pretend that I didn't find him attractive or picture his face between my legs. It'd been a hellish few weeks because I did find him attractive and I did picture him every night between my legs as I tried to pleasure myself. I'd already run through two sets of batteries. I was frustrated with myself because this reaction wasn't normal for me. I tried my best to ignore it, but every second I spent with Mason solidified that he was indeed getting to me.

"We had a meeting at eight to discuss your appearance at the charity function, remember?" I said as I followed Mason into the kitchen. I sat on a stool and watched him reach into the cabinet and pull out two mugs.

His back muscles pulled and flexed as he moved. I liked when he was turned around because I could admire the view as much as I wanted and he couldn't see me. A perfect time to check out the merchandise without having to hear his dirty mouth.

"You know the stove is reflective, right?" he said as he turned around and grinned. Well, damn. All these weeks I'd been staring at his arse thinking I'd been stealthy. Showed what I knew.

I shrugged. "You're practically naked." I opened my bag to pretend that I was looking for something. "Can't help that I appreciate the male form," I mumbled.

"I can show you what practically naked looks like," he teased as he walked towards me, running his fingers across the seam of his underwear.

"Enough. Gimme." Reaching out, I took my cup of coffee as he sat across from me. "So, your coaches have noticed a great improvement with your game. Your stamina's back and no screw-ups," I said, shuffling through some papers.

Mason smiled. "Excellent."

"Now that you aren't partying and screwing anything with a vagina, we need to get you a date for this charity event. I saw some footage of you and your ex. You guys were great. What was her name?" I asked nonchalantly.

He clenched his jaw as he took a sip of coffee. All of his muscles tightened, like a pulley I was afraid would break at any second. I tried not to notice his reaction, but Mason was generally pretty carefree. This was a side of him I'd never seen before.

"Rachel," he said as he stood up and went to the sink to put his mug in. The cup was full and I watched him pour the contents down the drain.

"That's practically murder." I stared at him as he turned around.

"What?" he asked, looking around his kitchen.

"That coffee, what did it ever do to you?" I held my mug

and inhaled the sweet scent. Coffee was my life. I drank way too much, but it kept me going. "It needs to be cherished. Worshipped, stroked, and cared for." I took a sip.

"Are we talking about coffee or my dick?"

I nearly choked as Mason blinked at me. I loved that about him. When he was being crude he didn't always grin or laugh afterwards, because he was usually being serious.

"Coffee." I set it down. "Back to what I asked. What happened with Rachel, anyway? I know how the media misconstrues everything. I could use some background to know what I'm working with, and Oliver won't tell me a damn thing." I relaxed in the chair. I'd been trying to get in his good graces to find out about Rachel, curious as to why any woman would leave Mason. He seemed to have all his shit together when he was with Rachel, and despite my immunity to male advances, Mason seemed to be a contradiction to that rule.

He gripped the side of the counter, his eyes burning with anger. "It doesn't fucking matter. It happened. End of story." He let out a frustrated breath.

I fought the urge to reach out and move his hair out of his face. He needed someone to tell him he wasn't ruined; maybe a bit misguided, but deep down he was a good guy.

"All right." I put up my hands in defeat. "You need a date for Saturday's event. Which is two days away. And not one of those whores you used to mess around with." I knew he had a phone full of women who he could call on a moment's notice. I was thankful that I hadn't had any encounters with any of them.

Mason let go of the counter, the colour returning to his hands.

"A date? I don't date," he said as he walked back over to me.

"Okay, I can find someone for you. Not a problem. I think it will be good for your image. Take a lady out, treat her right. Show the media a different side for a change other than your tongue down someone's throat," I said, gathering my stuff to head out. I slung my bag over my shoulder, trying not to steal one last glance at his abs. "I'll see you tomorrow to help pick out your suit."

I turned the knob for the door and opened it slightly before a large weight hit it.

"You come with me Saturday," he whispered close to my ear.

"What?" I looked up at him and blinked excessively. Me go with him? I was going to sit it out. I didn't want rumours to spread about Mason and me. Already we'd had to issue a statement that I was his PR rep and helping with some things. Apparently, the press immediately assumed Mason was screwing any woman by his side.

"You know what I need to seal this deal that I'm a changed man. You come with me."

I shook my head. "Bad idea. Everyone will think we're together."

"Ah, love." He touched my cheek. "What's wrong with that?" he said with the cheesiest grin on his face.

"Everything. I'm a professional, and I can't have myself connected to you in any way that could insinuate anything romantic or that we're sleeping together." I huffed and pulled at the door. It didn't budge. Damn, he was strong.

"I didn't say anything about sleeping together. But if you insist." He reached down to his boxers again and started to pull them down.

I grabbed his hand to stop him. "You're incorrigible."

"I've been called worse. Just professional. No funny business." Mason smiled and I swear my knees almost buckled.

Okay. Even through everything I'd been taught, and all the times I'd watched women in my shoes make the same mistake, there was something about a barely dressed Mason that did things to me. Hell, a fully dressed Mason did things to me. I was in desperate need of some quality time with my battery-operated friend, to buzz away the thoughts of him. I fought back a smile. That was how I was going to spend the rest of my day. *Note to self, you need more batteries.*

Mason did have a point. I could go as a professional and make sure he didn't screw things up. Leaving him to choose someone would be a bad idea, and honestly, I didn't have the time. I had clients in New York that I had been neglecting due to being here. And because of the time difference, I worked crazy hours to keep them content.

"Fine. Professional only. If anyone asks, I'm just there in a professional capacity, nothing more."

"Got it." He nodded. "So tomorrow I'll have my driver come get you at ten and we'll get my outfit."

"Perfect." I pulled on the door again. "Can you let me out, please?"

"Only because you said please." He opened the door and I stepped outside, turning back around to say goodbye. Or to look at him one last time. It was a win-win.

I sighed, waving goodbye as I hightailed it to my car. Clutching my steering wheel, I let out a scream.

"Idiot!" I yelled. "I shouldn't have said yes." My mind had been nothing but a jumbled mess since I'd arrived. Not just my mind, but my body. Everything vibrated whenever Mason was around. I hated it with a fierce passion because no matter how hard I tried to fight it, giving it time, trying to pleasure myself, it didn't work. All I could think about was him.

His reputation was something I knew inside and out. Fuck, I'd been hired to fix his image. Yet all of that seemed secondary to the person I'd seen over the past weeks. While I had gotten nowhere with what happened between him and Rachel, I knew that there was more to Mason St Patrick than everyone knew. Maybe, just maybe, the booze, women, and fighting masked a pain so deep that he hid it from the world. All I knew was that I had to wrap this up faster than I'd anticipated, because the more I was around Mason, the less control I seemed to have.

Chapter Five

MASON

I shut the door and fought back the urge to do a little dance in my underdaks. I finally got Delaney to go out with me. Okay, well kind of. She would be working and it would be professional, but over the past few weeks she'd been loosening up around me. Becoming more comfortable. I knew I had to seduce her, show her a side of me that no one had seen. I intended to do just that. It'd been a while since I was interested in a woman for anything more than one night. Where the hell did I start?

"Oliver, I need you," I pleaded into my phone.

"*You* need *me*?" He snickered. "I want it to go down in the history books that on this day, Mason James St Patrick—"

"Oh stuff it. Come on. Help me, mate. I need to plan something for Delaney."

My request was met with silence.

"Mason, you better not be screwing with me. She's a good woman, not like these groupies who hang around and suck you off whenever you want."

I laughed as I paced my floor. My nerves were in overdrive. This had to be perfect. "Seriously. I haven't wanted to screw anyone else since she came around."

"She's your PR rep. She's trying to change your image. You can't screw anyone or she'd castrate you."

I plopped down on the couch. "I know, but it's more than that. I like her. I like the way she tries not to stare at me. How when she smiles it stretches across her face and lights up her eyes." I paused, picturing her doing yoga and those pants that hugged all the right parts of her. "And I love the way her arse looks in those stretchy pants."

Oliver laughed. "There's the Mason I know."

"I'm serious. She agreed to go to the charity event with me Saturday. Professional terms, of course, but I know deep down she likes me too. I just need to show her that I'm not a man whore."

Oliver scoffed.

"Okay, so I was a man whore. But I don't want to be anymore. Rachel ruined me. Left me when I needed her the most because I worked too much and didn't give her enough attention. I was too busy trying to make a life for us. For our future family." I ran my hands across my couch to try to find my words. "Delaney makes me forget what happened and have hope that maybe I can love someone again."

Oliver sighed. "All right. I'll be over in an hour and we'll plan a day for tomorrow that will make any girl swoon."

I grinned. "Thank you. I owe you."

"You've owed me since high school. I'll collect someday. For now, I'll just keep racking them up," Oliver added before hanging up.

It was true. Oliver had been there for me since I could remember. I caught some kids roughing him around in high school and felt bad for the bugger. I told them to fuck off and since that day, we were inseparable. He was smart. While I wasn't dumb, I leaned towards sports, especially footy. When he saw me play for the first time he wrote up a five-year plan and started marketing me. He's the reason I'm a professional footy player. He had the vision and I had the skill. We made a perfect team.

***

"Holy fuck. I'm nervous," I announced.
Oliver laughed as he handed me a sheet of paper. "Here's the itinerary for the day."

I clutched the paper. "Itinerary?" I scrunched my nose at the map of my day.

"Delaney is organised. She'll appreciate it. Trust me." He smiled and smacked me on the shoulder. "Open doors, tell her she looks nice—"

I rolled my eyes at Oliver's lecture. "I'm not an idiot. I know how to take care of a lady," I stated.

He raised his eyebrow before breaking into uncontrollable laughter.

"Okay. It's been a while for you. Just didn't want you to pinch her nipples and think that's appropriate," Oliver said jokingly. I punched him in the arm.

"Fuck off." I scowled.

He put both hands on my shoulders. "In all seriousness, good luck. Delaney is a good woman."

"You know her so well. Why didn't you go after her?" I tensed. Maybe he'd had a fling with her.

"No. We're just friends. I've had my mind set on someone else," he replied as he moved away and pulled out his phone.

I snapped my fingers, the realisation of who it was coming to me. "It's Celeste, isn't it? You always had a thing for smart women. Isn't she some big-shot doctor now?"

"Yes. Now fuck off." He gave me the finger and I chuckled, shutting the door behind me.

I was a little rattled because I wanted everything to be perfect. It'd been years since I'd taken a woman on a date, especially a woman who tried so hard to resist her feelings for me. Smiling as I glanced at the itinerary Oliver had helped me make, I slipped into the back of the limo, my confidence rising. It was time for me to woo the ever-loving shit out of Delaney Matthews and show her I was a man capable of something other than a quick screw.

Chapter Six

DELANEY

Pacing up and down my hotel room, I thought of all the reasons why I shouldn't go. I could tell him I had gastro. That would work. I'd just pulled out my phone to type out a message to Mason when there was a knock at my door.

"Dammit!" I muttered, grabbing my bag and opening the door.

"Hello, love." Mason leaned against my doorframe. Jeans gripped his thighs and a T-shirt moulded to his body. I wanted to be the doorframe or the T-shirt. I'd even be the jeans, just to feel his legs pressed against me. I looked down at the floor, cursing myself for not cancelling sooner. It wasn't going to be easy to resist his sex appeal. But did I want to resist? I wasn't so sure anymore. The rapid beat of my heart against my chest made me second-guess why I was resisting him. *Oh yeah, he's my client and a man whore. Ding ding!*

"Hey. Where to today?" I pulled up the notes on my phone. "I have a few designer places that we can go to and—"

He ripped the phone from my hands and shoved it in his pants pocket. I lunged for it and he grinned.

"You can go in and fetch it if you want," Mason taunted. I rolled my eyes and had to hold my hand back for fear it'd go digging around for my phone.

"I need it to do my job." I held out my hand.

"I'm your primary job right now, so I need your undivided attention today, okay?" Mason asked.

I crossed my arms over my chest. "Okay. What for?"

"You're too stressed out. I've got plans for us today. Shall we?" He held out his hand.

His outstretched hand called to me. If I took it, I was giving up control. My body ached at the thought of giving in to Mason, letting him kiss every inch of my body and ravish me with his mouth. I knew he could use it. He'd had enough practice for the both of us. I liked being in control; a regimented schedule was what had kept Mason on track these last weeks, but somehow the thought of throwing that out the window for just a few hours turned me on.

"Stop overthinking everything. Take my hand and trust me."

I looked into Mason's eyes and was met with an expression that made my breath hitch in my throat. Even though there was a lot about Mason that should have made me run in the other direction, the man standing before me was different. He was changing, and that was enough for me to take his hand and allow him to take the lead.

"Do you trust me?" he whispered, his hand still outstretched.

"The only thing I don't trust is oatmeal cookies."

He looked at me and tilted his head to the side.

"What?" he asked, letting out a small laugh.

"I hate oatmeal cookies. If you don't look close enough they look like chocolate chips. You take a bite expecting one thing, and bam, raisins. That's where my trust issues stem from." With that, I placed my hand in his.

He gripped it tight and ran his thumb across the top of my hand.

"Don't worry. I'm a chocolate chip," he said seriously.

"Duly noted," I replied with a smile.

We walked hand in hand down the back corridor of the hotel. Something about it seemed so normal, like I wasn't walking with the biggest footy star in Australia. I didn't know the side of Mason everyone else saw. I just knew the man, and he was fantastic and funny. I closed my eyes as I realised what I was thinking. I brushed it all aside and took my hand from his as he opened the door to exit the hotel.

"Your chariot," Mason said as he motioned to a limo stretched across the street. I glanced up at him as my eyes widened.

"Mason, this is too much. We're just supposed to be going to a few stores."

He opened the door for me and I slid inside. There was champagne already open and chilled. The leather seats felt like butter against my body and I sighed, letting my head roll back against the seat.

"Nothing's too much for you. You deserve the world." He sat next to me, placed his hand on my knee and caressed it. That simple motion sent my body whirling with want and need so deep I feared I'd strip down right there and give all of myself to him. I still couldn't figure out if that was a bad idea or not.

My mouth hung open. Was this Mason? The smart-mouthed, dirty-humoured man I was used to? I wasn't sure which one I liked more, because this side of him was fucking hot. Everything I'd been taught and held true to my character seemed pointless now. I was kind of growing to like this man in front of me.

"Catching flies?" he asked, slowly closing my mouth with his hand. He opened a compartment and pulled out a container. I took the minute he was distracted and not being totally swoon-worthy to roll down the window and watch the familiar sights of Sydney fly by as we drove. In all the weeks I'd been there, I'd never visited the places I remembered from my childhood. I worked myself into the ground and never gave myself any time to just live. Maybe Mason was onto something.

"Close your eyes," he requested. I turned to face him and was met with the most devilish smile.

"What?" I wrung my hands together in my lap. He was going to kiss me. I couldn't let that happen. I'd be like putty in his hands with the way my mind and body were right then.

"Relax. I want you aware when I kiss you." He leaned closer to me, his mouth close to my ear. "Because I will kiss you. But not now, love, so close your eyes. Remember what I said." He inhaled. "Trust me."

And I'm wet.

I let his words sink in. Everything was happening too fast. Mason had gone from being annoying and a certified man whore to sweet with a mix of sex. I loved all sides of him, and that scared me the most. He'd asked me to trust him, and even though everything I knew about him told me that he was going to be nothing be trouble, I closed my eyes.

I focused on my breathing as I listened to him fiddle with something.

"Open your mouth," he asked again. As I slowly opened, he gently put a spoonful of something so light and airy into my mouth that I moaned.

I opened my eyes. Mason stared back at me, his smile turned into a seductive smirk. The fire in his eyes didn't make me shift. I loved when he looked at me because it was like I was the only woman in the world.

"What is that? It's so good." I moaned again, bringing my hand to my lips.

"Pavlova. My mum used to make it." There was melancholy in his voice and I found myself wanting to know everything about Mason. What was his family like? Had he had a good childhood?

My tongue grew heavy in my mouth and I swallowed. It felt like knives running along my throat.

"Wait, what kind of fruit is in that?" I asked. Mason's eyes widened. He shuffled for the bowl and opened it, looking inside.

"Just meringue, but it has kiwi and peaches on top."

I brought my hand to my throat as I felt it closing.

"I'm deathly allergic to peaches," I whispered, the pain becoming too much to bear.

"Ah hell." Mason banged on the divider between us and the driver. "Hospital. Quickly, please."

"In my purse. My EpiPen," I managed to get out.

All I remembered was Mason telling me it was going to be all right. The only plus to passing out was that in my dreams there was a shirtless Mason. And that was enough to make me smile.

Chapter Seven

MASON

I was going to put a hole in the floor if the doctor didn't come tell me what the hell was going on. Delaney had passed out in my arms, and I'd followed the directions on the EpiPen and injected her in the thigh. I almost puked as it dug into her skin, but when I heard her let out a staggered breath I knew I'd do it a thousand more times.

"Damn. Is she going to be okay?" Oliver ran around the corner and brought me into a quick hug.

"I don't know. They haven't come out yet. I screwed up." I hung my head.

"Mason, you couldn't have known. It's not your fault."

I'd opened my mouth to protest when the doctor came around the corner.

Playing for Keeps

"You're Mason St Patrick, aren't you?" the doctor asked with a smile.

"Yes. Not the time to be star-struck. Fucking focus," I ground out. My voice was about two octaves too high but I didn't care. Oliver squeezed my shoulder to keep me level-headed because right then I was anything but.

I took a deep breath and asked, "How's my girl?"

The doctor raised his eyebrow. "She's fine. You can see her whenever. You saved her life with the EpiPen. Hey, um, can I have your autograph?" He put what I assumed was Delaney's chart underneath his arm. What didn't he understand of what I'd just said? I was about to punch him square in the face when Oliver came to the rescue.

"How about I send you some autographed gear, Doctor? To show our appreciation for all you did for Mason's girl," Oliver said as he put his arm around the doctor's shoulders. He winked at me as the doctor talked animatedly to him. Once again, Oliver had saved me.

I rushed to Delaney's room, avoiding the whispers and stares of all the nurses. All I cared about was getting to her and seeing with my own eyes that she was okay.

"Delaney?" After gently knocking on her door, it then creaked open. She was lying back in the bed, her eyes shut.

"Hey. Some date I am, huh?" She gave me a small smile.

I pulled up a chair next to her and took her hand in mine.

"You said date." I grinned.

She fidgeted and tried to sit up. "Oh, I didn't mean…. I just—" Her stammering made me laugh.

"It was a date." I pulled the itinerary from my pocket. "I

had a whole day planned."

She looked over the plans and I saw tears glisten in her eyes.

"Hey. What's wrong?" I scooted her over on the bed and slid in next to her, pulling her close against my chest.

"Nothing." She looked away. Gently, I took her chin and moved her face in my direction again.

"It's something. Tell me," I said softly.

She sniffed. "No one's ever done anything like this for me. Thank you."

I gave her a sad smile. "Stick with me and there'll be plenty more where that came from."

Stiffening, she sat up and held out her hand.

"Can I have my phone? This is going to be a nightmare." Back to business. Pulling it from my pocket, I gave it to her.

"Jesus. Apparently, I'm a druggie now. And the press is here. My boss is going to kill me," she murmured. She patted down her hair. "How do I look?"

I jumped from her bed.

"What?" she asked.

"This has to end. They are so fucking annoying, making up damn stories about people. Not you. They won't mess with you." I looked out the window at the press that lined the entrance to the hospital. "I'll find every one of them who said you were a druggie and—"

"It's okay. Take a breath. You can't storm the entire city and punch people because of me. I messed up by agreeing to go out with you," Delaney said.

I stopped pacing and stared at her. "Don't. It wasn't a

mistake. We both wanted it."

She looked at her phone as it vibrated in her hand, the message causing her to scowl.

"I'm getting discharged in a bit. You go home and I'll go to my hotel. We can't be seen together. Not after all of this." Her eyes flitted back to the window, avoiding my stare.

"Delaney, I—" I moved towards her and she put up her hand. I wanted to tell her what she meant to me. How I was falling for her.

"We have to protect your image. Until I can debunk these rumours of me being a druggie, it's best if we aren't seen together."

"I don't care what they say. I am taking you home and taking care of you," I stated.

"Oliver can do it. Now go," she pleaded. "Please." Tears glistened in her eyes again. Why couldn't she just let me take care of her? I didn't care about the press or any of that shit. All I cared about was her.

"Go! I'll fix this. It's what I do best," she added with a small smile.

She was pushing me away because of some stupid information that wasn't even true. I was immune to the press now. They'd captured me at my worst and I let it roll off me. But Delaney wasn't used to being on this side of things. She worked from the sidelines and always followed the rules. This mess was killing her. She was doing what she thought she had to in order to protect me, her client. Leaving her with the tears and stubborn attitude, I stormed out of the room and ran right into Oliver.

"What the hell," he said, rubbing his shoulder.

"She's pushing me away. I had her. And then—boom." I made an explosive motion with my hand.

"It's her job to make sure your image is sound. This makes it harder. She could lose her job, Mason," Oliver reminded me.

"She can come back home where she belongs instead of prancing around New York City!" I yelled. A few heads turned. I ground my teeth together. Oliver just stared at me. "And who cares about her job. I'll take care of her," I whispered.

"Then show her. Don't give up so easily."

Oliver slipped into Delaney's room, leaving me with his advice. I was going to show her. I wouldn't give up that easy.

Delaney was going to be mine.

Chapter Eight

DELANEY

Oliver dropped me off at my hotel and I sent him on his way. I didn't want to be alone, but Mason's best friend keeping me company wasn't the best idea. Even though I'd told Mason to leave, I wanted to feel his body next to me in bed, his hands stroking my hair as he told me it was going to be all right. It was my job to fix his image and now, I might have ruined everything.

I stripped down and crawled into bed, letting the coolness of the sheets envelop me. I wanted to wallow in my own self-pity just for a few hours before getting my shit together and fixing this nightmare. I'd screwed up. I'd let my emotions take control, something I always avoided for this very reason, and Mason was paying for my mistake.

I must have fallen asleep because the sound of knocking at my door startled me awake. I reluctantly exited the bed and wrapped the robe hanging from the door around my body.

"Yes?" I said as I opened the door. One of the hotel staff was standing in front of me with an armful of stuff.

"For you, Miss Matthews."

"I'm sorry, you must have the wrong room. I didn't order anything."

He glanced at the note in his hand. "It's from a Mr St Patrick. May I put this down, ma'am?"

I stood there blankly with what I was sure was shock on my face. "Oh yeah. I'm sorry, please come in," I finally said.

He laid the bags on the couch and latched the door behind him when he left. I leapt over to the bags.

First, I unzipped the large garment bag. I gasped, running my fingers across the long, stunning red dress with a dangerously high slit that screamed Mason. I squealed and opened the shoebox. A pair of high-heeled beaded black shoes glistened back at me.

"Oh, you're good, Mason." I slipped them on; they moulded to my feet with perfection. I strutted around the room, stopping at the mirror to admire how they looked. They made my legs longer and shapelier, and I knew they'd go nicely with the dress.

I went back over to the packages and saw two jewellery boxes. I ran my fingers over the top of the blue Tiffany and Company boxes, the smile never leaving my face. I wasn't the type of woman to be bought, but I didn't think that's what Mason intended. I never really dressed up, other than my suits and boring outfits for work, and looking at these things, I knew I'd feel like a princess.

I opened the jewellery boxes. Two beautiful diamond-studded heart earrings and a matching bracelet shone back at me.

I fell onto the couch, overwhelmed by the gifts Mason had sent. I pulled out the envelope that had my name scrawled across it.

I'm sorry for how things ended between us today. I had no intention of practically killing you. Although, it could have been a ploy to get in your bed. I mean, I did end up snuggled next to you.

I know the press are being fuck heads right now, but you know what I say? They can all go to hell. The press has been a thorn in my side since I started playing footy. It's the one part of the game I hate, always being under their microscope. I got used to it, though, and I realised when you asked me to leave that you've never been on this side of the camera.

Tomorrow at six, my driver will come pick you up. Please give me another chance. We can fix this mess, together.

I know you feel a connection with me. I see it in your eyes when you let yourself look at me. Just don't go living in your head and blaming yourself for what happened. If anyone is to blame, it should be the fool who made you eat peaches.

Wear the dress, the jewellery, and please don't forget those shoes. Or you can just come in the shoes. That'd be just fine with me.

Give me a chance, love. I promise I won't let you down
Yours if you'll let me be,

Mason

I clutched the letter and leaned back against the couch. I did have feelings for Mason. But now that I'd accepted it, I was more confused than ever. Where would it leave us? I lived in New York and he lived in Sydney. I wasn't sure if I was willing to put myself out there for someone when I didn't even know where it would go. It was too late, though; I had already fallen. I just needed to figure out how far I was willing to go.

Chapter Nine

MASON

I was proud of myself. I hadn't even asked Oliver for help with Delaney's surprise. I went to the stores myself, picked out everything that I thought would look amazing on her, and hoped that it would be enough to convince her to give us a chance.

It was seven and there was no sign of her, and my driver wasn't answering. Currently, I was knee-deep in people who were bragging about how much money they donated and how they were the biggest sponsor. The only place I wanted to be was with Delaney. She'd made her choice, though, and that wasn't me.

"You okay?" Oliver came up behind me and handed me a drink.

"I'm good. Did she leave?" I asked as I took the drink from him and placed it on the table. It was non-alcoholic; all I wanted was some rum to drown my feelings.

"I don't know. She won't answer my calls. I doubt she did. She's not one to run. She'll finish out her contract."

I nodded. She'd just ignore me in every way possible.

"I thought we had something. I put myself out there for the first time, and nothing." I shook my head in disbelief at my stupidity.

Oliver sat down next to me and let out a sigh that held all of my frustration.

"Hey, Mason. I've missed you."

I looked up just as a blonde snaked her arms around my shoulders. I blinked at her, trying to remember her name.

"Lisa. From the game in Melbourne." She smacked her gum annoyingly.

"Right." I undid her arms. "Sorry. I'm not interested."

She pouted. "You're all alone. I can keep you company."

"He said he's not interested. What about those words don't you understand?"

I turned around and there she stood, my Delaney. The red dress was accentuated by her long dark hair that was pulled into an updo. Tendrils fell around her face, kissing her cheeks. The slit was high up her leg. The shoes glistened on her feet, causing my dick to instantly harden.

That was all small in comparison to the fact that she'd come. She was there.

"You came," I said as I stood up, and she wrapped her arms around my waist.

"I did. I mean, I couldn't let the dress and shoes go to waste." Her cheek was pressed against my chest but I couldn't miss the smile in her voice.

"You look beautiful," I added as I stepped back to look at her again.

"You have good taste." She motioned to the dress and shoes.

"I do." I brought her in closer, brushing my lips against hers. Oliver cleared his throat and mumbled something about heading to talk to someone. I didn't care; I was finally kissing Delaney, something I'd imagined for the past few weeks. It was better than I'd dreamed. Her soft lips were easily coaxed open with my tongue. She melted against me as my hands roamed her body.

"I can't wait to get this dress off you." My words were met with a giggle.

Ed Sheeran's "Give me Love" played and Delaney swayed to the music.

"Want to dance?" I asked as I held my hand out for her. Without a second thought, she put her hand in mine. We danced, murmurs of our relationship buzzing around. I had a big interview the next morning that Delaney had arranged to explain my behaviour, and I would make it clear that Delaney was my girl. There would be no more Lisas, no more blow jobs in the locker room—unless Delaney wanted to, of course. Mason St Patrick was officially off the market.

***

GOING *South*

The night died down. I'd spent most of it wrapped around Delaney on the dance floor. Where normally I'd be piss drunk and balls deep in some random chick, this was far better.

I brushed the tendrils of hair out of her face. "Come home with me," I whispered.

Her eyes widened. "To your house? To do what?" she asked as she tucked the same piece of hair behind her ear.

"Stuff," I said as I raised my eyebrow.

"Like sex?" she asked, and I choked on a laugh.

"I won't say no to sex. But I just want to be with you. It has been a while, though." I adjusted myself. A blush formed on her cheeks when she realised what she did to me.

That blush was quickly replaced with Delaney's normal sass. "It's been a few weeks. I think you'll survive." She rolled her eyes.

"I have survived, but only because I've been waiting on you." Before I let her reply I kissed her again, slipping in my tongue and grabbing her neck. I couldn't control how badly I wanted her anymore. Now that she'd let me in, I was never letting her go.

Breathlessly she pulled her lips from mine. "To your house, then," she said with a smirk.

I told my driver to step on it and we made it to my house in record time. All I knew was that if Delaney didn't stop fidgeting in the seat next to me, I'd have to keep her still by pressing my body against hers.

"Why are you so nervous?" I asked, grabbing her hand as we made our way towards my bedroom.

"I haven't been completely honest with you," Delaney said.

I dropped her hand and turned to face her.

"Oh God. Don't tell me you're married or something." My mind went to some dark places. That was it. That was why Delaney was so hesitant to go out with me. She had some guy at home. Probably kids….

"No! No!" she screeched. "I, um…." She took off her shoes and placed them on the floor by the bed.

"Bloody hell! Spit it out, woman!" My heart beat erratically in my chest. What the hell wasn't she telling me?

"I've never had sex before, okay! I'm a virgin." Her chest heaved. I tried to fight the smile that ached to spread across my face. I would be the first and last to make her come.

I closed the distance between us and brought her into my arms. "That's the hottest thing any woman's ever said to me."

"It doesn't bother you that I've never had sex with anyone before? I don't know what I'm doing." She looked down at the ground.

"Look at me, love." Slowly, she brought her eyes to mine. "It will be my pleasure to show you what to do."

She grinned. "Stop talking and kiss me. Show me how dirty you can be, Mason," Delaney murmured.

"I won't deny it," I replied as I played with the straps of her dress. "I'm a dirty man who's done some awful things. But since I met you…. You make me want to be better." A tear escaped Delaney's eye and I brushed it away.

"Now let's take this off you." I moved behind her and slowly unzipped her dress. I fought back the urge to take a bite out of her arse on display before me in just a G-string. She didn't have a bra on; her back was completely exposed to me.

I brushed kisses on any part of her naked skin I could, and she moaned and writhed in pleasure.

"Easy." I led her to the bed and laid her down. Her nipples hardened as I shimmied down her underwear.

"You're perfect," I whispered against her ear.

"To you I may be perfect," she said with a sigh.

"And that's all that matters."

She put her hands above her head, showcasing her round breasts to me. I wanted to bite the hell out of her nipples, but I figured I'd save that for another night because there would be many more nights with Delaney.

"I'm feeling slightly underdressed," Delaney said with a sly smile. Quickly, I tossed off my clothes as she leaned over and gathered up her heels.

"Woman, you're a minx." I groaned as I watched her seductively put back on her shoes.

"I do recall you wanting me to wear just these." She stood up, naked but for her heels, on display in front of me. I was a lucky man.

It was official. It wasn't a matter of what I was missing, but who, and it was Delaney Matthews.

I knelt before her, and she gasped as I spread her lips and slowly lapped my tongue between her wet folds. Fisting my hair, she pushed my mouth farther against her as I nibbled and tongued her clit. Falling onto the bed, I held her down as her body shook around me, her cum spilling into my mouth. I licked up each bit of her, not wanting a drop to go to waste.

"Holy fuck," she murmured. I thought she'd be exhausted, but she arched her back as she moved her hands down to touch herself.

"What do you want, Delaney? Tell me what you want." I looked down at her as she spread herself open and slid her fingers in and out.

"You inside me. I need you inside me," she said breathlessly.

Opening my bedside drawer, I ripped open a condom and rolled it on.

Positioning myself on top of her, I hovered for a moment, letting our bodies mould together.

Delaney looked at me, a hesitation—almost a fear—in her eyes.

"It will hurt for just a minute. I'll be gentle." She nodded as I positioned my dick at her centre. Heat radiated off her, and I slid in as she clenched her body around me.

"Relax." I put some of my weight on her so I could whisper in her ear. "I won't hurt you."

"I know. I trust you," she said.

"It's about damn time." Slowly, I slid in and out as she finally started to relax around me.

"Go faster," she demanded. I moved my body up and looked down at her.

"Are you sure?" I asked.

"Yes. You feel so good." She pulled me down, and my dick thrust inside her. She was tight, her pussy wrapping around my cock like it was made just for me.

"Oh God, Mason. Don't stop."

The sound of my name sent me over the edge, my body tightening as I released inside her. It was unlike any orgasm I'd ever experienced. Usually it was fast and I couldn't get the woman off me quick enough, but this was different. My dick twitched inside her, filling the condom to the brim with my cum. Delaney's own orgasm swirled around me, grabbing me just as she had the moment I first saw her. Watching her lose control, finally letting herself just feel and be, put a smile on my face.

I slid off her, carefully removed the condom, tossed it aside, and brought her close against my body.

"Are you okay?" I asked as I smoothed down her hair.

"Yes, just a little sore and tired." Her voice was barely a whisper as her eyes shut.

"Okay, love. Let's go to sleep." Turning over, I clicked off the light and brought her back into my arms. I listened to her heart beating, the little sounds she made in her sleep. I finally had Delaney Matthews, and I was never letting her go.

Chapter Ten

DELANEY

I stared down at Mason, the muscles expanding across his chest. I was no longer a virgin. I'd given it to him because these past weeks, I'd grown rather fond of him. I was so fond of him that I had to leave. It made no sense to run instead of talking this through with him, but even though I was a PR queen, when it came to me? Yeah, I had no clue what I was doing. Now I was mixed in with Mason's life and had no idea how to fix it.

I couldn't make him choose. We didn't have a history that tied us together. There was nothing that would make him choose me. I had my job in New York and he had his footy career in Australia. I could move back home to Australia and get a job, but damn, I was afraid. Afraid of all the feelings that happened so quickly for a man I barely knew. I wasn't well versed in how to handle my own shit, so leaving seemed best for me to gain some insight, step away from Mason and hopefully get my head on straight.

I placed my dress, shoes, and jewellery on his couch. Slipping into a pair of his shorts and T-shirt, I left a note that I hoped would explain my thoughts.

Mason,

I'm sorry I left without saying goodbye. The past few weeks have been interesting, that's for sure. I couldn't resist your charm, your carefree nature. Okay, mostly I couldn't resist your rock-hard abs.

You're a good person. I'm not sure what Rachel did to hurt you, but you deserve someone who can see all the things that I see. The man who has a sensitive side, who is looking for something more than just a quick screw.

Thank you for giving me these past weeks that I won't ever forget. You've changed me. I hope I changed you.

Yours,
Delaney

Fighting back the tears, I went to my hotel to pack and head to the airport, scheduling myself to catch the next flight to New York. I thought of what Mason would say when he saw the note and realised I was gone. I didn't want him to come after me, yet part of me did. What woman didn't want to be chased after? I knew that wasn't Mason, though. He was set in his ways and so was I. That's why leaving was for the best.

My phone buzzed with messages from Oliver and Mason. I deleted them all without looking at them. I had to stick to my guns. Within a few hours, I was at the airport, ready to leave Mason behind me.

"Checking in for the flight to New York City, please." I pulled out my driver's licence and slid it across the counter.

"Hey, it's you!" the woman next to me exclaimed, showing me her phone. My picture was there, with the headline "Mason's Newest Girl Toy" underneath. I pulled out my own phone, looking up the interview Mason was supposed to have that day.

I froze in place, unable to keep my eyes off the screen. I turned up my volume and listened.

"Mason St Patrick. Thank you so much for agreeing to join us today." Tess from Channel 10 Sports sat across from Mason in their studio. This was his big interview. What we had been preparing for. This was his chance to explain his behaviour, the drinking and fighting that started to impact his game.

"My pleasure, Tess." The way he said her name made her smile, and I knew he was trying to work his magic. It pissed me off because I cared for him. I wanted him to only talk to me like that. But I was leaving. Running from my feelings and any complications because I had no idea what the hell to do, which gave me zero right to be pissed off.

"So, the reason we're here today is to talk about how you've been spiralling. Drinking. Women. Fighting. Those are some lucky women, by the way." She giggled. The damn woman actually giggled.

Mason glanced over at someone and shook his head as he

stared down at the notecards in his hand.

"Well, to be honest…." Mason looked away from her again, out to the side. I assumed Oliver was over there covering for me and providing him with the guidance he needed.

He put the notecards down next to him and my heart nearly jumped out of my chest. He was deviating from the script. "I had my heart broken."

I gasped and put my hand to my mouth.

"Oh. I'm so sorry. Let's talk about her. What was her name?" I watched a small smile flit across Tess's face. She was going to make this work for her. *She's good.*

Mason leaned back and looked right at the camera. "Rachel, my ex-girlfriend. She wanted a normal life with a husband who worked nine to five, and I wanted footy. I was doing what I loved but also trying to prepare for our future. It wasn't the life she wanted, so she left."

I placed my hand over my heart, unable to tear my eyes away from Mason. His words were sincere, tears glistening in his eyes. And I was doing the exact same thing Rachel had.

"Why explain now? Why not before?" Tess asked. *Good question.*

"Because I met someone who made me remember what it felt like to want something beyond sex. Now she's running too." He looked right at the camera.

"Does this woman happen to be the new lady we've seen hanging around? She's your new PR rep, right?" She glanced down at the paper. "Delaney Matthews. She works for Improving You in New York."

Nice plug for the agency. Thank you, Tess.

Mason smiled. "Delaney Matthews. Yes, that's her."

Tess nodded. "She's into drugs, right? That must be difficult to manage."

Mason clenched his fists at his sides. "No. And I want everyone to stop spreading that rumour. She had an allergic reaction to peaches," he yelled.

Tess shifted in her seat. "I'm sorry. Where is she now? Shouldn't your PR rep be with you?" she asked.

"She's gone back to New York." God, the hurt in his eyes damn near killed me.

"Go after her!" someone yelled from behind the cameras, and Mason smiled.

"Go after her, huh?" He smoothed the stubble on his chin. Then he looked right at the camera. The look in his eyes was one I'd seen before when he got an idea in his head that he intended to follow through on. *Oh fuck.*

"What woman doesn't like to be chased?" Tess said with a smile. Before I could blink, Mason was gone, the camera following him as he ran out of the studio.

"And that, my friends, is Mason St Patrick, star player for the Sydney Roosters. He's on his way to win his girl back. Stay tuned."

I panicked, realising that must have been recorded earlier.

"Do you know when that was recorded?" Shoving my mobile back into my bag, I turned to face the lady who was next to me, but she was gone. I grabbed my bags and rushed back through the airport. Why was I such an idiot? I should have never left. I wanted Mason. He wanted me, and I'd just done to him what his ex did. I wouldn't leave him. I couldn't.

"Going somewhere, love?"

I stopped and turned around, coming face-to-face with Mason. There were cameras everywhere but I didn't give a shit. They could watch for all I cared. The PR rep in me screamed to not do this in front of them, but the woman in me wanted this, the Hollywood-worthy moment when everything came together and the whole world watched.

The woman in me won out. I stayed.

"I was going to go back home to New York City. Then I realised this is my home now." I moved closer to him, dropping my bags.

"Oh really?" he said with a grin.

"Yep." I traced the outline of his abs through his shirt. "My mind kept freaking out this morning about how we would make this work. But hearing what happened with Rachel, it all kind of clicked. I'm not her. I don't care what I have to do to make this work, but I don't want to leave you." I felt his stomach suck in at my words.

"Well good, because I don't want you to leave." Grabbing my waist, he pulled me against him.

"Then I'll stay." Crashing my lips down on his, I claimed Mason as mine.

The cameras snapped and I smiled, resting my head against Mason's chest. It was different being on that side of the camera, but I could get used to it. Regardless of what side I was on, it was what I knew.

"Does this mean you're off the market, Mason?" a reporter asked, the cameras flashing.

"Yes. He's off the market," I answered for him, sliding my

hand in his.

"Didn't you just meet? Isn't this soon?" The reporter shoved the microphone in Mason's face. Apparently she wasn't happy with my answer.

He looked down at me and pressed a kiss to my forehead.

"I play for keeps. And this woman right here is what I've been waiting for." He flashed his signature smile.

A collective "aww" sounded throughout the airport. There wasn't a dry eye, including my own. I didn't know what the future would bring. I didn't have an itinerary, a handbook, or rules on how this would play out. Excitement coursed through me at the possibilities of the beautiful life I knew I'd share with Mason. Because this life was full of surprises, and I had captured one of the best ones—love.

The End

Upside Down, Back to Front

BY MEGAN LOWE

Dedication

To all the Aussie larrikins and everyone who has helped make Australia great, in particular the St Kilda Football Club, thank you for creating such a wonderful place to call home.

January

This isn't summer; it's the depths of hell. Thirty-five degrees—that's ninety-five in American—and so humid you can hardly breathe. Welcome to summer on the Gold Coast, Australia's party capital. It's also my home for the next year.

Study in Australia, they said. It'll be awesome, they said. Sure, it's a heck of a lot cheaper than attending college back in the States, but what they failed to mention, especially to a girl from New England, is that this part of Australia doesn't do cool and comfortable. It just does hot. Which is what it is right now. *Really* freaking hot! I saw on the news that in a town not far from here people were frying eggs on the road! I mean, it was so hot they could use the road surface as a way of cooking food! I'm a long way from home, Toto.

I shouldn't complain, though. The coffee shop I'm working at is right on the beach, and I can see the blue water of the Pacific Ocean from my spot behind the counter. The aqua water, golden sand beach, and refreshing sea breeze sure do make a difference from the green forests of my home state of Vermont. And then there are the guys. One definite upside to this stifling heat is it makes shirts very much an optional extra for the bronzed men who live on the Coast, as it's affectionately called.

I've been here for three weeks now and aside from the heat, there's not much I don't like. Sure, some things are lost in translation—sometimes it feels like Australians speak another language—and getting used to looking for cars coming from the opposite direction takes some getting used to, but I haven't been hit by a bus yet, so yippee! Other things are just downright weird. I'm looking at you, Vegemite—insert shudder here—but I can deal with that. What I can't deal with is the absolute god standing in front of me. If it weren't already hot as Hades in here before, I'd think the temperature was all due to him.

"G'day," he says, a massive smile on his face and that relaxed, easy-going nature all Australians seem to possess oozing out of him like sweat is pouring off me.

"Argh," I garble.

His eyes twinkle. They're a sea green and I don't think it'd take much for me to get lost in them. "How ya doing?"

In the past three weeks, I've also become accustomed to the Australian love of mangling the English language. I just nod dumbly.

"A bit hot out, hey?" Again I nod. "I'm Sam. What's your name?"

"Er, Georgia," I manage to squeak.

"Nice to meet ya." He offers me a calloused hand. I take it in mine and gasp at the electric shock that runs through me when we touch. My eyes flick to his face and he gives me a wink. Does that mean he felt it too?

"Where're ya from, Georgia?" he asks as he leans against the counter separating us.

"Er, Vermont?" I say like it's a question. What the hell is going on with me? The heat. It has to be the heat. It's finally gotten to me, and this hallucination is my brain's last hurrah before I slip into a coma and die. Or maybe it's just wishful thinking as I make a total idiot of myself in front of the hottest guy on the planet.

"Yeah? Is it as hot there as it is here?"

I snort. Further proof I'm making a complete fool of myself. "Not even close." Hey! A sentence! That's better. I'm making progress. Now to continue it.

"So, do you like things hot?"

And there go my panties. I swear to all things holy I'm about to combust. Not good. This is *so* not good.

"Ah…," I say before swallowing loudly. Sam just laughs.

"Do you like it here?" he asks, giving me a reprieve.

"I haven't been here long, but what I've seen, I like." *That's it, Georgia. Focus on the mundane. You're good at that. You* like *that*.

"How long have you been here?"

"About three weeks."

"Here for uni?"

That's Australian for college. I nod.

"Nice."

"Do you go as well?" Maybe I might see him around campus. It'd be nice to see a familiar face.

Please, who am I kidding? I'd probably drop all my books whenever I saw him, like the klutz I am.

"Me? Nah, I'm a chippie." He runs a hand through his sun-bleached light brown hair.

"A chippie?" Does that mean he eats a lot of chips? Judging from the six-pack abs on him I can't see that being the case.

"Yeah, a tradie."

I shake my head.

He laughs. "I'm a carpenter."

"Why didn't you just say that?" I ask, resting my hand on my hip.

"I did!"

"No you didn't, you gave me some Australian gobbledygook."

He shrugs. "It's more fun that way."

I roll my eyes. "So what can I get you?"

"A large flat white to take away, please." I marvel at that sentence. Two weeks ago it may as well have been German. Now I know it's a coffee with milk and a small amount of foam, or froth as they call it here. Take away means to go. How anyone can drink anything hot in this heat I'll never know, but the café does a roaring trade.

Australians. I tell you, they're a little strange but I kind of like them that way.

"Four fifty, please."

Sam hands me one of the blue notes that I'm pretty sure

is ten dollars. The money they use here is really pretty, a nice change from boring green. I open the register to retrieve Sam's change. There are only red and yellow notes, which are twenties and fifties, so coins it is.

"Er," I say as I look at the pile of metal coins in front of me. I grab two of the small gold ones, a big gold one and one of the hexagon shaped ones. I'm double-checking to make sure they're right when Sam chuckles.

I give him a bashful smile. "Sorry. The notes I've got the hang of, but the coins take a little more getting used to."

"You'll get it."

"Thanks. It'd be easier if the sizes made sense. I mean, why is the most valuable the *smallest*?" I ask.

He shrugs. "No idea. Just the way it is, I guess."

"It's weird."

"It's Australia. We do a lot of weird things here."

"I'm beginning to realise that."

"So, you got any plans for Australia Day?" he asks.

"Australia Day?"

"Kinda like your Independence Day."

"Oh, when is it?"

"Thursday."

I pause for a second while I think. "I don't think I'm doing anything."

Sam looks at me and tilts his head, weighing something up. "What time do you finish here?"

"Huh?" I'm confused. What the heck is happening here?

"You gotta stop work sometime, so when is that?"

"Why are you asking me this?" I ask, suspicious.

He shrugs. "Why not? You seem like a nice enough bird."

"You're calling me poultry?"

He shrugs again. Ugh! That is *so* frustrating. "Would you prefer sheila?"

"My name is Georgia."

He laughs a hearty laugh that warms my already overheated insides. "I know it is. Sheila is Aussie slang for a woman." He gives me an appreciative once-over. I felt my cheeks heating, so knew they would be glowing.

"So what time do you get off?"

Any minute now is the first response that comes to mind as I press my thighs together. What is wrong with me? Ten minutes in this guy's company and I've turned into a floozy. It must be the heat. It *has* to be the heat. That's the only explanation. Maybe that's why Australians are so peculiar; too much long-term exposure to temperatures the human body isn't equipped to survive in. It would explain a lot, or even just the existence of Vegemite.

"Look, I just wanna take you out for a drink and a bite to eat. Nothing sinister, I promise."

I look at him again. He's tall, like six three-ish, built like all the guys are here—that is, a solid wall of muscle—with sun-bleached light brown hair and those sea-green eyes I want to dive into. He doesn't look like a serial killer, but then what do serial killers look like? It's not like they have a sign on their forehead warning unsuspecting Americans. He gives me a pleading look.

I sigh and look at my watch. "I finish in twenty minutes."

"Awesome. So would you like to go for a drink with me?

Maybe a bite to eat too?"

With a deep exhale, I say, "Sure, why not."

His face lights up. "You sure? I don't want you to feel like you have no choice or anything." I arch a brow at him. "Okay, so I *really* don't want you to say no, but if you don't want to go out with me, that's cool."

I smile. "No, I want to go."

"You sure? 'Cause I don't want you to think I'm one of those guys who—"

"Sam," I interrupt.

"Yeah?"

"Let me finish up here and we can go, all right?"

He takes a breath. "Yeah, okay."

I give him his coffee and he sits down to drink it while I finish my shift.

I go over to him when I'm done. "You ready?"

Sam's eyes are fixed on my legs before slowly moving up my body. Now that I'm no longer hidden behind my apron and the counter, he has an uninterrupted view. I don't know what he's so enamoured by, I'm not that impressive. Taller than average at five nine, I have chestnut hair and hazel eyes. I've dated in the past back home, but I can't say I've ever fallen in love. At least I don't think I have, and it's something you'd know, right? Not that I'm planning on falling in love with Sam. That'd be crazy. For one, we only just met, and two, I'm only here for a year. Where can anything go in that time?

We exit the café and walk along the beach. I don't know if I'll ever get used to the skyscrapers here; it's one of the biggest differences between the Coast and home. In Vermont we don't have anything taller than 124 feet. Here, that's tiny. Q1, which is the jewel of the Gold Coast skyline, is over a thousand feet and is the tallest building in the Southern Hemisphere. Sure, it stands out, but not by much.

"It's pretty impressive, huh?" Sam asks, looking at the skyline.

I nod. "And so different from Vermont."

"Yeah?" I nod again. "What's it like?"

"Small. We're the second-least populated state and the sixth smallest in area."

"Wow."

"Yeah."

"So this is different."

"A lot. But I like it here, even if it feels like I'm burning in the pits of hell at the moment."

"Not used to the heat?"

"And then some. Vermont shares a border with Canada, so heat isn't really our thing. What about you?" I ask. "Were you born here?"

He nods. "Yep, Gold Coast born and bred."

"You've never lived anywhere else?"

"Nope. Don't really want to either. The Coast has everything I need."

"You don't want to travel and see the world?"

"Oh I'll travel, but the Coast will always be home." I nod. "So how come you came here, anyway?" he asks.

I shrug. "College back home is expensive. Plus, you know, experience, something different."

"Uni's not expensive here?"

"Not as much as it would be if I stayed in the States. I only have three semesters left, so I thought why not try something different and save my parents a bit of money while I'm at it?"

"Huh."

"Did you go to college?"

"Me? Nah."

"You didn't want to?"

"I'm not so much for studying, more of a physical kind of guy."

"A fry, is that what you called it?"

He throws his head back and laughs. "You mean a chippie?"

"Yeah, that's it. You're like a contractor, right?"

"We call 'em tradies or tradesmen."

It's my turn to say, "Huh."

We walk in comfortable silence for a bit.

"So where do you wanna go?" Sam asks as we approach Surfers Paradise.

I shrug. "I don't know. Where's good?"

"What are you in the mood for?" he says, smiling.

"Burgers?" I ask.

"Oh yeah? Is Maccas okay?"

"Maccas?"

"Yeah, McDonald's."

"What did you call it?"

"Maccas."

"Why?"

"Just what we do. We like to shorten anything we can."

"Why?"

He slings an arm around my shoulders and I try not to melt in a puddle at his feet. "I've been told it's endearing, George."

I stop and turn to face him. "Do *not* call me George."

He flashes me a smile. "Okay, I won't call you George, but I *am* going to have to give you a nickname."

"Why? No, wait," I say before he opens his mouth. "Let me guess. It's just something you do."

"Got it in one, babe," he says, winking at me before leaning in and capturing my lips.

February

In the three weeks Sam and I have been dating (I tried resisting him, I really did. I mean, except for not kissing him; let's not get too crazy here because he's a *great* kisser) I've made a lot of adjustments. It's not a bad thing; I feel like this whole other world has been opened up to me now that I'm with him.

That first day we went for burgers and sat on the beach. Sam tried to educate me on the proper way of ordering a burger, with beetroot and egg like the locals do, but that's just one adjustment I won't make. Since then we've spent a lot of time at the beach, walking up and down the coast, exploring the tidal pools, splashing in the water. I asked Sam if he could teach me to surf. I mean, what Australian doesn't know how to surf, right? His answer? "Fuck no, babe. There's sharks and blue bottles and jellyfish in there!" So we're mostly beach bound, which I don't mind.

I also don't mind barbeques—or "barbies"—on the beach; they're one adjustment I will happily make. For Australia Day Sam and I met some of his friends—mates—Macca, Jacko, Smitty, and Bluey. For some reason Bluey is called Bluey despite having a head of red hair. It doesn't make sense to me either, but to the guys it does. We all got together and had a barbeque on Burleigh Beach. Afterwards we sat on the hill and watched the fireworks. It was an incredible night. Sam sat behind me, his arms around me, chin on my shoulder.

Life here is so different than my life in Vermont. At home I was quiet and reserved. Sure, I had friends, but I was never really close to anyone in particular. I had a couple of boyfriends but none who stole my heart, not like Sam is doing. He's so sweet with me. A real larrikin—that's Aussie for a cheeky troublemaker—when he's with the boys, which I enjoy, and sweet and attentive when we're alone, which I love. I'm still not loving the heat though, even if I am getting a nice tan from all my time spent outdoors lately.

Like where I am right now, although Lord knows why. Currently I'm watching Sam play cricket. Yes, you read that correctly, cricket. That weird almost baseball-like game but slower, less exciting, and just generally more polite. In truth it's a bit boring, but I like watching Sam get all hot and sweaty, even if I think it's unnatural to dress teams of men in white outfits they never get dirty. I mean, what the heck?

But I like being here. The café gave me shifts during the week when I don't have class, so my weekends are free to watch Sam's matches. Plus, it gives me a great opportunity to study in the Queensland sunshine, slathered in fifty-plus sunscreen, of course. Queensland is the skin cancer capital of the world, so wearing sunscreen here in summer is a definite necessity. Whoever invented cricket and decreed it to be a summer sport obviously never had to endure an Australian summer.

The wind picks up and I have to scramble to keep my papers from flying everywhere. I look to the sky and see deep purple clouds gathering over the mountains.

A few hours later, the game ends, and not a moment too soon. Fat drops of rain start falling seconds before we get to Sam's ute. I made the mistake of calling it a truck—and going to get in the wrong side—and was promptly corrected. A truck here is an eighteen-wheeler; the average tradie drives a ute or utility vehicle.

Yeah, I speak pretty good Aussie now. That's Aussie pronounced Ozzie, not Au-see; that's also vitally important, apparently. When it comes to how you refer to things, a *lot* of things are vitally important. Bris-bin instead of Bris-bane, Mel-bin not Mel-bourne, to-mah-to not to-may-to, capsicum not peppers, soft drink not soda; all of these have been added to my American/Australian dictionary, though for the life of me I can't pronounce aluminium the way they do. It's just not happening.

Within minutes of leaving the field the rain is pelting down. Thunder is crashing while lightning lights up the sky. The windshield wipers are going flat out, and Sam is hunched over the wheel.

"Oh my God! This is insane! Should we pull over?" I ask. Even though Sam's complex isn't far from the cricket field, right now I can barely see three feet in front of the car.

"Nah, she'll be right. It's just a little storm."

"Little storm? Sam, you can barely see the road!"

He hears the panic in my voice and looks over at me.

"Eyes on the road!" I screech, and he chuckles.

"Don't worry, babe," he says, and squeezes my knee. "It'll be okay."

"This is ridiculous."

He shrugs. "It's a typical Queensland summer storm."

"Well I don't like it." Seriously, it's scary stuff! The wind is howling, the trees are bending at what I swear are forty-five-degree angles, and the thunder sounds like it's right on top of us and is going to crack the sky open.

"It's okay. We've still got a bit before it hits us fully."

"What do you mean 'hits us fully'? It seems to me that it's hitting us pretty fully right now!" I know Aussies are known for their laid-back attitudes, but this is taking it to another level. Sam's hand is still resting on my knee and he gives it a squeeze again.

"Almost there," he says as he turns into his street. He pulls into the space in front of his condo, turns off the car, and looks at me. "You ready to make a run for it?"

I look out the windshield and if anything, the rain seems to be coming down even harder, something I wouldn't have thought possible. I steel myself and nod.

"On the count of three, open your door and run, okay?" I nod again. "One, two, three." I throw open my door and dash for the stoop. It's only a few yards but I still get soaked.

"Oh my gosh!" I say as we reach the safety of Sam's front door.

"Brr." He shakes his head like a dog, spraying me with rain.

"Sam!" I squeal.

He just laughs and rushes at me, capturing me in his arms.

"You're all wet!" I try to escape his hold.

"So are you." He raises his eyebrows.

"Huh?"

He nods to my chest and I look down. My top is soaked and sticking to my skin, showing both my lace bra and my hard nipples. I gasp and try to cover myself. Sam just chuckles and lets me go to unlock the door.

"Come on, let's get dry."

We traipse through the house, going upstairs to his room and the bathroom beyond.

"You hop in the shower and I'll find some dry clothes for you to put on," he says.

"Thank you." I rise onto my toes and give him a chaste kiss.

"No worries." He winks for good measure.

I turn on the shower and get out of my sopping wet clothes. I've never experienced weather so wild and fierce before. Of course, I've endured a heck of a lot of snowstorms in my time, but these thunderstorms? They're something else. I step into the shower and let the water rush over me.

It's strange—even though it's raining, it's not cold. It just... refreshed everything, I guess. It's like the storm is cleansing everything.

I hop out and find Sam has left some clothes on the bathroom counter for me. I'm drowning in them, but at least they're dry. He's sitting on the bed when I leave the bathroom.

"Better?" he asks.

I nod. "Much, thanks."

"No worries. Lemme hop in there for a quick sec. I'm pretty sure I reek after the match."

"Take your time. I'm sure it was hard work just standing in the field all day," I reply.

"Hey, I'll have you know it takes a lot of effort to stand around *and* look good while doing it."

My eyes move down his body, taking in his tanned, muscular form. He's right; he *does* look good.

"You right there, babe?" he asks, a smug look on his face.

"Huh?"

"I'm just gonna grab a shower, if it's all right with you?"

"What? Why wouldn't it be okay with me?"

"You seemed to be enjoying the view, that's all. Wouldn't want to deprive you of it."

I smack his arm. "Go have your shower."

He laughs but swaggers away anyway. While I wait, I lie on his bed and open my Kindle. The great thing about living in Australia, at least for the moment, is getting book preorders fourteen hours before America, which usually means I can be finished before it's even available in the States. Be jealous, book nerds!

I hear the shower turn off and a minute later Sam appears in the doorway in nothing but a towel. We stare at each other for a minute before a clap of thunder sounds like it's about to break the house in two. I cower and Sam rushes to me, pulling me into his lap.

"Hey, it's okay," he says, rubbing a hand up and down my back.

"That was close."

"It's okay. We're inside. Everything will be fine." He kisses my forehead. I relax into his touch and listen to the beat of his heart while the storm rages outside.

After a while he breaks the silence. "You okay now?"

I lift my head and stare into his sea-green eyes. "I'm more than okay."

"Good." He moves so we're lying down. I snuggle into his chest, his arms tight around me, our legs tangled together.

"You don't get thunderstorms in Vermont?"

"We get storms, just not so extreme. And if they are they come with snow."

He nods. "They can get pretty violent here."

"They may be scary as all get out," I say, drawing circles on his chest, "but it's also kind of beautiful. It feels like everything is being washed clean."

"Mmmm," he agrees.

"This is nice," I say after a few more minutes have passed.

"You know what would make it nicer?"

"What?"

"This." He leans over and kisses me. First he nibbles on my lips before swooping inside, his tongue owning my mouth. I moan, my hands cupping his face before one slides to his back, the other at the base of his neck, keeping his face connected to mine. As the kiss wears on, Sam shifts so he's on top of me, my legs spreading so he fits between them. A hand moves under my shirt, heading to my breast. He pulls back when he realises I'm not wearing a bra.

"No bra?" he asks.

I shrug. "It was wet."

"What about undies?" I give him a smile that encourages him to find out. He moves down my body, kissing the skin exposed where my shirt has ridden up. When he gets to the waistband of the shorts I'm wearing—I think he called them stubbies once—he pauses. I nod and he pulls them down.

"They were wet too?" he asks when he sees me bare before him.

"If they weren't before, they would be now," I say, shocking the heck out of myself. When did I get so bold? He must be rubbing off on me. I'm suffering from more heat-induced Aussie psychosis.

"Is that so?" The smirk on his face is a mile wide. I bite my lip and nod.

"Well then," he says, pulling my shorts off, "I guess I better help you with that, huh?" He settles between my legs.

I'm just about to reply when his tongue laps at me for the first time. "Oh!"

"Mmm," he mumbles as he licks me again.

"Sam." I moan as I bury my hands in his hair. He alternates between licking my juices and nibbling on my clit. Eventually he adds a finger, then another, before I'm seeing stars.

He's resting on his side facing me when I open my eyes again. "Hey there."

"Hi," I reply shyly.

"Enjoy that?" I nod. "Good." He leans over and kisses me. I can taste myself on his lips, something I thought would gross me out, but I'm intrigued to discover it's the opposite.

I swing my leg over his hip and he rolls us so I'm on my back again, the towel he's still wearing doing a poor job of containing his erection. I reach down to undo it and he pauses.

"Are you sure? If you don't want to we can just pash. I don't mind."

"Pash?"

"Yeah, you know, kiss, make out, whatever."

"Oh." It's sweet that he's doing this, but I don't want sweet right now. I sit up and strip off his shirt. "I'm sure."

His eyes are wide as he looks at me and swallows audibly.

"Do you have something?" I ask as he sits and stares at me.

"Huh? Oh yeah, hang on." He scrambles across the bed to his bedside table, opens the top drawer and retrieves a foil square. He rips it open and rolls the condom on.

"You sure about this?" he says as he positions himself on top of me.

I reach up and cup his face. "Yes, Sam, I'm sure."

He leans down and kisses me while sliding into me at the same time. It's been a while since I was with someone—the only other one, actually—, so it's a tight fit.

"Holy fucking shit," he grits out.

"What? What's wrong?" I ask.

"You're so goddamn fucking tight."

"Oh. Sorry. I've only been with one other guy, and he wasn't nearly as big as you."

"Nothing to be sorry about, babe," he says as he starts to move, and I let out a moan. "You feel so fucking good."

I moan again and wrap my legs around his waist, pulling

him deeper into me.

"Fuck, babe."

"Mmm." I throw my head back and arch off the bed. He reaches down to rub my clit and I come within seconds.

"Sam!"

He continues to thrust into me before throwing his head back, yelling my name and collapsing on top of me.

"Damn, that was good."

"Mmm," I agree as I run my fingers up and down his spine.

He rolls off me and goes to the bathroom to clean up. When he comes back he pulls back the sheets, opening them so I can slip inside. He joins me a second later, pulling me to his chest.

"You okay?" he asks as he strokes my hair.

"Perfect."

We stay like that for the rest of the afternoon as the storm eventually passes, leaving sunshine in its wake. Maybe they aren't so bad after all.

March

The day I thought would never get here has arrived: the end of cricket season. I've tried to like it, I really have. It's just so... I want to say boring, but for Sam's sake I'll go with slow. But I'm a good girlfriend and go to every match I can, even if I have no idea what's going on or don't even pay that much attention. As a side note, my grades are pretty spectacular right now.

We're at Sam's local (that's his local pub) with Macca, Jacko, Smitty, and Bluey for a Sunday sesh (a Sunday afternoon drinking session, something I've definitely embraced), just relaxing and enjoying the Aussie way of life.

"You ready for footy?" Macca asks Sam.

He nods. "Fuck yeah. I've been dying to smash someone for ages."

"What's this?" I ask.

"Footy's starting up soon," Sam says, rubbing my leg.

"Footy?"

"Yeah, Aussie Rules," Jacko says.

"Aussie Rules?" I ask. "It isn't one of those crazy tackle games you play without pads, is it?" All five guys look at me like I'm crazy.

"Babe, you just spent six weeks watching the only game we play *with* pads," Sam says.

I shake my head. "You're all crazy."

"Nah, we're tough," Bluey says, and flexes his biceps.

"It's not dangerous, is it?" I ask Sam quietly.

He cups my face. "No more than any other contact sport."

"That doesn't help." I lean into his touch.

"Here," Smitty says, and hands me his cell— sorry, *mobile* phone.

I tap the screen and a YouTube clip starts playing. It shows teams of men in sleeveless jerseys and tight shorts running and jumping, kicking and passing an oval ball around.

"This is Aussie Rules?" I ask, intrigued. If nothing else, I could get into it purely for the uniforms, and the chance to see Sam in one, but it looks interesting as well, a real game of skill.

"That's how *real* men play footy. None of that pansy-arse wearing a shitload of protection bullshit for us," Macca says.

"You play this?" I ask, turning to face Sam.

He shrugs. "Yeah."

"So what do you think?" Jacko asks.

I look at him and smile. "Looks like I'll be sitting on the sidelines watching you guys play footy."

"Yeah!" they chorus, and Sam leans over and kisses my cheek.

I'm kind of excited, to tell you the truth. It's funny; I never pictured myself being with a jock. At home they're all full of themselves and treated like gods. Here, everyone either plays a sport or watches it, and if anyone gets a big head about it, they're immediately brought back down to earth. It's good; it helps maintain an equal society.

"You sure? You don't have to, you know. It'll be winter, so it won't be warm like it is now."

It's fall right now, which means instead of ninety-five-degree temps, it's down to around eighty, a real reprieve.

I cup his face this time. "I'm from Vermont. The cold doesn't bother me."

He smiles a brilliant smile. "That's good, 'cause it might be cold when we go camping."

"You're going camping?" Bluey asks.

"Yeah, just down to Byron."

Sam asked me a couple of weeks ago. We're going down to Byron Bay, which is the easternmost point in Australia.

"Nice," he says, nodding.

"Yeah," Smitty agrees, "but watch out for drop bears. It's the season for 'em."

"Drop bears?" I ask worriedly. I'm really starting to like this country, but the sheer number of dangerous and deadly animals is overwhelming and frankly a little concerning.

"Yeah, drop bears," Macca confirms. "They didn't tell you about 'em when you first got here?"

I shake my head. "What are they? Are they dangerous?"

"They can be," Jacko says.

"What do they do?"

"Well," Bluey says, sitting back in his chair and sipping his beer, "they're kinda like koalas but bigger and more ferocious."

"Yeah," Smitty joins in. "They hang out in gum trees but if they see someone walk past and look up, they drop on their faces and maul 'em. People have been cut up pretty bad. Plus, it's their mating season right now. All that humping, it gets 'em all riled up and they're extra vicious."

"Are you serious?" I ask them before my gaze settles on Sam. He nods and shrugs.

"Oh yeah, we're totally legit," Macca says.

I narrow my eyes at him. "I don't believe you. I've never even *heard* about drop bears before."

"It's not something we like to advertise," Smitty says, and takes a sip of his beer. "Plus, they kinda damage the reputation of koalas because they look so similar, and we have all those snakes and spiders and stuff, so it can get a little overwhelming. We usually only tell backpackers when they go out of the city."

"I still don't believe you."

"That's your choice, pancake," Jacko says. Ever since they found out Vermont is the leading producer of maple syrup in the US they've been calling me "pancake" or "pan" or "cake." "But if one of them happens to latch on to that pretty face of yours, don't come crying to us."

I look back to Sam. "It'll be fine," he says, and squeezes my knee.

"Oh, and look out for mozzies," Bluey says.

Macca must see the stricken look on my face. "It'll be fine. Just roast some marshmallows or something and take repellent."

"Oooh, can we make s'mores?" I ask.

"What are s'mores?" Sam asks, a genuinely puzzled look on his face.

No, everything is *not* going to be okay.

***

Against my better judgment, I find myself watching as Sam pitches our tent.

"Are you sure there aren't any drop bears here?" I ask, shielding my eyes as I look up into the trees. While I'm pretty sure the guys were joking, just in case they're not I don't want to take any chances.

"She'll be right," Sam says. The guys say this a lot, I've noticed, and I still have no idea who "she" is.

"Be honest with me. Are drop bears real?"

He comes over to me and takes me in his arms. "We'll be fine, babe. There's nothing for you to worry about."

"You didn't answer my question," I mumble into his chest.

In response, he chuckles and runs his fingers through my hair. "I'll keep you safe from anything and everything that comes at you."

We spend the rest of the day wandering around the town and at the lighthouse. Apparently it's a good place for whale watching, but it's too early for them.

For dinner Sam cooks a "sausage sizzle," which is grilled sausages and onions wrapped in a piece of bread. I couldn't get any graham crackers here or find anything similar, so s'mores are off the menu.

Later that night we're lying in bed—Sam combined two sleeping bags to make one big one—when he breaks the silence. Not that it is silent. There's a ton of strange noises, but I'm trying not to think too much about them or what they could be.

"So how have your first three months here gone?"

Sometimes it's hard to remember that I've only been here that long. Sometimes it feels much longer, and other times, much shorter.

"They've been good," I say as I rub circles on his chest. My head is resting there too, and one of his arms is around me. "At first it was kind of difficult to get used to things here—everything is back to front, or so it seems to me—but I think I'm getting the hang of it."

"Mmm," he agrees. "So what's been your favourite thing so far?"

There're so many things that come to mind. The food, the beaches. We went to one of the amusement parks the other week, a hike in the hinterland before that. But nothing compares to where I am right now. I lift my head so I'm looking into his eyes. "You," I say simply.

His answering smile is blinding. "You're my favourite too."

"Really?"

He nods. "You're refreshing, different than most of the

girls around here, and I really like spending time with you."

"I like spending time with you too. I feel like I'm a different person here."

"Why's that?"

I shrug. "All I know is being here in the fresh air and sunshine, it makes for a brighter outlook on things. It's easier to be happy when everything isn't as serious as it is back home. Everything is so laid-back. It's nice, relaxing."

"Especially when you have a hot fry wrapped around you."

I shove him playfully as he laughs. "Very funny."

"So you like it here?" he asks. I nod. "Maybe even love it here?" he asks almost shyly.

I get the feeling we're not talking about Australia anymore. I swallow. "I think I already do."

"Yeah?" I nod. "I love it here too," he says.

"We're not talking about a place anymore, are we?"

"Nah, babe." He brings my head back down to his chest.

"So did you just say you love me?" I ask after a few minutes, unable to stop myself.

His chest bounces as he laughs. "Yep, and so did you."

"Technically I said I love it *here*. There was no mention of you anywhere in that conversation."

He laughs again. "If you want to play it that way, babe, then that's fine, but you and I both know what just went down here and it wasn't me."

"Huh?"

He lifts his hips and I can see his erection tenting—ha!—the sleeping bag.

"Oh."

"Yeah, so you still gonna stick to what you said before?"

"Um," I say, biting my lip. The arm that's around me moves from my shoulders to my butt, where he begins to massage my cheeks.

"You gotta let me know, babe. Wouldn't want anything to get lost in translation." His hand slips between my legs and I know he'll find my panties damp.

"Mmm." I moan and try to move so he's where I need him most.

"So what is it, babe?"

"You! It's you, all right?" I say, not able to take the torture.

He smiles a triumphant smile before taking my lips in a punishing kiss.

Oh, and we didn't get attacked by drop bears, in case you were wondering.

July

I'm not happy. I was told winter was coming, you know, like *Game of Thrones*—which is on at the very friendly time of 11:30 a.m. here, thank you very much, HBO. But winter has *not* come. The high during the day has yet to dip below seventy and it doesn't look like it will anytime soon. Even at night it only gets down to fifty. I have a closet full of winter clothes that are about as useful as a broken thong—the things you wear on your feet, not under your sexiest little black dress. So all my coats and jackets will be staying where they are. Though I do have to admit that it is kind of novel to be running around in the middle of winter in only a light sweater. It makes those hours spent on the sidelines watching Sam all the more pleasant.

As a bonus, I *actually* like Aussie Rules. It's fast and exciting, with constant movement, even if some of the terms are a little weird. Speccy? Clanger? Hanger? Torp? But all of that is forgotten when presented with Sam in his uniform. A tight, sleeveless tunic that showcases his tanned, muscular arms and toned body, and tight shorts that show off his perfect butt. Makes it more than worth my while to come and cheer him on. The only thing missing is a pumpkin spice latte, but they don't do that here.

"You ready, babe?" Sam asks, slinging an arm over my shoulders before bending down to kiss me.

When I first arrived here I never even entertained the thought of finding someone to have a relationship with, let alone fall in love with, but I have. I guess it's true when they say you find it when you're not looking for it. But what happens come January? I'll be going back to Vermont and he'll be here…. My heart constricts at the thought of being without him, but soon, five months soon, it'll be our reality.

"You okay?" he asks.

I nod and wrap my arm around him, giving him a squeeze. "I'm with you, so I'm perfect."

"Yeah?" He doesn't seem convinced. "You looked a little sad for a minute there."

"Just thinking about home. I'm fine now, though."

He bends down so we're eye to eye. "You sure? Is there anything I can do?"

I cup his face. "You're doing it."

He smiles and kisses me again. "Come on, we gotta hit the road."

We're going to an actual AFL—that's the pro league for Aussie Rules—game tonight and I'm excited. Even though the

Coast has its own team, Sam doesn't support it. He supports a Victorian team, St Kilda. I googled them and they seem to be... I'm going to go with unlucky. They have one premiership (like the Super Bowl) in 144 years and the most wooden spoons (I figured out that meant bottom-placed finishes) in the league's history. But the one thing that's always mentioned in all the articles I read is loyalty, heart, and determination, which is something I can get behind.

We get into the stadium and it's a real family atmosphere. There are bands playing and heaps of kids running around, kicking the balls they've brought from home with their friends. Before going to our seats, we stop by a concession stand and Sam buys us each a meat pie and a beer.

"You had one of these before?" he asks, opening the bag the pie is in and squirting ketchup all over the top.

I shake my head. To be honest, I don't know if I want to; I've heard bad things.

"Well you're in for a treat. There's nothin' better than a pie and beer at the footy." I raise an eyebrow sceptically. "Trust me," he says, and shoots me his panty-melting smile. I want to raise the issue of drop bears but I don't want to sound like an ignorant American, so I don't. Instead I sigh.

"Fine."

He hugs me to his chest and plants a kiss on the top of my head. "My missus, my team, a good game, a beer and a pie. What more could a guy ask for?" At first I was a little taken aback at being called his "missus" but I quickly worked out it didn't mean he was proposing; it's just what girlfriends are called here. There's honour in being someone's missus, and

I'm more than fine with that.

With food and drink in hand, we make our way to our seats and dig in to our meal. I'm a little unsure of the pie at first, but the flaky pastry quickly wins me over. Add to that the thick gravy inside and it's pretty good. When he's finished eating, Sam slings his arm around me and cuddles me to his side.

"So how was it?" he asks when I finish.

"It wasn't bad," I say, grinning.

"You thought it would be?"

I shrug. "I've heard bad things."

"When have you ever had bad food here?" he asks.

I stop and think about all the amazing food I've had since I arrived—lamingtons, Anzac biscuits, Golden Gaytimes, pavlova, Tim Tams (oh my God, Tim Tams). Then I remember. "Vegemite."

"We've had this discussion. You were doing it wrong!" He chuckles. He made me some Vegemite toast not long after we got together and it was actually really good. Hot toast, loads of butter and a light layer—we're talking a quarter of a teaspoon, maybe less—of Vegemite on top.

"Okay, I'll give you that."

"Thank you," he says smugly.

"But you're right, the food here is pretty awesome." I'll miss it when I leave, but I don't say that part. Why is everything reminding me of home today?

I snuggle closer to Sam and sip my beer. The game is really good. The difference in skill between the games I watch Sam in and the guys on the field is vast, which you'd expect. The Saints end up comfortable winners—at least I think they are.

Games that regularly score over a hundred points are normal, if not expected. The points differential can be huge, sometimes well over a hundred or as small as one. It's definitely exciting; "a real shoot-out," I heard someone describe it as once. The crowd really gets into it too. For a relatively small number, they make a lot of noise, yelling and shouting and abusing the referees. It was a really great experience.

"Thank you for bringing me here," I say to Sam as we board the bus to take us back to the car.

"No thanks necessary. It was my pleasure to hang out with me missus and watch the footy." He leans down to kiss me. After a minute he pulls back, both of us breathless but with massive smiles on our faces. Home might be on my mind today, but five months is still a long time.

September

Against all odds Sam's footy team made it to the playoffs, or finals as they call them here. What's even more incredible is the fact that they managed to win, which is how I find myself in the pub with thirty rowdy footy players, all of them well on their way to inebriation. Not that I can blame them; winning a "grannie" or grand final is a big thing.

"Here she is," Sam slurs as he comes over to me, slinging an arm around my waist and pulling me to him.

"How's it going, champ?" I ask him, and his face lights up.

"I like it when you call me that."

"It's the truth, isn't it?"

He nods slowly, like the movement is too much for him, and I chuckle.

"Yep," he says, popping the *p*, "'cause we smashed 'em."

This time I laugh out loud. "Yes, you certainly did."

"You know why we did?"

"Because you're the best?"

"Well yeah, but nah. It's because you're my good luck charm and I love you."

I look down to make sure I haven't melted in a puddle at his feet. Outwardly Sam is your typical Aussie bloke. He's a little rough, tough, and strong, but when I'm around that takes a back seat and he's sweet, loving, and caring. In a way he's kind of a metaphor for Australia. The landscape itself is harsh and rugged, with its stifling heat and dangerous animals, but when you get here the people are so laid-back and friendly. It's a land of extremes, but one I've come to love.

I stretch up to kiss him. He tastes like beer and ketchup. "And I love you."

He meets my gaze and I can see the power of his words in his sea-green eyes. "This year has been so incredible. I've never met anyone like you, Georgia."

"Me either," I whisper.

He leans down and captures my lips again, his tongue exploring my mouth, our bodies pressed so tight together I almost can't tell where he begins and I end. Before we can get too carried away, Macca, Jacko, Smitty, and Bluey interrupt us.

"Oi! There'll be none of that. There are impressionable young eyes around here," Jacko says. Sam and I break apart but he keeps me close, hugging me to his chest.

"Yeah? Where?" I ask.

"There," Jacko replies, pointing to a group of girls huddled in the corner of the pub. I've seen them around; they're at every game, hoping to snag one of the guys.

"They don't look so impressionable to me." It's true; they don't. Even though the nights are cool at the moment, they're still dressed in tank tops and booty shorts, hardly the outfits of girls who are looking to keep their virtue intact.

"They're impressionable because they see you, pancake, with our man Sam here, suckin' face and bein' all lovey-dovey and they start thinkin' we're all like that," Macca says.

"Like what?" I ask, genuinely confused.

"*Committed*," Smitty says with a shudder. I'd ask if they were pulling my leg (aka yanking my chain), but I know these guys well enough by now to know they're dead serious. I straighten from my slouched position against Sam.

"Sorry, guys. We'll behave."

"Much appreciated," Bluey says as the four of them stalk towards the bar.

"Come here, you," Sam says, and pulls me against him again.

"What about the guys and the impressionable minds?" I jerk my head in their direction.

"Fuck 'em." He swoops on my mouth again.

***

Hours later the impressionable minds have gone off in a huff, annoyed by the lack of attention, leaving me with the boys. They're singing loudly and boisterously to a song about a working-class man while Sam and I sway slowly on the dance floor.

"I meant what I said earlier," Sam says. He's sobered up a little bit, having stopped drinking a few hours ago.

"About what?"

"You being my lucky charm."

"Not about how incredible this year has been and how you love me?" I joke.

He squeezes me tightly. "You know I meant that. I mean it every time I say it."

I look up at him. "I know you do."

"I want to ask you something." My heart starts to race and my palms get sweaty.

He swallows and takes a deep breath before continuing. "I was wondering what the chances of you staying here next year would be?"

"Oh." So not the question I thought he was going to ask, but this is good. Better, even. Not that I don't want to marry Sam, but I'm young, he's young, and I'm rambling and panicking about something he hasn't even asked me. "Um, I don't know. My visa's only for a year," I say dumbly, still trying to calm myself down over my freak-out.

"I know, but I thought maybe you could see about getting it extended." He has a puppy-dog look on his face and it kills me. I want to stay as much as he wants me to, but I don't think it's likely to happen.

"I guess," I say. It's September now and I'm due to leave early January, so it doesn't leave a whole lot of time, but it'd be worth a try, if for no other reason than so I can stay with Sam.

"I mean, that is if you want to. If you don't, then that's

fine." The look on his face is so forlorn.

I cup his face. "Of course I want to. I'm just not sure if I'll be allowed."

His shoulders slump. "You could always come back to the States with me," I say in an effort to cheer him up.

"I looked into that. I can't go into the Green Card lottery because I didn't go to uni, for a work visa I need a job offer or to be *renowned*, whatever the fuck that means, and a student visa is just insane. I have to put the cash down upfront, and I don't have that kind of dough." Now it's my turn for my shoulders to slump. I knew American immigration rules were tough, but this makes it almost impossible.

"I've got my boss keeping an ear out for anything, but he's not optimistic."

I hate this. I knew when Sam and I started dating that this would happen, but back then it was something way off in the future. Now that future is almost here and it's tearing me and us apart. I don't want to leave Sam, don't want to leave Australia, but I know my chances of extending my visa are about the same as his are of getting to the States. I look up into the green eyes that have turned my back-to-front world upside down, and I know I don't want to leave him.

"There's no harm in trying, right?" I say, and try to smile through my pain. Sam's answering smile is bright, and I know I'd do anything for more of it.

December

Apparently the Australian government aren't romantics. I kind of guessed that, seeing as though it's 2017 and they *still* don't allow gay marriage, but I thought an American girl wanting to stay here and continue her education (and her relationship with a hunky Aussie chippie) would be allowed. According to the immigration department, however, it's not, and my visa expires on January 7. Both Sam and I are devastated, but what can we do? I've seen how they treat illegal immigrants here. We've been trying to spend as much time together and do as much as we can, but no matter how much we don't want it to, time continues to tick down. We haven't really spoken about what's going to happen once I go home—it's too painful—but we've both come to the conclusion that breaking up isn't an option.

I'm down to my last two weeks, which means Christmas is

upon us. It's so weird to be having a hot Christmas! I'd say it feels strange to not see any snow on the ground (fun fact, Sam at age twenty-three has only seen snow once, on a school trip to Canberra), but instead, it feels right. It only makes the pain of having to leave increase.

Christmas is held at his mom and dad's house. A herd of his cousins run around, the women inside, the men outside tending to the barbeque, bottles of beer in their hands. I'm watching the younger kids splash around in the pool when I feel strong arms come around me, his chin resting on my shoulder.

"A bit different than Christmas in Vermont, huh?" he asks.

I nod. "Just a bit, but I like it. It fits with the whole laid-back Aussie way of life."

"I never thought of it that way. I guess it kinda does."

I play with the heart pendant Sam gave me this morning. "I don't want to go home," I whisper, the tears I'm holding back burning the back of my throat. Being here with Sam's family, having them welcome and accept me so openly and quickly, and celebrating such an important holiday with them only tears my heart apart even further. I have loved every single minute I've been here, thanks in large part to the man wrapped around me. It seems so unfair that we've found each other but in a few weeks' time we won't be able to be together. In the eleven and a half months I've been here I've really come to love Australia, and not just because of Sam either. I love the climate (never thought I'd *ever* say that, but I do), the people, the places... just everything. It's like someone took an idea for paradise, added twenty-four million people, and set them far away from the rest of the world to make it that much more attractive and unique. I guess I should be grateful that I got to experience Australian life for as long as I have, but it's not a thought that's going to keep me warm when I'm back in the depths of a Vermont winter. I sigh and Sam squeezes me tighter.

"I don't want you to either."

We stand and watch the kids for a little longer before his mom calls us for lunch.

"Come on," Sam says, taking my hand and giving it a squeeze. "Today is all about happy, so let's not think of what's going to happen in two weeks. Let's go and eat ourselves stupid. We've got a major day of sports tomorrow to prepare for."

In my time here I've watched more sport than I ever did back home. Cricket, AFL, the Melbourne Cup horse race—or the race that literally stops the nation—occasional games of NRL (rugby league) and rugby union, plus V8 racing, cane toad races (yes, it's a thing), and a rubber duck race (for charity). I feel like I've seen it all, but at the same time seen so little. Sam gives me a wink before dragging me to the table. It's too hot to eat inside so we're sitting outside instead. A nice breeze is coming through, keeping the temperature bearable, also known as the mid to high eighties today. I'm trying not to think about the fact that I've just gotten used to the heat when in a few days' time I'll be going back to temps in the thirties and below.

An Australian Christmas meal is so different from an American one. Cold cuts of ham and chicken replace roast ham and turkey, salads replace vegetables, and a huge mound of shrimp is quickly devoured.

"Oh my God!" I say when I spot them. "They're huge."

"Haven't you heard?" Sam asks me. "Everything's bigger down under." He wiggles his eyebrows at me.

"I didn't know shrimp could get so big!"

"Uh-uh. *Prawns,* not shrimp. Contrary to *Crocodile Dundee*, Australians have *never* thrown a shrimp on the barbie. We have prawns, and this, my love," he says, grabbing one and thrusting it in my face, "is a king prawn, fresh off the trawler this morning."

"Well those *prawns*," I say, emphasizing the "correct" terminology, "look incredible, but how do you eat them?" They're all shells, whiskers, and legs.

"Don't worry, babe. I gotcha." He puts a heap on my plate and leads us to our seats at the table.

"Now, you're not allowed to become an Australian until you've learned how to peel a prawn, so here's your official lesson," he says. "First, you twist the head off. Second, peel away the outer shell and legs, including the tail. Third, take the vein out from along the back of the prawn." He cuts down the back and pulls the black string out. "Finally, dip in Thousand Island dressing and enjoy." He dips the prawn in pink sauce and motions for me to open my mouth, which I do. The prawn is sweet and salty, the sauce tangy, the perfect combination.

"Oh my God, that's so good!"

"Food of the gods right there," he agrees.

New England does some pretty good seafood, but nothing compared to this. I don't know if it's the prawn itself, the atmosphere, or the way it was fed to me, but whatever it is just makes everything taste so much better.

The rest of the day is spent lazing around by the pool with periodic interruptions for more food. It's perfect.

***

The next day, Boxing Day, is a major day in the Australian sporting calendar. Not only is it the day the famous Sydney to Hobart yacht race starts, but the Boxing Day cricket test also begins. Naturally, the day is spent on the couch, flicking between the two. Because of my imminent departure, Sam opted not to play cricket this season so we could have as much time together as possible.

"There's nothing like the G on Boxing Day," Sam says as we watch the bowler run in to deliver the first ball of the match.

"Huh?" I ask. I've gotten pretty good at understanding the slang here, but the only G I know is the tram that runs along the coast. "Do you mean the tram?" I ask.

"Nah, the G is short for MCG, or the Melbourne Cricket Ground."

"Oh."

"Yeah, the atmosphere there on Boxing Day, especially for an Ashes test, is second to none."

"What is an Ashes test?"

"Australia versus England."

"Oh. It sounds amazing. I wish I could've had the chance to go."

"Maybe in a few years when it's an Ashes summer again you can come down. We could do the whole tour—Brisbane, Adelaide, Perth, Melbourne, and Sydney. It'd be a great way to see the country too."

I love how he's not daunted by the fact the next Ashes isn't for a few years and yet he has no doubt we'll still be together then. It makes my heart swell with love. "I'd love that." Even though I know that there is so much time between now and then, the trip sounds like a dream and I want to do it, so I will. I love Sam and I want to be with him. Somehow we'll find a way.

"You know, I'm gonna try and see you too," he says. "I don't want you to think that you're the one who's always going to have to come here."

I cup his face. "I don't think that."

"Good, 'cause I'm looking at coming in June or July. Maybe I could be there for Independence Day. That'd be cool, right?"

"Any time I get to spend with you is amazing." I lean over and kiss him.

We made love that night, but instead of being sad it'll be one of the last times we're together, I felt hopeful. Sure, five or six months is a long time, and 9,641 miles (I googled it) is a long way, but I have faith Sam and I can make it. We *have* to make it; you can't be able to turn someone's world upside down if it's only a fling. No, such earth-shattering, perspective-tilting feelings only come with the real deal.

January

It's been almost three weeks since Sam and I bid a tearful goodbye. I waited until the very last second before going through the golden gates at Brisbane International Airport. Even now, when I close my eyes, I can still picture him pressed to the glass, watching as I ran to my gate.

It's a year today since we met and I've been trying to get Sam on Skype all morning, but he isn't answering. I stayed up half the night and into the early hours of this morning so I'd reach him before he went to work, but it seems it wasn't enough. I'm trying not to think about what this means as I lie in bed, watching the snow fall steadily outside my bedroom window. It's funny, a year ago I would've killed to be back in the cold, and now I'd kill to be back in the humid heat of the Gold Coast. Just another example of how Sam Thompson has turned my world upside down, even if he's ignoring my calls, the jerk. I go back to my Kindle and the book I was reading. For reasons that are going to stay nameless—*jerk*—I've been getting into a lot of books set in Australia. There's one in particular that I really love, about this motorbike racing family with terrible luck in love. The first book's called *Breaking the Cycle*; you should check it out. I've just immersed myself in Reed and Bria's world when the doorbell rings. Slowly I extricate myself from my mound of blankets and make my way downstairs. The doorbell rings again when I'm halfway there.

"All right, all right, I'm coming!" I yell.

I open the door and just like it did a year ago, the sight of Sam standing before me turns my world upside down and renders me mute.

"Well? You going to let me in? I'm freezing my nuts off here," he says as he hops from foot to foot.

I nod and move so he can come in. The sight of my bronzed Aussie wrapped up in ski gear looks so wrong, but so right. In so many ways Sam and I are complete opposites, but for some reason we're exactly what the other needs in order to take our back-to-front worlds, turn them upside down, and make them feel like home. My home is wherever Sam is, and there's no place like it.

The End

Pineapple Dreams

BY ARIA PEYTON

Dedication

For everyone who believes in the pot of gold at the end of a rainbow.

I HAVE A CONFESSION TO MAKE.

Yeah, I know, who doesn't, right? But please, hear me out.

My name's Belle. I'm freshly forty and have never been in love. Yep, you heard that right. Never. You'd think by this age I would have experienced true love. Well… no. I haven't.

At one point in my naïve and sexually undereducated life I thought I was… and then I fell pregnant and he left faster than Usain Bolt timed at the Olympics.

The stupid thing is, I was twenty when this happened! But naïveté has no boundaries or age restrictions. If you don't know you're being played for a fool, then shit is going to happen. In my case, shit hit in the form of twin girls two days after my twenty-first birthday, and you know what? Spending that milestone in extra-long labour is no fun at all.

So from twenty-one with newborns, to forty with nineteen-year-olds, I have travelled the rough road of single parenthood. For my birthday this year, I wanted to actually travel on proper roads and go somewhere. Anywhere. Preferably away from the stagnant little life I've found myself stuck in all these years.

Don't get me wrong, I love my girls to Jupiter and beyond, but there's something stifling about having an almost non-existent support base and no time for myself. None of this self-discovery business I've heard the other mums talk about over the years. No breaks. No holidays past the borders of South Australia. Nothing.

I'll tell you a little more about how my stupidity landed me in motherhood with no backup soon, but for now I'm on holiday with my girls. A joint birthday holiday out of the state—finally!—visiting iconic landmarks throughout some of our great country.

***

For years, I've wanted to travel overseas, take my girls on an adventure of cultures and landscapes. As you can imagine though, I've never managed to do this. By the time I had myself established in a job that paid enough to go travelling and accrue sufficient annual leave, my girls had reached high school and their hellish study regime. I felt guilty for wanting to take them away from everything for a few months and have them miss out on their education—despite the excellent learning they could've done while trekking around another country.

Time whittled away like wood under a knife, until this year. With my fortieth birthday looming, and my twins, Ronni and Chrissy—Veronica and Christabel on official documents—

about to start university after taking a gap year to get out there and work, I wanted to finally grab life by the balls and go somewhere, experience something different, let my hair down for a change.

Grasping at straws, and possibly the last opportunity I may ever have to travel with my children, I decided to plan a holiday for us. A trip around part of Australia to see as many *big* things as we could.

So here we are, spending the summer holidays on a road trip through Oz. When we first started out, Ronni scoffed at what I had planned for us, and Chrissy gave me the biggest eye-roll I've ever witnessed, so large I'm surprised she didn't manage to see her own brain back there. Despite their occasional protests though, I can see their secret enjoyment in our trip. I mean seriously, what's not to love about a giant turnbuckle and propeller?

We've been through Victoria, New South Wales, and crossed the border into Queensland to spend a couple of weeks seeing every big thing we can. In addition, we've been to Australia Zoo to appease Chrissy and her love of animals, and we've seen as many art galleries as we can find to soothe the artist in Ronni.

But as we come closer to needing to make the journey home again, we're spending our final week in Woombye, the home of the Big Pineapple, as well as the Big Macadamia. Yum to both of those! And it's just our luck that a gallery, Queensland Zoo, and the pineapple are in walking distance of each other, and all are nice and close to the caravan park we're staying in. It's my pleasure to be able to indulge them both in what they love.

***

We cruise the town after settling into our caravan. It's easy to tell we're tourists from the southern end of the country. Everyone around us is tanned and buff. Okay, maybe not everyone, but certainly the local contingent we're paying attention to. Although our pasty white skin has finally browned a little on our road trip, it's still very obvious that we're not from around here.

We attract attention with the combination of our almost vampiric paleness and very clear burn lines. All right, I'll be honest, my *girls* attract the attention. They're young, gorgeous, and have sass. I'm just the frumpy-looking mum who never had the time to regain her pre-baby body no matter how hard she tried.

But that's okay. Kind of. All right, so I'm learning to accept it.

Instead of worrying though, I enjoy the view from behind my mirrored sunnies of all the hot young studmuffins who openly perv on my teens. I'm glad they're nineteen; otherwise the urge to bitch slap some of these guys would be stronger than it is now. Anyone under twenty-five can perv… okay, maybe thirty is the *absolute* max, but over that and it just gets skeezy.

Especially the ones clearly over the hill or with their wives. I glare over the top of my lenses at them.

At dinnertime on our first evening in town, we sit outside

a small but noisy restaurant-slash-café in the centre of town, enjoying the prospect of dinner and the still-warm air of summer. When our waiter comes around, it's my turn to feel like the skeezy perv. Or am I allowed to claim cougar status now?

My skin tingles with awareness as he stands next to me and hands out the small menus. His voice resonates within me when he reads out the daily specials, a smile on his face the whole time. The urge to kiss that smile surges through me, taking me by surprise. I thrust my hands beneath the table, gripping the chair tight to keep from launching myself at this unsuspecting young man.

As he smiles again and walks off, I realise I have absolutely no idea what the specials are. I heard none of the words, only the timbre and cadence of his voice. My view of his arse as he walks back through the door to serve someone else wavers when Ronni grabs hold of my shoulder and shakes the crap out of me.

"Mum. Mum! Yoo-hoo. Over here, space cadet."

I wrench my eyes away from the hunk who I hope will be back soon and glare at Chrissy first for her smart-arse words, and then at Ronni for shaking me.

"Do you mind?"

Ronni snorts. "Geez, Mum. Feel free to perv all you like, but do you think you can be a little bit subtle about it next time? You were starting to drool."

Chrissy snort-laughs—a snaughle—from the other side of the table, earning another scowl.

"Was not," I grumble, surreptitiously wiping my lower

lip. Just in case. This makes them laugh harder. I love being the brunt of their humour some days. Makes me feel freaking awesome. My inner sarcastic bitch is flipping them the bird as I shoot mummy daggers across the table to them. I may be forty, but I can still stoop to their level of immaturity at a moment's notice.

With a "Hmph" I pick up a menu and scan what's listed. But that's all I manage to do. Scan. Nothing sticks in my head because all I can see floating across the page is a set of magnificent blue eyes, the kind I long to stare into as I ride the owner into the sunset. I allow my thoughts to wander under the sheets, a fantasy never to come true, until I'm rudely shaken out of it. Again!

"What?" I snap at Ronni. Chrissy snaughles again and tries unsuccessfully to muffle it with her napkin. I pin each daughter with a stare, watching as their identical faces fill with mirth. "What's so fucking funny, you twits?"

Chrissy loses it laughing, pointing slightly to my right with one hand as the other slaps the table. I turn slowly, feeling the increase in tingles as I meet his gaze. His cerulean eyes are crinkled with his smile as he so obviously fights the urge to join my daughters in their chuckle fest. I want to glare at him too, just for taking their side, so I slide my sunnies down the bridge of my nose and pin him with *the look* every mother perfects when their children are young.

The intention to laugh leaves his face, his lips no longer stifling humour. Instead, he unconsciously licks the bottom one. The crinkles leave the corners of his eyes, only to be replaced by dilated pupils and a look I've only read about. But dammit, the moment is broken when Chrissy coughs rather loudly.

"I'd like to order the fettuccini carbonara, please, with a side salad, and a vodka raspberry."

Mr Smooth and Delectable nods, not breaking eye contact for extended seconds until Chrissy coughs again, this time with a laugh in it. Something flashes in his gorgeous eyes; regret, maybe? He taps in her order on his iPad and turns to Ronni. She orders too, and then all eyes are on me.

Fuck! I hadn't taken in anything from the menu, didn't hear the specials before, and have no clue what to order.

"And what can I get for you?" His sultry voice shivers through me, and as I open my mouth to give him a sassy answer, I find myself tongue-tied and stuttering. I swallow, trying to force the words from my throat to order my dinner. With a shake of my head, I grab my water, take a large gulp, and hang my head in dismay. I can't even speak around him. This is ridiculous!

Finally, I manage to croak, "What would you recommend?"

His smile lightens the pressure on my throat, and as he speaks, enticing me with promises of delicious morsels of food, my imagination runs wild, hearing that same voice make vows of hot nights and even hotter sex.

"That sounds great," I murmur, forcing the words past lips gone dry again. "Thank you."

I'm lost in thoughts of our to-die-for waiter when the object of my daydreams returns to the table, laden with plates.

"Your orders, ladies," he announces in his velvet tones. I

can't help but glance up at him over the rims of my glasses, meeting his eyes as he places my plate down. He drags a smile from me with his own grin, then walks off inside. By the time I turn back to the table, Ronni is already scoffing her dinner and Chrissy is inspecting hers.

With my fork in hand, I look down, hand poised to dig in. "What's this?"

My girls stop midchew and frown at me. "Wha ou mean?" Ronni garbles through a mouthful. "Ou ord'd ee."

"Yes, I know I ordered it. But what in the hell did I order?" I'm staring at the colourful mess on my plate in confusion. "Surely you have some idea of what this is."

Chrissy giggles through her food, then swallows before replying, "I think it was some kind of new-age fried rice. I think… I can't be quite sure. I was too busy watching you drooling over the waitstaff to take any notice of your food choice."

I can't help the scowl I aim her way, muttering, "Well you're no bloody help, then."

Ronni laughs as she wipes her lips on a napkin. "Pretty sure it's fancy veggie rice, Mum. But I have to admit, you were funnier to watch than to listen to him speak."

"Speak for yourself. I found his voice—"

"We get it. Mesmerising." I watch them drag out the word and make funny faces at me, rolling their eyes in an "I'm under hypnosis" type motion. Dickheads. I bred dickheads, seriously.

"Shut up, both of you." For anyone observing this table, I wouldn't blame them for thinking I wasn't their mother. I can't help the smile I'm hiding though. They really do act more like friends at times than my kids. I like the banter I'm able to share with them.

We eat in between comfortable silences and pleasant conversation. The food is delicious and despite my initial shock at not knowing what the hell was on my plate, I'm glad I went with his recommendation.

"How do you two feel about dining here tomorrow night?" I ask casually, popping another mouthful in and chewing slowly. I studiously avoid eye contact.

"Oh yeah, sure, Mum. That sounds great. Any particular reason you don't want to try another fine dining establishment?" There's humour in Chrissy's voice.

I wave my fork around airily. "No reason other than the food here is great. Thought we might try something different on the menu tomorrow."

Chrissy shakes her head at me as she scoops up her last forkful and points it at me, one eye squinting. "We're onto you, you know that, right?"

Giving her my "I'm totally innocent" look, I shake my head. "No idea." But there's a smirk there for her. We laugh together and are still laughing when Mr Voice of Velvet comes back to collect our plates.

"How was your meal, ladies?"

At our nods, he smiles briefly at my girls, and a little longer at me, before gathering the dishes. "Can I get you a dessert menu at all?"

Although the offer is tempting, and I really could do with some sweets, I glance around the table before speaking. "No, thanks. Not tonight." I grace him with a smile and hope to hell he's on tomorrow night. "Tomorrow, perhaps?"

I receive a blinding grin in response, which makes my chest flutter. I'm almost 100 percent sure I'm not having a heart attack, but something's going on in there. I nod once, struggling to look away from him.

When he leaves and our table is clean of everything but our drinks, Ronni slaps my arm, whisper-yelling, "He was *so* flirting with you, Mum!"

"Huh? What?" I'm gobsmacked. But if anyone is going to know what flirting is, it's my girls. I think they mastered the art in order to get their own way, score discounts in shops, and who knows what else, so I'm leaning towards believing her claim. "Really?" The blush that steals up my cheeks can't be stopped, so when he comes back with the bill, I'm bright freaking red. I just nod mutely at him.

"See! Totally flirting with you." Chrissy joins in the declaration. She looks at Ronni and they share their silent twin speak. They both nod and turn to me. "Okay, we'll come back tomorrow night. I'm curious to see where this goes."

***

The next day we get up early and go shopping at Sunshine Plaza. We all have a ball and spend way too much money, but it's so worth being able to kick back and relax about it for a change. We have lunch at Maroochy Surf Club, then stroll up the beach towards Cotton Tree, checking out the cool rock formations embedded in the sand.

I still have no idea what they are, but they look amazing. The views from my map app are even better than on the ground. Gotta love technology. Time flies by as we enjoy the sand between our toes and the wind in our hair. Naturally, Ronni complains that she'll have to wash the seawater out of her hair, but really, girl, live a little already!

It's past five when we set out on the return journey, and the girls fidget in their seats as we near Woombye. It's annoying me, all the constant wriggle and jiggle in the car.

"What's up? You two got worms or something?"

Chrissy snorts and shakes her head at me in the rear-view mirror. "Nup. Just wanna get to dinner."

I squint one eye at her in the mirror. "Oh yeah. And why's that?" I try to fight my smile at the prospect of seeing the spunky waiter again as I wait for her answer.

"I think you know why, Mum. I think you'd be jiggling too if you weren't driving."

Ronni chimes in with, "I wanna see if Mr Flirty ups his game tonight."

I can hear the laughter in their voices, and it makes me smile even as it sort of hurts. I can count on one hand how many times I've dated while they've been on this planet. And that's kind of sad if you think about it. It's a wonder my pink parts haven't cobwebbed over by now. And it's not for lack of trying either.

My darling daughters have tried to set me up with single dads, teachers, after-school carers, police officers, and anyone else they can think of who might date an on-the-larger-side mother of two. Coffee with whoever their choice of the week was has been about the extent of it, with only a few making it to an actual date. It makes me sigh, but I've resigned myself to being alone in this life.

That is until Mr Hot Stuff at the restaurant popped on by. Now my neglected pussy is craving some attention and responding intensely to him alone.

Which is a shame because, without asking, I know he's too young. And why the hell would he be interested, anyway? I dined with two very gorgeous young women last night who are obviously much closer to his age bracket. I hate that I'm suddenly jealous of my own daughters, but I can't lie and say I haven't wished a time or two to be that young again and actually able to have fun.

My hands grip the steering wheel as I fight the surge of emotion those thoughts bring. I wouldn't give up my girls for the world, but I'm allowed to wish I'd been a little more experienced and knowledgeable about such things before throwing my social life to the wind so early. I'm entitled to not want to be lonely for the rest of my life.

The café comes into view, making me wonder how I got us here in one piece when I wasn't paying any attention to where I was driving. I give myself a mental pat on the back for us all being alive, then find a car park nearby. We head into the café and find a seat outside again, quietly hoping we get the same waiter.

I'm not disappointed, and I think Ronni and Chrissy are pretty happy too. The smirks on their faces are damn obvious, their hands and curtained hair not hiding a bloody thing. I'm scowling at them as they giggle like ten-year-olds before I realise that there's heat emanating from someone beside me. I turn slowly, craning my neck up as I do.

It's him. He managed to get the menus on the table without me noticing. The smile on his lips makes my insides go gooey as our eyes meet. This man, as young and unattainable as he is, creates sensations within me that I'm not familiar with; the types of feelings I've only ever imagined from reading second-hand romance novels on the train to work each day now buzz through me. They spark heat and longing in areas thought long dead from disuse.

"Good evening, ladies. What can I start you off with tonight?" His velvet voice winds its way through my centre, undoing any semblance of poise I'd retained.

"Midori lemonade for me, please. Girls?"

"Vodka raspberry for me," Chrissy says, while Ronni orders a tequila sunrise.

"Sheesh, Ron, you planning on walking or rolling out of here tonight?" Chrissy asks her.

"Ha. Ha. Mum's driving, so I'm good to go."

I suck in air at her words, unnoticed by them as they laugh it up and start a conversation I tune out. I don't want to see the look on our waiter's face now, knowing that he is privy to our relationship. A feather-light touch on my arm snags my attention back to him, and he gives me a small smile. "I'll be back shortly with your drinks."

Disappointment fills me as he walks off to do his job. The angle of the sunlight catches on his tanned skin, highlighting the structure of his toned arms. I get a tiny peek through his work shirt as he moves, but it's so brief. I sigh at the impossible dream of having someone young and insanely good-looking being interested in me. Focusing my attention on the menu, I slip off into a world where love exists for me and I'm deliriously happy.

My girls pick up on my melancholy and order for me when he returns. I hear them asking for his recommendation like I did last night, so I'm sure to get another random dish for dinner. I can feel him hovering next to me, almost like he wants me to look up, but I can't. It hurts to be affected so much by someone so out of reach. Even the kick to the shins by one of my traitorous daughters doesn't budge me.

Dinner takes time, the crowd tonight being larger than last night, but it flies as my teens drag me into their conversation, chipping away at my misery. Before we know it, plates are being placed down on the table in front of Ronni and Chrissy. They glance at me briefly and dig in, hunger overriding the need to be polite, it seems. By the time I look up, he's gone again. I listen to a conversation had through mouths full of food, shaking my head at their manners, or lack thereof.

As I'm contemplating if these teens really are mine, a plate is set gently before me. A finger runs lightly over my arm and lingers, not actually leaving my skin. I can't help but look up this time.

"Enjoy," he tells me. There's still a smile there, lingering on his lips, but it seems not as bright as before, not as blinding. I push my sunglasses to the top of my head, snagging them in my hair, and meet his eyes. The contact seems to last a lifetime, when in reality it's probably mere seconds. His smile strengthens, in turn bolstering my own. The resting finger near my wrist strokes ever so gently, creating a concentrated spot of burning heat.

That finger sneaks down towards my own, and as I shift my hand to pick up my knife, I lift my pinkie slightly. There's tiny contact as his finger wraps around mine, a minute amount of time where the universe aligns for me.

And then the moment is over as he gives my pinkie a squeeze and turns away from the table, returning to his job. If I weren't seated already, I'd likely swoon as he glances back from the café's doorway, shooting another smile my way. I pick up my drink and have a sip through the straw as I watch him until he disappears from sight. When I turn my attention back to the table, I'm being stared at.

"Well, I think that answers that one, Chris," Ronni announces, picking up her cocktail and slurping it. My cringe is automatic. "I do believe that our darling mother is being hit on." Her grin is huge and apparently contagious, as Chrissy's face splits into a smile, too.

"I do believe you're right, Ronni dear. What are we going to do about this?"

At that, I freak out slightly. "Do? You'll do nothing. Every time you've attempted to set me up with someone before, it never worked."

"You ended up screwing the cop, didn't you?" Ronni mutters, at the same time Chrissy speaks again.

"Awww, come on, Mum. Besides, if we *do* nothing this time, then you'll end up *doing* no one. Again."

I raise an eyebrow at her, earning me her patented puppy/

kitten eyes. Puppy-dog eyes were never enough for her; she had to go and combine it with sad kitty eyes. The result is disturbing when you want to stand your ground. But I need to. They're dabbling in my life here, and if I'm going to fuck up this opportunity, whatever it may be, then it's going to be *my* fuck-up, not theirs.

I hold up a finger, halting her words but not her expression. It's pathetic, but in the funniest way. I can't help myself, I crack up laughing. And that laughter manages to attract attention. I really should learn to laugh quieter, but I just can't. It's big, it kind of booms, and it's definitely not for the faint of heart. But you know what? Tonight I just don't care. I couldn't give a shit if my laugh is big, or if people are looking over. I'm finally having fun with my children, my gorgeous nineteen-year-old girls, and living without restrictions.

It's such a freeing revelation!

And then, from inside the café, comes the man who makes me dare to dream again. The nameless waiter with gorgeous everything. As he serves the other tables outside, he gifts me with little glances, the occasional flick of his eyes in my direction. Even if this is just a bit of fun flirting, it gives me the hope that one day I'll find my happily ever after like most people dream of. If nothing else, he's given me hope.

***

The next morning I awake from dreams of our nameless waiter, a flash of arousal engulfing my tired body. In the years of unintentional celibacy, I've done my fair share of "rubbing one out." Now is one of those times when I wish I could do just that. But… kids. A scowl pulls at my eyebrows as my heated core cries out for attention. I desperately need relief.

Pushing back the sheet, I make an early trip to the bathroom, doing my business before jumping in for a shower. Wasting no time, I lather up and reach between my legs.

Showered and a damn sight more relaxed than when I woke, I break out the map of the town. Today we're going to the Big Pineapple. It's the perfect location really, since Queensland Zoo is on the same plot of land, and the art gallery too. We'll all be happy Vegemites in one trip. The last time I visited was when I was nine. It holds memories I've always wanted to rekindle.

I guess it's time to see if those memories hold up to the reality of now.

***

Everyone is up, showered, breakfasted, and ready to roll, so we head out. I don't think I've mentioned it yet, but we've cruised in classic luxury on this road trip. When my dad passed away, he left me his Ford XY GT sedan. I think it was his way of saying sorry for ditching me when I needed him most. It's in pristine condition and runs like a dream. The V8 engine rumbles like nobody's business, and chews through petrol like you wouldn't believe.

Off we go, thundering along the highway to the parking lot across from the iconic pineapple. It's already hot by midmorning and I can feel the sweat rolling down my back beneath my bra strap as we cross the overpass, watching the cars whizz along beneath our feet.

My admiration of the Big Pineapple is scoffed at by Chrissy, who just wants to get to the zoo. "All in good time," I tell her as I walk towards it. First on my agenda is to ride the plantation train before the heat becomes any worse. "Come on, let's go for a ride!"

I pay the money at the café counter and we find our way through to the platform where the train departs. I love it when I time things just right. We look out over the plantation while we wait.

"Are you going to climb the pineapple when we get back, Mum?" Chrissy asks.

With my insane vertigo at the damn Big Rocking Horse, her question is a reasonable one. "Yeah, why the hell not. I did that blasted horse. Nothing's going to stop me from climbing a pineapple." I grin at them both as the train pulls up and passengers disembark. An announcement rattles through speakers nearby. The voice is strangely familiar, but the distortion from the speakers and the noise from the passengers heading back inside make it hard to distinguish.

The next half hour is spent enjoying the up and down of the track, the rainforest, passing the zoo, and all the sights in between. I'm happily hot and a little windblown on our return, and eager to climb to the top viewing platform of the landmark structure.

Photos are taken, selfies are posted online, and we enjoy the tiny space as we look out as far as we can see. The breeze up here is cooling, and I put off descending the stairs as long as I can. Eventually though, thirst gets the better of me and I give in, going down to see about lunch in their café.

As we step out into the sunshine, I misjudge my footing, miss the last step, and stumble heavily, making a freaking spectacle of myself in front of strangers. I was always told not to worry about the opinions of others, but it's hard not to when people are staring at you like you're some kind of clumsy freak.

"Oh shit, Mum, are you okay?" Ronni is at my side in a flash, making sure I'm steady on my feet before she lets me go and steps back to assess the damage.

"I'm fine, Ronni, just a stupid trip."

"You almost fell on your arse, Mum. No stupid trip about it." Guiding me towards the gift shop and café, she starts brushing me down as if I were covered in dust and dirt. I'm forty and suddenly embarrassed by my child touching my butt in public.

"Oh my God, Ronni, can you stop that, please? I never hit the ground so there's nothing to dust off." She keeps going. "Get your hands off my butt, Ron!"

She laughs at me, continuing with her inappropriate touching. People are watching her as they come and go, curiosity in some gazes, humour in others.

I blush, wanting to crawl inside a hole. Embarrassment floods me as my face burns, the red hue creeping from my chest all the way to my damn eyebrows. As I'm dying from mortification, I hear a familiar masculine chuckle nearby. *Oh God! It's him!* That makes it even worse. My hands shoot up to cover my face, hiding from the hot waiter of the past two nights.

Ronni hits me across the bicep, sending my arm fat wobbling, increasing the wish for the ground to open and swallow me whole. Although, at the rate I'm going, I'll get stuck in the crevice and never get out in either direction.

I slide the brim of my cap further down over my eyes and wait for the clock to speed up, taking me out of this moment and into tomorrow. Of course, the universe doesn't hear my desperate plea. I know this from the excited yet hushed whispers coming from my two teens. It's a wonder they're not giggling maniacally. For the first time ever, I wish I could shrink like a cock in cold water.

"Are you okay there, ma'am?" His voice may be steady but I can see the damn smirk, and ma'am? *Really?* I groan at the same time Chrissy snickers.

"Ma'am. He called Mum ma'am!" They both lose it in a fit of hysteria, leaving me floundering before the hottest guy I've had the pleasure of meeting in... well, ever. I have the overwhelming urge to slap them both, but I'm sure that'll look like grand parenting in front of the hot stranger. At least I find my voice this time.

"Ugh. Don't mind them. Teenage freaks."

His deep chuckle sends those zings of something I haven't experienced down my spine. The more he laughs, the farther it travels. His voice at the café was one thing but oh my, that chuckle is another monster entirely. In minutes, my body is humming and all I want to do is lie down and ride the feeling to its natural end. Without warning, the laughing stops, from both my girls and the man who makes me sizzle.

Slowly, I peel my eyes open—*when the hell did I shut*

them?—and actually take notice of what's going on around me. My girls are staring at me like I've got two heads, and *he* is giving me a *look*. His eyes are hooded and the slight smirk on his lips is making the tingle deepen.

"What?" I ask, looking between the three of them. Chrissy shakes her head, eyes rolling like I'm dense, while Ronni crosses her arms over her damn perky boobs, grinning like an idiot. It'd be nice to have perky boobs again. I want to scowl at my stupid thoughts, but as my eyebrows dip, a light touch on my shoulder sends my heart racing.

"Nothing, ma'am. You look a little flustered though. Would you like to sit down for a bit?"

Mortification threatens to rise and laugh at my clumsiness, but is squashed by the glance Mr Doable gives me. It's different from the expressions he gave me at the café, and I can't quite decipher it. However, it seems my daughters already have. Despite their giggles and eye-rolls, when I turn back to them, gesturing for them to follow me, their wide eyes and shooing motions tell another story. Frowning, I mouth, "What?" Chrissy gives me her well-practised head shake, the one meant to tell me I'm an idiot, and strides over to me.

"Mum, he's hot, he's still eyeing you off, and offering for you to *sit down*. For fuck's sake, just go already!"

Her demanding whisper encourages one of my eyebrows to lift in question, earning me yet another eye-roll. Practically shoving me away, she takes a few steps back and crosses her arms again, foot tapping impatiently on the rough-sawn wooden floorboards. Seeing my indecision, Ronni flaps her hands at me too, the shooing motion reminiscent of trying to fend off mozzies.

I relent and turn away, checking over my shoulder that they'll be okay. By the time I turn, they're both giggling, heads together, shooting me looks and hand waves to move me along. Then they turn their attention to what's on the shelf in front of them, having already found some quirky souvenir I'll no doubt be buying them later. As I face the front to see where I'm going—since bashing into something now would be the icing on the cake—I see Mr Spunky waiting for me by a door behind the register.

As I pass customer service, he touches the small of my back, guiding me through the door. I can't help the involuntary flinch as his hand sends heat through me. He must feel my movement, because he withdraws the contact and the tingles stop. My shoulders sag and my head drops, along with any self-esteem I'd managed to regain by his apparent interest in me.

The seat against the wall looks comfy and I drop myself onto it, uncaring at this point of my life whether I appear elegant or like a heifer. With a quick flick, I drop my handbag to the floor and lean my head right back across the low backrest, resting it against the wall. When I take my hat off, hair sticks to my face with the incredible humidity here in Queensland, and I can imagine I look like a hot mess.

Great.

I finally manage to get in a small space with a hot male for the first time in *years* and I probably look like shit. Story of my fekking life.

I hear plastic snap and lift my head too fast from the wall, cracking my neck in the process. The world spins before me as my eyes adjust. Mr Spunkytrunks is offering me a bottle of water, the condensation on the outside showing me that it's icy cold and ready for gulping. Without any decorum, my grabby hands snatch the bottle and bring it to my forehead, rolling the cold plastic over my sweat-sticky skin.

The heat today makes me wonder why in the ever-loving fuck I brought us here in summer. Of all times of the year, bloody summer. Idiot!

With my eyes closed, I smooth the cold, condensation-wet bottle over my face and down my neck. A soft groan escapes me at the cooling sensation, which seems to elicit a slightly louder groan from the young man I'd almost forgotten is with me. *Ha!* That's total bullshit; I knew he was there. Slowly opening my eyes, I have to confess that I like what I see standing nearby.

As I continue to roll the cold bottle over my neck and top of my chest, I take in the fine specimen of masculinity that gives me tingles. Bronze from the Queensland sun, muscles galore adorning his sculpted biceps and pecs, and thighs that look like they could support… ahem… well, they look sturdy. His shorts hug those thighs, giving me a better look at the legs. I avoid glancing at the bulge for now.

I allow my eyes to scan farther down, coming to rest on the tattoos winding around his calves. A dragon curls its head around the right leg just under his knee, a foreleg and claws resting beneath its chin.

A husky chuckle brings my eyes slowly back up his body, not missing an inch of the delicious-looking man. The glint in his eyes and the smile gracing his lips brings that tingle up to a burn. He licks those lips as they roll in and out, a cheeky smile appearing on the glistening, kissable… *No!* Must not think any more dirty thoughts about—

"Like what you see?"

His voice. Oh my God, his voice does it for me every time he speaks. It's like chocolate-smothered cheesecake. Meeting his eyes, I can't control the slight nod. *Traitorous head!* And it seems that my tongue is in on the mutiny as it peeks out to wet my own lips, dry despite the water… which is still in my hand. Without breaking eye contact, I twist the cap off the bottle and gulp the cold water. It soothes the parched walls of my throat, the chill refreshing as it cools the burning desire within me.

Or at least I can wish it does. All it really does is give me a brain freeze.

Within seconds of guzzling almost a full bottle of ice-cold water, my head is throbbing and searing pain shoots through my temples.

"Ah fuck!" I swear, clutching my head as I shake it from side to side. "Fuck a fucking duck!" My foot joins in, stomping on the wooden floor, sending echoes bouncing in the small room. "The pain, the pain!" See, this is why I stay away from Slurpees and shit like that these days; I just have no damn tolerance for the things I used to. Damn aging sucks balls.

As I'm in the death throes of a massive head freeze, warm hands slip in under mine and a whispered "I've been dreaming of this for two days" feathers across my cheek before lips make contact with mine. Their caress is gentle, trialling the contact, but as the desire flaming through me increases, the head chill wanes and my passion kicks in. He must sense when I'm good to go, as the movement of his lips becomes less gentle, more urgent.

A groan vibrates in my mouth as my fingers tug on his hair. *When did my hands sneak in there?*

Who cares; the strands are long enough to grab, and smooth to the touch. I tug again, enjoying the effect it has on his kissing. Unable to help myself, I nibble on his bottom lip, tugging the stubble-edged flesh between my teeth.

Unlike previous men, this guy seems to like my lip nibbles and it spurs him on. The kiss becomes deeper, more passionate, and I suddenly find myself pulled up out of my seat and pressed hard against him. Hands are on my ample butt, pushing me closer to his ripped body, my soft and squishy to his hard and oh… *hard*. Swoon. Instinct has me grinding, pushing my pelvis as close to his as I can manage.

It's divine!

His fingers squeeze my arse, and mine are on their way to return the favour when a loud bang has us both jerking back. I lose balance, falling backwards into the chair, hair mussed, legs akimbo, and shooting daggers at the person who dared interrupt the first decent kiss I've had in years.

The interrupter glares straight back, tapping her foot on the floor and her finger on the watch on her wrist. Ronni huffs impatiently at me.

"You've had your fun, Mum. Now it's time to go. You promised we'd go to the art gallery today, and Chrissy wants to talk to the keepers at the zoo. It's getting damn hot out there and—"

I'm gobsmacked. Utterly speechless. "Your timing sucks

nuts, kid." The chair has decided to keep me, as when I try to haul my arse out of it, I just can't. I may have turned to jelly under the caress of expert lips. After several failed attempts, with my daughter waiting in the doorway, arms crossed, and Spunky McHard-on still standing in front of me, I huff in frustration and blow the sticky strands of hair out of my face.

Or at least I try to. Those fuckers aren't going anywhere in a hurry.

Crossing one leg over the other, I fold my arms over my large bosom and lean back. "Well, I guess you'll be waiting a while, Ronni. This chair doesn't want me to go anywhere." I give her one of my patented "mum" smiles; you know what I mean—the one that tells you you're not going to get anywhere by arguing with me at this very moment.

Rough pads gently stroke along the back of my arm, following the line of my forearm to my hand. His fingers curl around my own, linking them together. With a firm tug and mesmerising stare, he yanks me up out of the possessive chair until I'm standing right up against him. When I go to move away, he holds firm to my hand, stopping me in my tracks. I frown at him, trying again to leave.

All I get is a small shake of his head. His eyes move to the door and back to me. Repeats. I turn my head. "Ronni, take a twenty out of my purse and grab what you and your sister want from the shop." I shuffle my handbag towards her with my foot from where it sits on the floor. "Grab a couple of cold drinks too and meet me outside somewhere shady."

"You're shady at the moment, Mum," Ronni mumbles as she bends down to retrieve a twenty-dollar note from my purse. I feel my bag hit my ankle as she slings it back over to me, and the door soon shuts behind her.

Fingers thread through my damp hair and down my cheek. "Where were we?" he asks. After being crashed back into reality, I try to pull away from him, regretful that I have to leave, but also aware of the certainty that this isn't anything more than a delightful kiss on a summer's afternoon. A frown dips his brow when he sees my reluctance.

"Why so sad, pretty lady?"

"My name's Belle, and I'm no pretty lady." My voice is sad; there's no hiding it. He strokes my cheek again, thumb coming down to play across my bottom lip. I almost swoon at his touch, but I don't. Steeling my legs, I try to sidestep, but end up tripping on my bag instead. Down we go, me onto my fleshy butt, back hitting the floor hard, and the taut-muscled hottie landing perfectly in line with my hot and tingly lady parts.

For an accident, it couldn't have been planned better if I'd tried. Except I really have to go and I don't want to. I can hear my girls' voices outside the door, chatting to the other people in the shop serving the pineapple-shaped tourist trap.

"I have to go…." I look at him pointedly, wanting to know his name.

"Matt. My name's Matt." His lips are so close when he speaks, breath skating over my mouth. I want to bite those lips again, and they're so damn near. Near enough for catching.

My thoughts are lost in a trance as I pull my torso up off the floor to capture his mouth with mine. Arms wrap around my upper back, keeping me off the floor, and I reciprocate, wrapping mine around under his arms to clasp at his rippling muscles. If I had claws, they'd be deeply imbedded in Matt's shoulders right about now, and most likely needing a pair of pliers to be removed.

The kiss ends naturally this time, no interruptions by cock-blocking daughters. Speaking of which….

"I know I'd probably have your balls if you'd tried, but why in the hell weren't you trying to pick up my girls instead of me?"

Mouth working its way down my neck, he murmurs, "I'm not one for younger girls. Always had an eye for an older woman, but I can't have done too well this time with such a small gap between us."

"Flattery will get you everywhere," I gasp as he nibbles my throat. "But I think you're too young for me, Matt."

He lifts up, shaking his head at me. "I don't think so. Doesn't matter anyway. Age is irrelevant in the long run. Just passion and the commitment people share."

This conversation is getting deeper than I'm comfortable with. I may have had a hot make-out session with him, but I don't know Matt and he doesn't know me. I wriggle beneath him, feeling his erection pressing my hot spot. Dammit! I'm throbbing down there, ready for action. It's been so damn long.

I stop moving and meet his eyes. "I need to get up. My girls and I have places to go. It was nice to meet you, Matt." I manage to work my arms up from where they're wedged and hold one hand under his nose, palm out for a friendly shake. He glances at my hand and back to my eyes. His crinkle with amusement, as if I've done something funny, and instead of taking my hand in his, he dips his head and sucks on a finger.

Fireworks shoot through me at the erotic contact, sending my pelvis into another fit of unconscious grinding against his cock. His suction gets stronger and a moan escapes him. I'm so rooted! No matter what this guy does to me, he sets my body aflame. It's enough to drive any sane woman to the nuthouse. Teeth drag up my fingertip until he reaches the top, letting it go gently.

He leans in to kiss my nose and backs off, kneeling before me and offering me a hand with which to haul myself off the floor. When we're upright once more, I hold out my hand in the gesture I was aiming at just a minute ago.

"It really was nice to meet you, Matt. That was, um, fun." I plaster a smile on my face to cover up the disappointment trying to crowd in. Fun is fun, and usually never lasts. Unless it results in children; then the fun stays with you always.

I push aside the past and take a step back from what I wish was my future. My wayward thoughts have me stumbling but before he can help me, I've righted myself and am bending to grab my handbag from the floor. "I'm fine. Just a bit wobbly. Nothing new." I'm babbling and need to get out of here. Fast. Before I do something stupid. "Erm, bye, Matt." I give him a small wave and turn around, yanking open the door so hard it slams against the wall.

My steps are uneven and flighty as I leave, mumbling bye to the other cashiers and holding on tight to my handbag as I push through the doors and out into the small car park in front of the complex.

Out in the sunshine, I take deep breaths and calm my erratic pulse. Never in all my forty years of life have I ever reacted to a male of the species like I have on every occasion with Matt. Not with Ronni and Chrissy's dad, not with the few men I'd managed to be with since him, no one. Matt made my blood churn, my stomach whirl, and my heart race like it was running the Melbourne Cup.

I have to get away from here before my old arse does something stupid like march back in there and kidnap the poor guy. Heading to the car, I spot my girls lazing under the shade of the giant pineapple, sipping their drinks. When they see me, they gather their things and stand, dusting themselves off before beelining to meet me.

"Heads up," I call as I toss the car keys to Ronni. "Where do you want to go now?"

Her smile is huge and lights up the world. "Are you serious, Mum? I get to drive, *and* pick the place?"

I nod, happy to see just how ecstatic she is about the prospect. It's a rare occasion when they get to drive my baby. My gas-guzzling XY is my pride and joy, so it's a treat for them when I relinquish the controls. We cross at the pedestrian overpass to get back to the car, cracking open all the windows to let the heat out.

Absently, I slide into the passenger side, the vinyl searing a path up my backside. With a pained yelp and a little manoeuvring, I have the car seat cover back in place and the comfort increases. I relax in an effort to calm my still-humming body. Handing over control isn't so bad, since the gallery is on the same property as the pineapple and I'm not sure my shaking hands could get us even that short distance safely.

No more than a few minutes later, Ronni is pulling up out the front of the local gallery where she's been hanging to go since we started planning this trip. One of my girls is an artist, the other loves animals. And I just wanted to see the Big Pineapple again.

I still don't know why, don't understand the pull to go there, but if Matt has anything to do with that pull, well….

"Mum! Look at that sculpture. Isn't it amazing?" she gasps excitedly, pointing to a sculpture of… something. I have no idea.

"Go and enjoy it, Ron. Be free, be free!" I tell her, looking forward to taking in the gallery at a more leisurely pace.

Ronni drags her twin sister off to show her everything the gallery has to offer, and I watch them chatting happily as they disappear. The way people can create something from nothing constantly amazes me. I've watched Ronni turn empty toilet roll tubes into mini masterpieces with just a pair of scissors. I've been amazed at the three-dimensional animals she's made from a single piece of A4 paper. Those creations were when she was six years old, and the artistry has improved tenfold over the years.

Allowing the girls their freedom to roam between the gallery and the zoo, I wander off to enjoy the gardens and extensive bushland surrounding the large property. I'm lost in the beauty of the place when I sense a presence nearby.

Looking around shows me nothing though, and I go back to admiring the trees. Exciting, I know. But the way Mother Nature has created flora has always fascinated me; she's the original artist.

My hands are enjoying the rough texture of the bark when a set of hands on my hips makes me jump. I try to spin around but lips on my neck stop me, the telltale zing of energy telling me who is behind me. His voice confirms it, the rumble of his baritone zipping straight to my core.

Manoeuvring in his arms, I manage to face him, looking up into those soulful blue eyes of his. They're bright, accentuated by his tanned skin.

"Why me?" I can't help but ask. "With all the beauties you'd get around here, why me? Or are you playing me for a fool because I so obviously come across as desperate." My tone is condescending. No one would ever want me—mother to twin girls of nineteen, rolls of extra skin that have never shifted no matter what I've done, and fatty bits to boot.

He lifts his hand to caress my face, the touch already familiar and soothing. "There's something about you that draws me in. Your daughters are beautiful, but I can see deeper than that. I can see they get their beauty from you."

I'm flattered, but also sceptical. Don't guys just spout lines like this to get laid? It's been so long, I have no idea. Being out of the game for years, and starting off without a clue, has done nothing for my self-esteem or my knowledge. I just feel like I'm being sceptical for no reason, but on the other hand, I don't want to be suckered in by anyone. It makes for a lonely life.

My phone chimes with a text.

Ronni: Mum, where are you? Just want to let you know they're closing at 4.

My fingers swish across the screen.

Me: Be back before then. Just being one with nature.
Ronni: *Eye roll* Meet you back at the car then xxx
Me: Love you too.

I lock the screen and tuck it away in my pocket before looking up at Matt. His attention unnerves me and heats my passion all at the same time. It's confusing to say the least.

"I have to go soon."

When he doesn't answer, I get fidgety. My mother told me not to fidget as it distracted her, but I can't help it; he makes me do it. I'm nervous too, which makes it worse.

"Where do you live? Are you close by?" His voice is low and breathy, and it skims across my cheek as he leans in to my ear. When he finishes his question, he nibbles on my earlobe, sending a trickle of arousal downwards. I can't think, let alone answer as his teeth graze the side of my neck, down farther to my shoulder. That spot in between has me panting with need, a need left untended for too long.

When his hand skims down my body, touching my mummy tummy, I shy away. I've not been comfortable with that area since the girls were born. He doesn't withdraw his touch though. In fact, I'm pretty sure he moves closer, hand skimming over my tummy and down to the apex of my thighs. The back of my head connects with the tree trunk when I relax involuntarily at his caresses down there.

I hear a moan, and only realise it's my own when his

breathy chuckle fans against my neck, cooling the sweaty skin. "You like that?" he whispers in my ear. There are no words, just a noise that vaguely resembles a "Yes."

While I'm distracted by his breath fanning my ear, he slips his hand under my shirt and into the waistband of my stretch pants. My instinct is to pull away, to remove myself from his magic touch, but only because I'm unsure. Of myself, of him, of everything. This right here is foreign to me. My doubting thoughts are cut short when his questing fingers sneak into my knickers to reach my clit, circling it slowly.

His voice is raspy, broken, when he utters a short string of magic words, "Oh my God, you're so wet. I love it." Then he groans when my body responds to his declaration, sending more moisture to my cleft. While his fingers travel to bury in my pussy, his head snuggles into the crook of my shoulder, teeth grazing the skin in rhythm with his fingers.

My hips thrust, the pressure of his thumb on my clit becoming harder with the motion. I don't know how he's managed the angle, but it's perfect. With the next swirl of my pelvis, he hits both pleasure points, inside and out, and I'm suddenly pulsing in his grip, muscles grasping his digits tight. As my contractions subside, with the help of the gentle swish across my sensitive nubbin, he licks up my neck and whispers, "You never answered my question about where you live."

"Down south," is all I can force out of my mouth, brain too far gone with pleasure to think of anything more elaborate.

"I'd love to go 'down south,' but I need to know how far away you live, how far I have to go to see you again." He resumes his nibbles, but his question has doused a large portion of the flames he kindled. My body goes rigid. "What's wrong?"

I can't move my head back to see him, so I just answer, "Adelaide. We live down south, in Adelaide." He reels his head back faster than I'd like.

"Are you serious?" I nod sadly. "How far have you travelled to get here, get to me?"

Unbelievably, his hand is still down my pants, stroking softly as we chat. "We've been on the road for over four weeks. Went on a road trip to see all the big things we could before Ronni and Chrissy start uni next month."

"So," he says, swirling his fingers and thumb again, "how long are you in town for? When do you need to leave?"

I feel tears pushing their way out at his forlorn tone, and I just know that mine will match his. "By the end of the week."

"So soon?" His disappointment is breaking my heart, and the fact that we're leaving just makes the pain worse, which makes no sense. We don't even know each other.

I nod. "It'll take us at least a week to drive back since we'll make a few stops in different towns on the way. Probably take the more direct route across country rather than through the major centres." I'm trying to hold it together, I really am, but this moment we're stuck in is pulling me in opposing directions. "Plus, I'm only on leave from my job for six weeks. After that I need to be back there or risk losing my position."

It's his turn to nod now as he curls his fingers into a fist and withdraws his hand from my pants, tucking my T-shirt back into place on the way out. With a lost expression, he raises his hand to his face. One finger stretches out, reaching towards his mouth. The little-boy-lost look changes the closer the finger gets to his tongue, morphing into rapture when they meet. I can't help but be fascinated as I watch him suck his fingers clean of my juices, amazed that someone would do that.

I told you, my experience with guys is shithouse. I know nothing. Obviously!

His groan and rolled-back eyes tell me that he's enjoying my essence, and it reaches something else within me that I'd rather not acknowledge right now. Something born of deep longing.

When he's finished licking and sucking his fingers, he caresses my face with the other hand, tracing my cheeks and nose gently. "Before you head home, is it too much to ask for one night with you? May I have a night before you leave?"

It is delivered so sincerely, so passionately, that my only and immediate answer is "Yes."

We exchange phone numbers before walking hand in hand back to my car. I can't help but laugh when his eyes go round at the classic metal muscle my girls are waiting beside. It makes my happiness boundless when my beast is admired. When he's finished drooling over her, much to Ronni's amusement and Chrissy's bemused head shakes, he finishes his circuit of the car and wraps me in his arms. His chin rests on my head for a moment before he dips down to kiss me tenderly.

"See you tonight for dinner, then?" he asks playfully.

With a cheeky grin, I tell him, "I dunno. Maybe we'll go check out somewhere else tonight. Any recommendations?"

"Cheeky. See you later." With another kiss for me and a

nod for my twins, he's gone, and I'm left standing there like a lovesick fool until two loud coughs gain my attention.

"You done, Mum? Can we get going now? Everything's closing."

I toss the keys to Chrissy this time, giving her a chance to drive too. I sit and gaze out the windows as we go the short distance back to the caravan park before dinnertime.

Dinner in the café isn't as stilted as the past two nights, having a better grasp on this flirting thing. Matt sends cheeky grins and winks my way whenever our eyes meet, and I'm pretty sure I've never blushed so much in my life.

When he comes over with the bill at the end of our meal, he taps the paper as he asks, "You free in an hour?" Gorgeous blue eyes sparkle as I glance up, and in that moment of unspoken desire, I feel a boot connect with my shin. Resisting the urge to wince, I nod. His smile is blinding as he taps the paper again. "See you there in an hour, then."

Ronni and Chrissy high-five each other when he goes through the café door, and Chrissy passes a $20 to her sister.

"What the…?"

"We had a bet on when he'd ask you out," Ronni tells me.

"I bet on before dessert."

"And I wagered on after." Ronni smirks as she pockets the note.

Gobsmacked, I mutter, "I can't believe you placed bets on me." I'm still shaking my head at them as we leave, but I'm not too distracted to notice Matt's small smile and the finger tapping his wrist. I push the hair from my eyes as I grin back and nod.

***

Back at the caravan, my girls fuss about in the bedroom whispering to each other. They've done this many times before so I pay them no attention, instead opening an old book I brought with me. I'm enjoying the fluff storyline when they emerge. One look at their expressions tells me they've been up to no good. It's their version of the calm before the storm.

With one eyebrow raised, I assess their demeanour. "Well? What are you two plotting this time?"

Chrissy giggles as they pull their hands from behind their backs.

"Pretty dress. Where are you going?"

"Not us, silly. You. You've got thirty minutes, Mum. Let us doll you up."

I think I'm gaping at them. Like a fish out of water perhaps. No one moves for a good minute as I deem whether or not they're serious.

They are.

I place the book down and shake my head. With a small sigh, I tell them, "All right then. Do your worst."

With gleeful grins and bouncy claps, which make the van rock, they haul me off the couch and start their superfast makeover.

I feel like an idiot as I teeter in heels I'm not used to up to his front door. Hesitantly, I knock, the sound weak even to my ears. My doubts about being here crowd in on me until that door opens and I'm greeted by this heart-stopping, shirtless hunk.

Matt's smile lights up the dark night and my doubts scurry back into the corner where I hope they'll stay. He pushes the door wide for me and gestures inside without moving. His placement has me rubbing against him as I try to walk through.

I swear I hear a hissed inhale too, just before his hand connects with my fleshy arse with a resounding *crack*. I squeak at the unexpected contact, jerking my butt forward. His chuckle ripples through me, a physical reaction that doesn't seem to change.

When the door shuts behind me, I feel the atmosphere change as Matt closes the distance between us. His mouth descends on my shoulder, kissing and nibbling his way to my ear, where he whispers, "You didn't have to get dressed up for me, but I'm sure loving that you did."

The length of his hard cock rubs my lower back and I instinctively push back. His strong arms come around my waist, holding me tight as he grinds against me. A moan escapes and I let my head fall back to rest on his shoulder. Questing hands slide down to my thighs, grasping the dress. Air hits my skin as the fabric is hitched higher. Warm hands caress me, making me burn up inside.

"Oh God."

A growl reverberates on my neck, triggering a rush of wetness to my pink parts. I hear a voice moan Matt's name.

Oh right, that's mine.

He groans. "Do that again."

"Oh, Matt."

At his name on my lips, he pushes his cock harder against me. The hands under my dress start to wander, caressing my upper thighs and around to the front of my G-string—another of my girls' makeover treats. His fingers find the edge of the fabric and slide beneath.

I'm conscious of my weight as I use him to support my balance, opening my legs to grant him better access to my pussy. Tension helps keep me upright without leaning too heavily on him, but when he whispers "Relax" in my ear and pulls me closer, I succumb. If he thinks he can handle my heft, then so be it. When he copes just fine with me, I submit to his request.

His strokes through my pussy lips and the pressure of his thumb on my clit take me quickly to orgasm. I'm boneless, leaning to the side on wobbly legs. My panting is all I can hear in the front room of his place.

A kiss placed on my hair makes me feel cherished, although isn't it too soon to be feeling anything but lust?

His husky tone in my ear sends a shiver through me. "Are you cold?"

"Nuh uh," I reply. "How can I possibly be cold with such heat between us?" *Where the hell did that come from?*

Matt chuckles, rubbing his hands up and down my exposed thighs. "So it was me who made you shiver, then?"

"You'll get a big head making assumptions like that."

"How do you know I haven't already got one?"

Even in my woeful inexperience, I can hear the innuendo-loaded question.

"Ugh." I'm not yet able to produce a coherent sentence though, so I stick with a grunt and add in a moan.

"I know this is quick," he murmurs, "but I need to be inside you."

I nod, knowing he'll feel the motion of my head. In a daze, he moves us through the space until the solid feel of a mattress bumps my knees. I'm spun in his arms until we're facing and he kisses me on the nose before pushing me backwards.

I can't help the squeak that escapes as I hit his bed. Above me, I admire the surfer-blond god standing over me, muscles accentuated by tanned skin. My fingers itch to touch him and my mouth waters with the need to taste every accessible inch.

"If you keep looking at me like that, it'll be over too soon."

Unsure where the cockiness comes from, I sass, "Could be over before it begins if you keep standing there."

When he doesn't move, I sit up and tuck my finger into the waistband of his shorts. He sucks in a breath at my touch. Matt has no idea how wonderful that small sound is, how much it instils an unheard-of boldness to my next actions. I test the waters by running my fingers lightly up each side, scoring the skin gently with my nails. Looking up at his hiss, I like what's standing before me.

Hooded eyes, head tilted back, and hands fisting at his sides. The sight gives me all I need to go ahead. But my hands give me away as they tickle along the underside of his waistband on the way to the button and fly.

I'm shaking. And he feels it.

Strong hands, larger than mine, cover where they touch him. "Are you okay, Belle?" I nod, but he must see something—probably uncertainty—in my eyes. "Is everything all right? You're shaking."

I swallow, suddenly very doubtful of everything—his attraction to me, my ability to do this, the works. From sure to trembling in less than thirty seconds. Wonderful. I really am a loser.

A quick wriggle loosens my hands from beneath his and I do my best to escape his presence, ending up on the other side of the bed.

Matt speaks as I huddle on his pillow. "At the risk of sounding like a complete idiot, is there something I did wrong?"

I shake my head, unfurling myself enough to pat the pillow beside me. "I must be dysfunctional."

His little laugh, the one that doubts my words, earns him a glare. "Okay, you want to explain why you think that?"

I pat the pillow again. "Have a seat, Matt." When he's comfortable, I begin my story, all the while wishing I just had the confidence to sleep with him instead of boring him to tears with my tale of woe.

I start simple. "To cut to the chase, I'm an epic loser. I have no clue about men and never did." I pause for a second, wondering if I should keep going. A gentle squeeze of my fingers makes me glance up into the most beautiful set of cerulean eyes I've ever seen, and the compassion in them melts my heart. Maybe just softens it a little then. I take a deep breath.

"I vowed not to be a virgin by my twenty-first birthday." I sigh. "With that stupid vow came the predators. It was almost as if they could smell my loneliness and desperation on me, kind of like a lion smells fear. I'm guessing you'd know of the type, they wine, dine, they sixty-ahem… you know."

He nods solemnly as I continue. "Anyway, one of them found me wallowing in a pool of self-pity one night and schmoozed his way into my life. Six months later, after wheedling his way into my dreams and knickers, I was pregnant, ecstatic, and expecting promises of forever from him." I make a buzzer noise and snort. "Boy, was I ever wrong.

"Knocked up, dumped, and heartbroken wasn't good enough for the universe to saddle me with. When I found out I was expecting twins, I went on a downhill slide."

His fingers wrap around mine, bringing me back from reminiscing hell. "Didn't you have anyone to help you?"

"Only my dad. I bunked in his bungalow after giving up my room at uni and the last six months of study."

Matt's calming circles widen as my breath hitches. "Was there any way to finish off the year?"

I shake my head. "Matt, emotionally, I hit rock bottom. Only the fact that I had a roof over my head stopped me from being homeless. But only for a little while."

The circles with his palm slow, drawing out the time it takes to do a full circuit of my back. With a deep breath, I continue, "A week before I gave birth, he kicked me out. Told me that his girlfriend's teenage daughter needed the space more than me."

I swear, it's at this point that Matt actually starts growling.

"What an arsehole thing to do."

I shrug. "I could never prove it, but I'm positive it was the girlfriend's brainwashing that made him do it. She claimed her pussy was gold." Matt chuckles at this. "I got the last laugh though. I got his car and she ended up with nothing but a barren piece of land and a condemned house."

"So what did you do?"

"One of the girls who used to wax lyrical about her ah-mazing boyfriend in high school ended up pregnant, dumped, and pacing the halls of the same maternity ward as me. We rekindled a friendship over a mutual dislike of baby poo and shared a house for many years. Her and her boy, me and my girls. All went great for ages."

"But? What happened?"

"They grew up. Puberty hit, something changed between the three of them. They went from being the best of friends and living in each other's pockets to not being able to look each other in the eye. No one would explain what had happened, so Vicky took her boy and they moved out. Never saw them again."

"Have the girls ever said why?"

I shake my head. "Nope. Don't expect them to either. But a positive came from it. They know more about sex now than I ever did, and I can't find fault in that. If it stops them from being the idiot I was, then that's good."

"But if you hadn't been an idiot, then you wouldn't have them, would you?"

"True, but I always wonder what could've been."

Silence falls between us.

Matt breaks it. "Their confidence shows though. No matter what else happened, I think you did good with them."

I duck my head, embarrassed at the compliment. "Thanks."

A finger comes under my chin, lifting gently until our eyes meet. I think that's sincerity there as he tells me, "Don't shy away from me. I'm telling it to you straight." He kisses my nose and moves down to my lips. I must be in shock as I sit and wonder why the hell he's kissing me. I frown when he stops and leans back.

"What's the matter, Belle?"

"Why are you kissing me?" I'm honestly confused. "Why aren't you running for the hills and kicking me out of your house?"

His forehead meets mine when he lowers his head, eyes too close to focus comfortably. "Why would I run? Why would I kick you out?"

"Because I'm a pathetic loser who has twin teens and can count on one hand the number of sexual encounters in twenty years. Add to that, this"—I motion to my body—"astounding figure, and I can't understand what you're doing here." I push up off the bed. "I don't know what I'm doing here."

Panic at making a fool of myself claws up my throat until a large hand grabs my arse cheek. The shock is enough to shake me out of it.

"I can't put into words what you do to me or why I want you here, but will you let me show you?"

I hesitate, assessing those baby blues. The nod is easy, surprisingly so.

His kisses are slow, tender, thoughtful even as he takes my

mouth with his. This business of taking one's time for a kiss is new to me and I think I like it. Come to think of it, I believe I'd like any style and speed of kiss Matt gives me.

Our tongues parry in the combined space of our mouths, but it's not enough. I want more. I'm over being the hard-working wallflower who has no life of her own. I want to live. Want to experience. And I want to do so many naughty, dirty things to this gorgeous man.

My heart rate picks up as I take the initiative and deepen our kiss. It feels a little weird to be the one taking control, but I like it. Even if it doesn't last for long. Matt grasps my hips and drags me back onto the bed where he's kneeling.

As my feet hit the edge of the mattress, the impact against the side knocks my heels to the floor. They land with a solid thud. Their noise breaks some kind of spell and Matt stops. Eye to eye, I can see his pupils have blown out, the widest I've ever seen them. Without breaking our staring match, he runs his hands all over me, tickling, caressing, oh… searching for the zipper.

The sound of him pulling it down is loud in the small bedroom. The night air chills my overheated skin as he pulls my dress off over my head. As soon as there's bared skin, he seems to lose the iron control he had thirty seconds ago. As his questing fingers explore my padded frame, mine delve into the open front of his shorts. I must gasp when my hands wrap around his cock, as a rumbling laugh vibrates through his body. His eyes crinkle with his smile.

I murmur, "Seriously? Awesome." I can't even get my fingers to meet when I try to circle his girth. This is a good thing. This is the stuff of dirty books and Tumblr posts.

I push his shorts down until his fat cock springs free into my waiting hands. Caressing its length, I enjoy the silky-smooth texture in my palms. His groans speak to me, telling me what I need to know. Somehow I've made this man hard, and despite all my doubts and insecurities, I'm ready to do this.

With one hand grasping his length, I use my other hand to push his shorts all the way to his knees. Seeing his completely naked body, I fight the urge to cover myself, my inadequacy in comparison to his perfectly sculpted form is glaringly obvious. My arms are halfway across my torso when they're stopped.

"Don't." His tone is gentle, but the word is most definitely a command. He holds my arms away from my body and runs his gaze up and down. Everywhere Matt's eyes land, tingles spring up until I'm humming with arousal. How quickly can this man change my reactions? Matt releases one arm and runs his hand across my tummy, the same touch that made me shy away from him earlier. "You don't get how beautiful you are, do you? No concept that this here"—he rubs my belly—"is proof of the lives you brought into the world. You should be proud of it."

I'm speechless and I can feel the prickling in my eyes at his kind words. There's no chance to reflect any further as his hand still grasping my arm pulls it behind my back and yanks me close to him. Matt's mouth descends on mine, his tongue exploring thoroughly.

The sensation of slowly falling has me gripping his shoulder with my free hand as he lowers me to the bed. Following me down, Matt releases my arm and rests his hands on either side of my head, his weight pressing slightly. It's been so long since I experienced the glide of skin on skin. While I'm daydreaming about how good this is, Matt's retrieved a condom from somewhere and is kneeling between my thighs.

I'm fascinated by the way the latex stretches as he rolls it on, and I swear my mouth is watering at the thought of fitting that thing between my lips. But later. Pussy first.

In an unexpected burst of boldness, I reach down and rub my fingers through my juices, spreading the lips apart, waiting for him. With a groan, Matt lines up his cock and pushes forward slowly. This is heaven! I never thought I'd want to feel like a virgin again, but the way he stretches me makes it seem like it.

"Oh my God," I groan. "More, Matt. I want to feel it all."

Unable to wait for his torturously slow motion, I lift my legs and lock them around his hips. Heels digging into his butt, I push down, forcing him inside me faster. My back arches as he bottoms out, pleasure zinging through me. Pulling out slowly, he thrusts back in, and so it begins.

Pressure builds with each push and pull, the sheer width of him rubbing against every spot within me, bringing me closer to orgasm. Nothing can compare to the way my body explodes and the way my pussy grasps his cock so fiercely.

I'm still shuddering beneath him when he grunts on one last push. It's amazing and rather new that I can feel his cock pulsing when he comes. Instead of withdrawing straight away, which has been the sum of the few experiences before, he drops his head to my shoulder and exhales roughly.

"Fuck. That was awesome."

I can't help the chuckle at having sex deemed awesome. I'm kind of chuffed by it, to tell the truth.

"You know, laughing after mind-blowing sex has the potential to damage egos."

My laughter separates us as I reach up to stroke a finger along his jaw line. "I was just thinking that awesome is new and a 100-percent improvement on 'thanks for that' or 'perhaps we'll catch up again' that I've heard in the past."

Matt shakes his head. "I can't believe no one else recognised the treasure you are." He grins. "But then that's good for me."

After disposing of the condom, Matt acts as a big spoon, curling himself behind me. His comfort, his heat, and the way his chin rests on my head lulls me off to sleep easily.

***

The chime of my phone rouses me from slumber. I'm surprised to feel a warm body behind me and to see the sun peeking in through curtains. There's no stopping the grin that spreads across my face as Matt moves behind me, pressing his morning wood against my backside. I wriggle around until it slips between my legs, sliding easily in my slick heat. The head nudges my opening and I think nothing of it to push down.

I'm enjoying my stolen moment of bliss until my bladder reminds me of more urgent matters. Reluctantly I slide out of bed and go off to find the bathroom and my phone.

There's a bunch of notifications, including three missed

messages from Chrissy.

Chrissy: 9:00 p.m. Are you staying there tonight?
Chrissy: 11:37 p.m. Guessing you're sleeping over.
Chrissy: 7:49 a.m. We're going to explore the town on foot today. Relax and have fun. Xxx

I text back, fingers flying over the screen.

Me: Have fun, girls. I'll be back later. Xxx

I pad quietly back to bed, sliding in next to Matt. His cock is still hard, so I take it in my hand and pump slowly. He wakes gradually, groaning as he moves his hips in time.

"Good morning, gorgeous."

I blush at the endearment. "Good morning to you." I give his length a squeeze. "Waking up happy, I see."

His eyes open slowly until they meet mine. "Waking up like this every morning would make me extremely happy." Arching backwards so his dick is still in my hand, Matt manages to reach into the bedside drawer and retrieve a condom. With a smile, he passes it to me. "Care to do the honours?"

***

At least two hours and a growing pile of wrappers later, we're up, showered, dressed, and eating in his small kitchen. As I pick up my phone, my finger slips on the camera icon, opening the app. Without thinking, I raise it and snap a few pictures of Matt. One of them catches him midchew and he protests, trying to grapple the phone from my hand. I'm laughing so hard at his objection that he manages to snag it from my weak grip and starts scrolling through the photos.

Gasping for air, I manage a "Don't delete them!"

Instead of erasing them, he slides closer to me and holds up the phone, aiming it our way. "Smile, sugar."

I roll my eyes just as he takes the pic, and he keeps tapping that damn button as I pull faces at him. He even turns my face to his and snaps pictures as he kisses me.

The kiss deepens and the phone is forgotten. When a piece of his cereal ends up in my mouth, I pull away, laughing. I stick out my tongue with the rogue grain on the end and give it back to him.

Sexy moment broken, he picks up the phone to look through the gallery. I have to laugh at the silly faces, and secretly sigh over the one of us kissing. With a few taps, he says, "I need a copy," then keeps scrolling.

He comments on the photos as he scrolls, but something renders him silent. I glance over at him and then the screen.

"Why are they standing next to a giant poo?"

I snort, then laugh, almost choking on my juice. "Our trip has been all about Australia's big things. That was taken in Kiaima."

He continues to scroll, laughing at Ronni's expression when she first approached the giant piece of excrement. When he gets to the banana, I tell him, "That was at Coff's Harbour. And oh my God, you should've heard the filth they were spouting there." He flicked to the next image of the girls' rude gestures. "And at Wauchope…."

Matt laughs. "The bull! Big balls comments, am I right?"

I nod, putting on the face of unimpressed mum. This just

makes him laugh harder.

Together we revisit my holiday in reverse order, until we get to the first photo I took of Ronni trying to take a peek up the kilt of the Big Scotsman in Adelaide. When he asks where that is, his face falls. It's so far away from here.

Matt scrolls back up to the ones of us together and puts the phone down. His arm curls around my shoulder and he pulls me close, planting a kiss on my head. We stay like that a little while until he declares, "Let's enjoy the time we have together, then. There's a town to explore."

***

There's a certain comfort in having my hand held as we walk through town, even if it is completely foreign to me. On the way, we run into Chrissy waiting outside a shop, so when Ronni exits the store, the four of us continue together.

By mid-afternoon, we're ready to hide in the shade. Back at Matt's, I grab my keys and open the car to air out. As I'm hugging him goodbye and making plans to catch up at his work tonight, his landline rings. He releases me with "I'll see you tonight" as he darts inside.

"We'll be there!"

He blows me a kiss as the door closes, leaving us in his driveway.

"Let's go, lovelies. We'll hit up the ice-cream shop on the way back to the van."

At dinnertime, Matt's not there and we're served by someone new. On the way back to the van, I stop past his place to touch base with him, but the house is dark and no one answers. I call his mobile, but get no response there either. Attempting to wear a brave and unaffected mask, I take us to the caravan and spend the evening finding out about the twins' day.

In the back of my mind nags the horrid little voice telling me I've been duped.

***

We have two days left here before we have to leave, and I won't bring their holiday down by being a sad sack. My mood barely improves by morning, but I'm determined to let them enjoy what's left of our break. I indulge Ronni in whatever else she wants to do, and the day after that we do what Chrissy wants to do.

Both nights we dine at the café, and both nights I suffer without Matt there. I ask another of the waitstaff, but no one knows where he is. Even worse than that, the young woman I have the misfortune of asking gives me a look as if to tell me I'm not worthy of his time, even if he were here.

That crushes my spirit completely. I feel used and taken for a fool. This is not the way I want to feel at all. So the following morning when we need to leave, I pack us up with a forced smile on my lips and get on the road.

Ronni's in the back seat through this leg of the trip, playing with my phone when a message comes through.

"Who's that?"

Silence.

"Ronni, who's messaging?"

"Just a telemarketer, Mum."

I glance at her in the rear-view mirror and shrug. That shit wastes my time.

It takes four days to get home; the desire to take our time and explore each town has left us all and the consensus is to just get home and start fresh. Starting uni after taking a gap year is becoming a reality for them, and I no longer seem to have the drive to do what I've done for so many years.

As a personal assistant to a CEO, there are long hours, demanding bosses, and a to-do list longer than I am tall. Even though I haven't heard from Matt since he blew me a kiss at his front door, Adelaide no longer holds my attention. After a taste of what's out there, I find I want more than being stuck in an office from dawn to dusk.

Despite not wanting it to, my mind keeps skipping to my delectable waiter and the short time we spent together.

When I step back into the office on Monday morning, the first place I go is the boss's office to hand in my resignation. For no one other than me, my life is going to change. When they can't convince me to stay, management organises an advert for the job and I begin to make a comprehensive list of everything my job entails.

By the end of the day, I'm exhausted. On my way back to the car, my phone rings. On seeing the screen, I hesitate. The ringing stops and then starts up again. This time I pick it up.

"Hey, Belle." He sounds so damn sad.

"Matt, are you all right?"

"Not really. That call I went inside for was my mum telling me my grandma had died. I left straight after the call."

My heart breaks for him. "Oh, Matt. I'm so sorry."

"Thanks, Belle. Just hearing your voice makes me feel better. I could've done with you this last week."

"Why didn't you call me, then?"

"I drove three hours to be with family, and it wasn't till I went to call you that I realised I'd left my damn phone at home."

After his explanation and sincere-sounding apologies, we hang up. My step is lighter as I go to the car.

With no time to talk on Tuesday, Matt stalks me via text, sending me funny memes and things that brighten my stress-filled day.

By the weekend, we've managed to have a conversation or two, but they're both cut short. Saturday and Sunday are his super-busy days at both the pineapple and the café, so brief late-night calls suffice. By the end of the second week back to the daily grind, I'm completely over it all. The sporadic contact with Matt is keeping my positive thoughts intact, but I'm missing his smile and touch so badly. The urge to jump in my car and drive till I reach him is so strong. But I can't.

***

Ronni starts university in two weeks, and Chrissy starts her internship with the Adelaide Zoo and Monarto Open Range in a few days. I have no intention of disrupting their lives just so I can move, but each day I'm without his smile, his voice, and his touch is another day I go slowly insane.

I want him with a passion I never expected to feel, never thought someone else could feel for me. People do long-distance relationships, and I have no clue how they manage it. I am going nuts.

At the end of another short call, he clears his throat a few times to break the quiet, umming and ahhing. "Would you ever move up to Queensland?" he enquires softly.

This takes balls to ask, and I honestly don't think he would have if there wasn't something there from his side. I'd move there for sure, but many things would need to be sorted first. "In a heartbeat, but it would take me a good six months to tie all the loose ends and be able to move." I let him absorb that for moment before I ask, "Would you ever move to South Australia?"

I'm going to take his silence as contemplative, rather than stage fright or the phone equivalent. "Yeah, I would. But like you, things would need to be tied up first. Jobs, house, and all the little things."

When tonight's phone call is over, I curl up on my favourite seat of the couch. Dreams of Matt fill my mind, so I'm suitably annoyed when Chrissy wakes me from slumber, her voice high pitched and urgent.

"Mum! Wake up, please, wake up!" The frantic tone in her

voice triggers my motherly instincts and within seconds, I'm awake, looking around the room with bleary eyes for a fire or flood or something else catastrophic. When I focus on her face, the expression there doesn't quite match the urgency in her tone.

"What's up, Chrissy? Where's the fire?"

For a second, it slips, and I see excitement sneak through the cracks in her façade.

"What's going on? I saw that smile you're trying to hide."

She reaches down and yanks me forcibly off the couch, pulling me down the hall to the front door. A frown dips my brows. I'm so confused. It's like she's kicking me out of my own home!

As we near the front door, I see a pile of luggage near Ronni, who's placing her bag on the side table. "Where are you going?" I ask her, more confused now than a minute ago.

"Nowhere if I have a choice," replies a voice I dream of every night.

"Matt?" It comes out as a choked whisper. I must be dreaming still. He's not standing in my front entryway, appearing from behind Ronni. Disbelief is written all over me, and it's not until he approaches, eyes locked to mine, that I start to believe this is a dream. Dream come true perhaps as he wraps me in his strong embrace and squeezes me for all he's worth.

Tears hit his T-shirt as I cry with sheer happiness that he's here, in my house, in my state, and hopefully, in my life.

I hear Chrissy and Ronni retreat to their rooms, leaving us alone.

Matt strokes the hair from my face, cupping my cheeks with his hands. His lips meet my forehead in a kiss that makes my insides melt and my knees go weak. Staring up at him through teary eyes, I study every detail of his face, his ocean-blue eyes, the scruffy stubble on his cheeks and chin, the sun-bleached blond hair sticking out from his head like he's been running his hands through it constantly.

"How…? Why…? Talk to me."

"I think Ronni's been a bit concerned." He smiles down at me. "She's been… um… messaging me since before you got back."

"Ronni!" I yell as jealousy and shock zip through me. Matt must see it in my eyes because his palms are suddenly firmer on my face, and his eyes are blazing.

"She replied to my text when you were on the road and it was meant to be a surprise, but when she told me you were so sad, that's when I rang you. She's been doing what she can to get me down here faster. I'm here for *you* and no one else. You should be thanking your daughter, not envying her." His little chuckle should piss me off, but it doesn't. It just makes me crave him more, makes me realise how much I've missed his smile, his eyes, and his chuckle.

I reach up and run my fingers through the tangled mess, massaging his scalp as I go. Unable to maintain this distance, I grip his hair, bringing his face in line with mine. The kiss starts off gentle, the reacquainting of two souls, but then the embers ignite, catching quickly on the bone-dry tinder of time apart. Together we create a flash fire of desire, burning hotter than it did when we met.

Before I disrobe us both at the front door, I walk us sideways into my bedroom, conveniently located a few feet away from our current location, kicking the door shut behind us.

When the meeting of flesh occurs, it's equivalent to all the very best fireworks descriptions I've ever read. The epic sensations caused by his thrust and retreat make stars appear before my eyes, and the heavens should be singing his praises right now.

This is my perception of love. The connection of souls whose need to be together overrides distance, circumstance, and age. The knowledge that the other will go to whatever lengths they can for their beloved. And of course, the explosive sex that glues them even more securely.

So when his hard and deep thrusts while biting my neck cause me to convulse in the best orgasm ever, I declare my affection for him rather loudly. "Fuck, I love you!"

In the afterglow as my body lies like a limp noodle on my bed, sweaty and thoroughly exhausted, Matt curls himself around me and trails patterns over my skin with his fingers.

"Did you mean it?" he asks, a touch of uncertainty in his voice. I don't need to ask what he means, so I nod.

Meeting his gaze, I raise my hand to his cheek and cup it. "Yes, I meant every yelled word. I've never been so sure about something since the girls were born and I knew without a doubt that I'd love them to the end of time."

"I know it hasn't been long, and some would say it's way

too fast, but I love you too, Belle. More than I thought was possible."

The next kiss is full of promises: hot nights, snuggles, support, Christmases, birthdays, and so much more. Of everything you could ever want in a partnership.

But there's one thought that pops into my mind as we're lying comfortably pretzelled in each other's arms. My eyes widen and my mouth gapes open in surprise at the question I haven't asked before now.

"How old are you?"

The End

Crazy

BY KOLLEEN FRASER

Dedication

For all the crazy girls, shine like the magical unicorns you are.

Chapter One

WEDNESDAY, DECEMBER 7, SYDNEY, NSW, AUSTRALIA
12,493 KM FROM VANCOUVER, BC, CANADA

Another wave of panic rushes through me, causing me to grip the armrest until my knuckles turn white.

"Ma'am," a voice says from somewhere beside me. She has a nice voice; her accent is twangy, like the Australians I've seen on TV. But it doesn't change the fact that I'll most likely die if I leave this seat.

"I'm not crazy," I blurt, making me sound manic. I just don't want to leave this plane. I don't want to be here in this place where everything will try to kill me.

"Ma'am, do you need assistance exiting the plane?" she questions. I can sense from her tone that she thinks I'm crazy.

"It's not that I hate Australia. But I've read dozens of

articles that confirm that as soon as I go out there," I say, pointing to the door, "Australia *will* kill me. I don't have survival skills! Once, I saw a spider in my laundry room. I was too afraid to kill it so I shoved a blanket under the door. I didn't do my laundry for a month."

"I'm sure you'll be fine. It's not dangerous in the city. Millions of people live here. Survival skills or not, ma'am, we need you to exit the plane," she states with authority before nodding to her co-worker. Crap on a cracker, they're going to call security. I've seen Wentworth; I wouldn't last a day.

"Jeez, okay. I'm going!" Taking a deep breath, I stand on shaky legs and exit the plane into Sydney International Airport, aka the gateway to my doom.

Like everyone else on the planet, I am well aware of the dangers awaiting me in Australia. Though it looks pretty in pictures, I never in my life thought I'd be standing in a country that has an entire Netflix series dedicated to all the ways it can kill you.

How did I find myself here, you ask? It all started with a phone call from my pain-in-the-arse baby sister, Lizzy.

TEN DAYS EARLIER
SUNDAY, NOVEMBER 27, VANCOUVER, BC, CANADA
12,493 KM FROM SYDNEY, NSW, AUSTRALIA

"Elizabeth Grace! Where have you been hiding all week? Mom called me, she was so worried. You know how we worry with you so far away. You aren't going in the water, are you? Because they have these tiny octopuses you can fit in your palm, and that's when it kills you."

"Kat, stop," she says, laughing. She never takes my warnings seriously. Lizzy floats around riding unicorns on clouds and rainbows without a care in the world, while I scramble around her trying to keep her safe.

"Sydney is so amazing, you wouldn't believe it. I'm in love with everything Australian."

This is the point where I tune out. I can't listen to her tell me the reckless things she's doing down there without me looking after her. She's twenty, which apparently makes her an adult and allows her to do whatever the hell she wants. The day she was born, I appointed myself as her guardian. Even at a young age I was always there to pick her up or make sure no one was mean to her. Mom and Dad tried to talk her out of going for a semester away, but they never wanted to rein her in. They're content to let her live her own life. It's nonsense.

Interrupting, I ask, "Have you started packing?"

"Haven't you been listening? Kat, I may never leave."

"Don't be ridiculous. You can't simply adopt a new country. You have a visa and it expires in exactly sixteen days. Your butt better be on the plane, young lady."

"Ugh, don't 'young lady' me. You are only five years older than me. We're looking into ways I can stay. Please be happy for us."

We… us. With a deep sigh, I collapse into one of the comfy reading chairs in my bookstore, Indie Uprising. We opened last year and it's my second home, a book nerd's paradise. I bang the phone against my forehead three times before finally asking the dreaded question, "Who's we?"

Bless her precious heart, my sister is a lover. She falls in love every day with a million things and people.

"Blake, of course. Oh, Kat, he's just so wonderful. He has the deepest blue eyes, like the ocean, and soft blond hair. He plays in a band."

"Of course he does," I say, rolling my eyes. She has a type: beautiful blond men with blue eyes, a sexy tan, and about three brain cells rattling around their heads in a haze of bong residue.

"Don't be like that. This time it's different. I love him. He's everything to me. The thought of leaving him…." She sobs uncontrollably. I hear a quiet knock on the door and a murmur of voices. *He* has come in to comfort her. Okay, so he might not be a total moron.

"Look, Lizzy, I'm glad you found someone to play with while you're there, but you could end up in real trouble if you don't come home when your visa expires." I try to reason with her.

"They'd have to find me. They can't send me home if they can't find me. Blake's band is going on tour down to Melbourne and I'm going with them. Don't ask me to walk away from the best thing that's ever happened to me," she says defiantly.

"This is insane! You're going to end up in jail thinking like that, letting some loser musician tell you what to do. I'll drag you back myself if I have to."

Her gasp is audible. "Why did I ever think you would

understand? You don't love anything! You can't stop me. It's not like you would ever have the balls to come to Australia."

"You bet your patchouli-loving hippy arse I will if it means I keep you from throwing away your future on some idiot with a guitar!"

"Then come and get me." And she hangs up.

Hangs up on me! I swear, if our parents had brains in their heads they would have handcuffed her in her room. There is no way I can tell them about this; they would call the police or send her money to hide out. They were never much for setting boundaries.

Five days later, I have my passport and a visitor visa and one hell of an expensive last-minute plane ticket to Sydney that leaves Monday night. Oh my God, I'm going to Australia in three days. I rush to the bathroom just in time to lose my lunch. I'm going to die.

***

MONDAY, DECEMBER 5, VANCOUVER INTERNATIONAL AIRPORT, BC, CANADA 12,493 KM FROM SYDNEY, NSW, AUSTRALIA

As I board the plane, I curse the day my parents let Lizzy study a semester abroad in Australia of all places. Where tiny jellyfish can kill you, and spiders the size of a chihuahua eat squirrels, for Christ's sake.

"Are there squirrels in Australia?" I ask the man next to me. Without answering he puts his earbuds in and pretends to fall asleep. Well, someone forgot their manners at home.

Fifteen hours later, here I am, in the land down under. Forced out of my plane of solitude and thrust into a hectic airport. Where it is hot as hell. Or at least it looks hot from inside the terminal. I haven't worked myself up to leaving the building quite yet. I texted Lizzy, telling her I was here. She hasn't answered. So I sent her an email and Facebook message just in case. I have her address on campus, but I was hoping she could come pick me up. I saw a documentary once about cab drivers who pick up women, drug them, and sell them into human trafficking. I'd make the worst captive; I have a nervous bladder.

I almost made it out the door a couple hours ago; I could smell the air, but then some jerk elbowed me in the boob when he pushed his way in front of me. It rattled me and I had to regroup in the ladies' room for a while. I'm ready this time.

From inside the terminal, I scope out the weakest-looking driver in the row. One I could easily take down, if need be. Australia, here I come. With my chin up, I walk out of the air-conditioned terminal into the sweltering heat. I open the car door, toss my bag in, and say with confidence, "I need to go to the Darlington suburb, Darlington Road at Golden Grove Street, please."

"Yup," he says, pulling out into traffic.

I check the address on the paper to make sure I told the cabby the right one; so far, so good. I'll grab her and handcuff her to me until our flight leaves. Easy-peasy. I sit back with an exhausted sigh, watching the city pass outside my window in a blur until what I assume is her dorm comes into view.

"Be careful out there," the driver says as I step outside.

"What the hell does that mean? Are there snakes nearby?"

He shakes his head, mumbling, "Fuckin' Yanks."

"Hey, Mr Rude Guy, I'm Canadian. What kind of customer service is that?" This guy. Sheesh. How'd he like it if I called him a Kiwi? I heard that that annoys Aussies, but I'm too scared to say it to his face.

He drives off without another word. The sooner I get her and leave, the better.

Chapter Two

WEDNESDAY, DECEMBER 7, SYDNEY, NSW
APPROX. 860 KM FROM MELBOURNE, VIC

Curling my hand into a tighter fist, I bang on the door again. I've been at it five minutes, and no one has answered. No Lizzy, no roommate. I get out my cell and call her again. Nothing. Banging my head on her door, I grumble, "I swear on all that is holy, I'll beat your ass, Lizzy!"

A door across the hall opens and a six-foot tanned god stands before me in nothing but a pair of basketball shorts. I stare at the defined muscles on his naked torso, which quiver as he talks. "You looking for Lizzy? She and Blake are in Melbourne with his band until next week."

I stare at him for a few silent moments, letting his words

sink in before collapsing on the floor, crying, "I'm stuck in the world's most dangerous place alone. I'm going to die in some back alley in Sydney from a spider bite, and she pisses off to Melbourne. That's great, just great. Now what the hell am I supposed to do?"

He stares at me with wide eyes, almost as if he's unsure if he should console me or call the cops.

"I'm not crazy! I'm just… lost," I say between sobs.

"Want me to call Blake's mobile? She's with him, yeah?"

I jump up, hugging him. "Oh my God, that would be awesome. Thank you."

Taking out his phone, he waves me in as he dials a number and waits for an answer. I take him in. He's tall, a good foot taller than I am, with shaggy dirty-blond hair and deep blue eyes. My heart says he's sexy as hell, while my head says he's nothing but trouble.

"Blake, is Lizzy with you? Yeah, some girl is here looking for her." He glances at me.

"Her sister! Kat," I offer.

"Her sister. No, I'm serious. She's standing right in front of me freaking out."

I smack him in the arm. "Hey!"

"Ow, jeez. She's abusive too. Just put Lizzy on the phone."

He hands it to me and I immediately launch into her. "What in the damn hell are you thinking? Oh, that's right. You don't think, do you, Lizzy? I told you to stay in Sydney. I told you I would come and make sure you get on that damn plane!"

"I can't believe you're here," she says quietly. "I never thought you would come, Kat. I'm sorry I wasn't there. You shouldn't have come. I told you I wasn't leaving and I meant it. Go home, Kat."

"Are you high?" I ask, outraged. I can hear the guy snickering behind me but ignore it. "I'm not going to let you throw your life away over some guy. Our flight leaves in five days. You will be on it with me, even if I have to drag your unconscious body behind me."

"Holy crap, are you for real?" The question comes from behind me. I turn and lock on to the blue eyes of the sex god.

"Excuse me? Do you have a problem?"

"Other than some crazy Yank making a scene? No, not at all."

Gasping, I exclaim, "I'm Canadian, you dick. Can't you see I'm distraught!"

"I bet it doesn't take much to get you all hot and bothered," he says with a sexy smirk.

"Kat!" Lizzy's voice pulls my death glare away from the hot Aussie jerkwad. "Who are you yelling at?"

"I don't know, the guy from across the hall, the one who phoned you. He said I'm making a scene! What the heck kind of thing is that to say to someone who's upset?"

She giggles. "His name's Liam, Kat."

"Liam?" His eyes meet mine. "Yeah, that's him," I grumble.

"Look, I'm stuck in Melbourne for the next week. Why don't you come down here and we'll talk about it. I'm not saying I'll come home with you, but at least we can spend some time together while you're here."

"How on earth am I supposed to get to Melbourne?"

"You can fly, silly."

"Fly? I barely made it here!" I say, my voice coming out livid and high-pitched. I turn to Liam and he's already shaking his head with his eyes closed.

"Liam can give you a ride. He's headed down tomorrow," Lizzy states.

"He could be a murderer. I can't just get in his car," I whisper into the phone, hoping Liam doesn't hear me.

"He's Blake's cousin and best friend, and a dear friend of mine. You'll be fine!"

Liam must have pieced together our conversation because his eyes are wide and his hands shoot up in surrender as he shakes his head.

There is rustling on the other end of the line, then a deep voice speaks. "Kat, this is Blake. Could you please pass the phone to Liam? We'll see you soon."

With a smug smile, I pass Liam his phone. "Blake would like to talk to you."

He snatches it out of my grasp. Pressing it to his ear, he paces in front of me a couple times, listening to whatever Blake is telling him.

"Hell no! I'm not spending nine hours in a car with her. She's clearly insane."

"I'm not crazy!" God, I feel like I say that too much.

"Fine! But you owe me for this," he says before hanging up. "Lizzy said you can stay in her room tonight." He walks into the kitchen and starts rummaging through a drawer before turning back to me, holding out a key. "This will get you in. We leave tomorrow. Be ready by ten."

Taking the key from his outstretched hand, I get a zing

when we touch, and it causes me to gasp. "Thank you."

Heading across the hall, I unlock the door and enter Lizzy's home away from home. I wander around the small space with its bright colours and smells that remind me of my baby sister. I set my suitcase on her bed, taking out some comfy clothes. I've been dreaming of scrubbing the fifteen-hour flight off me for hours.

After my shower, I scour her kitchenette for something to eat. Nothing. Frustration, jet lag, and low blood sugar are too much to handle, and I curl up on her couch and cry like a baby. What have I gotten myself into? I don't even know where to get a decent dinner. Starvation wasn't what I thought I'd die of down under, but I guess it's the way I'll go.

A couple hours later, knocking interrupts my self-pity.

"Who is it?" I ask, my heart racing at answering a door in a strange city.

"You only know one person in this entire city, so who do you think...." His sigh is audible through the door. "It's Liam, from across the hall."

"Oh." I wipe frantically at my tears before opening the door. "Hi."

"You okay?"

"No. Why do you care?"

"Look, I'm trying to be nice, okay? We're going to be stuck in a car all bloody day. I thought we should at least have a conversation. And I know for a fact that Lizzy has no food in her apartment," he says, holding up a greasy fast-food bag.

"Sorry, come in. I'm a mess."

"Not exactly the trip you planned?"

"Not at all," I say, clearing a spot on the couch for him to sit. When I look up, he's standing in the middle of the room looking at me with his arms open wide for a hug. "What are you doing?"

"I know that look. That is an 'I'm lost and need a hug' look."

I look at him sceptically before relenting. I crash into his arms, crying. He smells so freaking good, all spicy and warm. It soothes my soul, and after a few minutes my heartbeat starts racing from being pressed against him. My hands slip around his neck and sink into his silky hair. His hand drops lower on my back, causing my breath to catch as he tangles the other one in my hair. I pull back enough to gaze into his crystal-blue eyes. I lick my lips, wishing he would kiss me. He watches the movement with hungry eyes.

"I'm starving," I say quietly, reluctantly trying to break the spell. His eyes widen. "How Lizzy can survive with no food in her apartment is beyond me. I thought I was going to pass out," I say as I snag the delicious-smelling, greasy bag off the table.

"She steals our food, that's how," he says, swiping the bag back after I've taken out a burger and fries. "Much like you, it seems."

Around a mouthful of food, I groan. "So good. You couldn't eat all of that yourself."

"I'm a growing boy," he says, patting his stomach.

"You look fully grown to me," I blurt, then cover my mouth, shaking my head.

He winks and sits next to me, digging into the other burger

and fries.

"Thank you, Liam."

"You're welcome, Kat."

When I'm so full I could burst, I sit back and close my eyes. "I'm gonna kill Lizzy."

"Give her a break. She's in love."

I snort in response. "What kind of excuse is that? People do stupid things all the time and blame love. It's nonsense. Love shouldn't excuse you from rational thought."

"You've never lost your head and done something crazy and irresponsible because of love?"

"Never! Lizzy's the one who lives in the clouds. My feet are firmly planted on the ground, thank you very much."

"That explains it," he says, putting his trash back in the now empty paper bag.

"Explains what?" I ask, confused.

"Why you're so uptight. You've never been in love."

Outraged, I stand up, grabbing the garbage and storming into the kitchen where I open and slam a few cupboards, trying to find the one containing the bin. "Just because I haven't ruined my life over some hot guy I'm uptight?"

Liam comes and takes the trash from my hand, opens the cabinet under the sink, and throws the trash in before looking back at me. "Point made. You need to get laid."

Taking a step away from him nervously, I ask, "Is that what this was? You thought what, that I'd fall into bed with you because you brought me food and pretended to be nice for five minutes?"

Liam, looking confused and livid, responds with, "What?

No, don't be crazy."

"I'm not crazy!" I scream at him. Okay, so that wasn't the sanest response. Maybe jet lag makes you violent and full of rage. I close my eyes, trying to calm down. "Sorry, I'm just tired and we have a long day tomorrow. Maybe you should go."

With a sad smile, he nods in agreement. Before he closes the door behind him, he says, "I'll be across the hall if you need anything. Goodnight, Kat."

"Goodnight, Liam."

Chapter Three

THURSDAY, DECEMBER 8, SYDNEY, NSW
APPROX. 860 KM TO MELBOURNE, VIC

A relentless pounding in the distance wakes me from a dead sleep. Instinctively, I smack my hand in the direction of my alarm clock, but it doesn't connect with anything but air. I sit up, confused, lifting my sleep mask to look around the room. "Aww, crap. It wasn't a nightmare." I fall back against the pillow. The banging starts back up again, startling me. "What the hell is that?"

"That would be someone banging on the door for the last twenty damn minutes!" a voice calls from the other side.

I stumble out of bed and open the door. "Jeez, Louise,

you're going to break the damn door down. What is your problem?"

"Right now? A crazy, five-foot-nothing *Canadian* with an attitude problem and a chemical imbalance who was supposed to be ready to leave half an hour ago."

"I'm not crazy! You are so rude."

"It's still early. After nine hours in a car with you I may decide to upgrade to *offensive* before the day is out. Now get your shit. We need to get on the road if we want to make it there by tonight."

"Fine!"

"Fine! Be outside in ten minutes or I'll leave without you."

"Ugh! You're evil." I slam the door in his face and go about getting ready. Before I go outside, I shoot a text to my best friend and co-owner of Indie Uprising, Crystal.

Me: I'm alive. How's the store? I'm about to leave on a long-ass road trip to Melbourne with quite possibly the rudest man in Australia. I might not make it. Love you.

Her response is almost instant.

Crystal: The store is fine and you're not going to die! Is he hot?

Shaking my head, I reply.

Me: NO!

Then a minute later:

Me: Yes… shut up! <3

I can almost hear her laughing at me.

Crystal: Have fun! Give Lizzy a hug for me.

Maybe after I throat punch her. Liam starts banging on the door again. Lord have mercy, he's like a dog with a bone about his schedule.

Between knocks, he says, "For. Fuck's. Sake. Get. In. The. Car."

I swing the door open and walk past him pulling my suitcase without saying a word. I can remain silent for nine hours, easy.

Outside on the street, I see a convertible sports car, but nothing else. This can't be his car. He looks homeless. Okay, maybe not homeless, but definitely scruffy and not like he could afford a car like this. Maybe he stole it.

He pops the trunk, placing my suitcase and his duffle inside with a cardboard box labelled Becca's, and a guitar case in the back seat. Climbing behind the wheel, he lowers his sunglasses. "Last chance. You in or out?"

"I'm in," I say, opening the door and settling into the seat. It's a nice car. Should be a comfy ride.

We ride in silence as we leave the city limits. My eyes sweep over the passing landscape, so different from the mountains and lush forests of home.

Liam's voice interrupts my daydreaming. "You don't like me very much, do you?"

"I don't know you. But no, not really."

"Why not?"

"You're not my type."

"What exactly about me screams not your type? Because I am, in fact, exceedingly handsome and charming."

"Ugh... and humble. Don't forget humble."

"So what is my great invisible flaw?"

"I don't have time to go over the list with you. Can we just leave it at that?"

He laughs long and hard before answering, "Oh no, this is way too interesting. There's a list?"

"What, are you so conceited that you doubt anyone could find enough flaws for a list?"

"No, I'm fascinated that you stayed up all night thinking of reasons not to sleep with me. Did you touch yourself?"

I groan in response. "You suck."

"Is that on the list? 'Liam sucks.' Because that's kind of vague. Come on, let me have it," he says, rubbing his hands together.

"You've got blue eyes," I offer.

He laughs. "That's the worst excuse I've ever heard. I can't control that shit. How does any guy get past your walls and near that icy heart of yours? What've you got against blue eyes?"

"You're getting nowhere near my heart, mister. I don't know. Blue eyes, blond hair— it screams entitled sociopath," I say with a shrug.

"Sociopath? Wow." He nods slowly. "Not gonna lie, that hurt a little."

"You wanted the list. I was just doing what you told me to."

He smirks, wiggling his eyebrows at me. "Well then, if you're doing as you're told…."

"Ugh, it's better when you don't talk." My curiosity gets the better of me and I have to ask, "So who is Becca?"

"No one I want to talk about."

"Just another notch in your bedpost, I assume."

"You don't know anything about me."

"So, enlighten me. Is she your ex?"

"Yeah." His tone implies he isn't interested in my line of questioning.

"Is she in Melbourne?"

"Canberra. It's on the way, sort of."

"Won't it be awkward showing up at her place with a girl?"

"Not as awkward as it was when I walked in on her banging some guy on my couch."

"Ouch. Sorry." I have no idea what to say to that, so we continue in silence. Poor Liam. I know that kind of betrayal all too well.

Chapter Four

THURSDAY, DECEMBER 8, RACING PAST WELBY, NSW
APPROX. 764 KM TO MELBOURNE, VIC

In a desperate attempt to find some common ground with this man I'll be sharing a car with for the next eight hours and fourteen minutes—according to Google Maps—I grab my cell and open my music app to the playlist I made for the long flight. All I need is a good playlist to turn my mood around.

"I made the perfect playlist. You're going to love it," I say excitedly.

"Let's see this so-called perfect playlist," he says, pulling over to fiddle with my phone. His nod of approval as he scrolls through my favourite music makes me all warm and fuzzy. "You and Lizzy have a lot of the same music."

Once satisfied with his song choice, he presses Play and hands me back my cell before pulling back onto the road.

As Sam Hunt begins singing "Make You Miss Me," Liam sings along. The deep timbre of his voice is smooth and sexy, enveloping me like a warm hug. He has a beautiful voice. I try desperately to keep myself in check; it would be way too easy to fall for a guy like Liam.

I get inspired and scroll my playlist for the perfect song, "Make you Smile" by Elle King. Liam smiles as he listens to the lyrics, and a kind of musical truce settles over us as we sing our way down the Hume. That is, until Miley comes on.

"Hell no. Not that song."

"Oh hush. Even people who hate Miley love Miley. Plus, isn't she an honorary Aussie since she's with one of those sexy Hemsworth brothers?" I ask with a smile, then lean over to his side and sing "We Can't Stop" about five inches from his ear. I put my seat back, lift my hands in the wind, and car dance through a great song.

I love road trips. The open road, great music—it's pure bliss.

"I won't be long. You can walk a bit and grab some food," Liam announces, taking the next exit, which is marked Canberra.

Desperate to stretch my legs, I don't argue. "A stretch would be perfect. After three hours in this car, my arse is going numb." Then I realise stopping means getting out of the car. I wonder if there's anything capable of killing me in Canberra.

Instead, I ask, "Anything fun to do in Canberra?"

Liam shrugs, then says with a smile, "Lots of tourist stuff.

The parliament buildings, National Museum, and art gallery, and of course, the sex shops."

My eyes go wide; he can't seriously think I'd go in a place like that with him. "Like *sex shops,* sex shops?" I ask, wary of his answer.

"Is there another kind of sex shop I'm unaware of? You seem like you could use a laugh, maybe a BOB."

"I have one, thank you very much."

Liam bursts into laughter, banging on the steering wheel. "I knew it! How big? How many settings?"

"Oh my God. I'm not answering that," I say, completely mortified that I'm talking about my sex toy with a stranger.

"I could just snoop in your luggage."

"I didn't bring it! What if airport security stopped me and searched my bag? I'd die of embarrassment."

"You care too much what people think. You should just let go. Have some fun."

It takes a bit longer than I expected to get to Canberra. I'd complain about the extended detour, but getting closure from an ex is delicate business, and I don't want to poke the bear. After pulling into the driveway of a small house, Liam turns the engine off and sits in silence for a few moments before exiting the car, taking the box from the trunk, and walking up the path to the door. Shortly after knocking, a small brunette comes into view. They exchange a short conversation before he pushes the box into her hands and walks away. Leaving her staring at him, and me.

He starts the car and drives off in silence.

"You okay?"

"Fantastic. Good riddance," he says with no emotion. This is obviously affecting him more than he's letting on.

Liam turns into a sex shop parking lot.

"What are you doing?"

"Having a much-needed laugh and giving you a chance to stretch your legs."

"Why on earth would I go in there?"

"To buy a boyfriend, of course."

I duck down. "Keep driving!"

"I thought you needed to stretch your legs?"

"Yeah, but not in here!"

"Fine, stretch your legs over there," he says, pointing to a park not far from where he parks the car.

"I'm going in." He gets out of the car and walks into the store. I clamber out and walk to the park across the street. I'm dying of curiosity, but I can't make myself go in.

Liam wanders out a few minutes later, holding a big bag and wearing a devastatingly handsome smile so large I want to throat punch him or kiss him. Are all Aussies this hot? I mean seriously, is this a national secret?

"Whatcha got there, Liam?" I ask him. My stomach rolls nervously, thinking about what he could've bought.

"Oh... a few things," he says, barely containing his childlike glee over whatever he's hiding. "Catch!" He tosses me a massive vibrator, already vibrating at high speed.

I scream, fumbling the device a few times before catching it. I toss it back at him. He's laughing so hard when it hits his chest that he almost falls over before throwing it back at me, shouting, "Stop throwing your dirty vibrator at me, lady!"

This time I'm ready. I catch it and run after him, smacking him as hard as I can with the sex toy. He tackles me to the ground and we roll around a bit, laughing our arses off.

Lying there in the grass with the sun warming my skin, I smile.

"I knew it."

"Knew what?" I ask.

"That you weren't as stuck-up as you pretend to be."

My stomach hurts. I haven't laughed this hard in so long. Propping myself up on my elbow, I smile at him. "I'm really not that bad."

"Neither am I."

We stare at each other until I calm the fire in my stomach and resist the urge to kiss him.

Liam stands, reaching out to help me up. Once I'm upright, he brushes the grass out of my hair, then tucks a piece in behind my ear.

"Let's grab some food and hit a couple tourist traps before we go."

We decide on lunch at this amazing restaurant called the Cupping Room and then wander through the wisteria on the grounds of Parliament. I'm in awe of its beauty. "This place feels magical," I say, snapping as many pictures as I can.

"Here, let me take a few," he offers, holding his hand out. I eye him sceptically but relent; what damage can he do? He's professional, taking some nice shots of me with the pretty purple flowers all around me. "Can't go to Australia and not do at least a few tourist-type things while tracking your sister down like a bounty hunter."

"Ha ha. I'm not tracking her down. She invited me! Ass," I sass him, snatching my phone out of his hand and putting it back in my purse.

"We better get back on the road or we won't make it to Melbourne until midnight."

"Ready when you are. Thanks for this, Liam. I never really thought about doing much when I got here, except finding Lizzy."

We walk back to the car in companionable silence. With full bellies and enough caffeine in our systems to kill a moose, we continue our drive to Melbourne.

***

Glancing at the speedometer, I see he's speeding. I try to keep my mouth shut, I really do. I manage to ride in silence for another ten minutes, until I can't hold back any longer. "You're speeding."

"We have a long way to go, Kat. I'm speeding carefully."

Before I can come up with a witty retort, the flashing lights behind us prove my point. I smack his arm, yelling, "I knew this would happen!" Panic rises quickly as the officer steps out of his car, walking towards us slowly. "They aren't allowed to carry guns, are they? I mean, I thought it was like England here. They aren't armed and itching to fire, are they?" The tone of my voice is now so high it can only be heard by dogs.

"They carry guns, yes. Calm down before you pass out."

The officer steps to Liam's side, but before he can speak I blurt out, "I'm Canadian."

Liam is shaking his head, trying to hold back a laugh. The cop doesn't see the humour and asks, "Have you been drinking?"

Unable to shut up when under stress, I continue. "I told him to stop speeding, Officer. He wouldn't listen to me, said he was speeding carefully. Can you imagine?"

"No, ma'am, I don't believe I can. Can I see some ID, please?"

Dumping my purse out into my lap, I root around for my passport, and a buzzing noise draws everyone's attention. It takes me a moment to realise it's the BOB. Before he can recognise it, I throw it from the car in a panic.

"Ma'am, what did you throw from the car?"

"You are a goddamned black cloud of doom, woman," Liam says, banging his head on the steering wheel.

"Did you throw narcotics from the car, ma'am?" the officer asks in a voice that demands submission.

Realising I just made things so much worse and he probably thinks I threw drugs out of the car like some desperate crack whore on the run, I quickly try to explain. "Drugs, no! This is all your fault," I say to Liam.

"Littering is taken seriously in Australia, ma'am. It's punishable by—"

I launch out of the car and into the nearby brush, trying to find it. "Don't arrest me, please. It's not drugs, I swear. I'm way too law-abiding to ever even try. Well, that's not true. Once at Missy Cramer's Halloween party, I got high, but that was years ago, and I ended up puking in her bathtub." I locate the vibrator and mentally prepare to introduce BOB to the police officer.

"Watch out for snakes," Liam mumbles, chuckling.

A scream worthy of an Academy Award escapes me as I scramble off the ground, throwing BOB at the officer, who catches it as it buzzes back to life. Liam bursts out laughing, as does the police officer, while I scurry onto the hood of the car.

Staring at them in disbelief, and realising his joke, I gasp, "You are the devil! And you, Officer, you should be ashamed of yourself. I could have hurt myself."

They both offer me a hand in getting down, mumbling apologies and having the decency to look contrite. With only a warning, we're sent on our way with BOB tucked into the centre console between us.

Chapter Five

THURSDAY, DECEMBER 8, HUME HIGHWAY
339 KM TO MELBOURNE, VIC

"If everything goes as planned, we should get into Melbourne by midnight. Only four more hours basking in my presence."

I'm about to sass him when the car starts swerving all over the road.

"Fucking tyre blowout," he announces as he pulls over. "We'll need to find a repair shop in Albury. We can't go all the way to Melbourne on my spare." He gets out his phone, to call a tow truck, I assume. I stand there, in true girl form, and kick the offending tire.

"Will this damn drive ever freaking end," I mumble to myself. "I swear Australia is conspiring against me. It wants me to die out here from a rattlesnake bite or a kangaroo mauling."

"There are no rattlesnakes in Australia," Liam states with his phone pressed to his ear, talking to roadside assistance, probably. Good, no rattlesnakes, but he didn't argue with getting my arse kicked by a kangaroo. I look around the car nervously, wondering if they can sneak up on you.

"Shit!" Liam curses loudly when he hangs up. "The shop's closed until morning. I can put the spare on, but we're fucking stranded until we can get a new tyre."

"Seriously? What kind of country is this?" I scream to the heavens. I know I'm being ridiculous blaming all of Australia for our troubles, but it makes me feel better.

A while later, we park in front of a motel in Albury, with the address of where we can pick up his tyre in the morning. After checking in, we agree to meet in the pub for dinner and a much-needed drink.

I rummage through my bag to find the only dress I packed. I spend more time than I should making myself look pretty for Liam. *Why, so he can reject me?* I shake off the negative thoughts. There will be no rejecting. Tonight, I'm going to do something crazy for the first time in my life—I'm going to seduce him.

I take out my cell and text Crystal.

Me: Flat tire on the road to Melbourne. We're stuck in this cute little city that reminds me of home until morning. How's the store? Did the signing go okay?

Crystal: Bow chicka bow wow. Stop worrying. The store is fine, and the signing had a great turnout.

Me: Girl, I'm going to meet him at the pub in a few minutes!

I take a quick selfie and send it to her so she can approve my outfit choice.

Crystal: You look sexy! Go get 'em, tiger. Wrap it before you tap it!

Me: Eek! Text you in the morning!

Sitting at a small table in a packed local pub, we devour the deep-fried pub food and beers set in front of us. Liam is looking so damn sexy in his black T-shirt and jeans that hang low on his hips.

"Can I get six shots of tequila and two more beers?" he asks me. I nod.

"Whoa, that's a lot of tequila."

"Three are for you. Let's do this."

I down the shots, then laugh at the surprised look on his face.

"Damn, that was pretty sexy."

I smile at him, loving the warmth spreading through my body. "Baby, you ain't seen nothin' yet." I'm already slurring. I'm a cheap drunk, always have been. Tilting my head to the side, my curiosity gets the better of me. "How old are you?"

He looks surprised but smirks before asking, "How old are you?"

"You're not supposed to ask women that!" I say, feigning offence.

"You asked first."

I give in. "Twenty-six."

Liam smiles at this, raising his glass. "Me too."

He is so sexy. I'm going to climb him like a tree.

The evening progresses with more drinks until a happy fog sets in.

I'm a giggling mess as we walk back to the motel. Liam does a fine job of keeping me upright most of the way, but a misstep outside my room causes my hand to slip under his shirt unexpectedly. I gasp at the searing heat of his skin against mine.

Liam presses me against my door, his hands cupping my arse. I grind myself against him, moaning, "You feel so good."

His lips graze my neck and without warning claim my mouth with more passion than I have ever felt in my life. I lose myself in him. Struggling with the door, I manage to get it open without breaking our connection.

Liam walks us backwards until my knees hit the edge of the bed. He stands there staring at me for a moment before pulling his shirt over his head. The moonlight from the window dances across his skin. Unable to hold back any longer, I trail my fingertips over his skin, and his stomach muscles flex under my touch. God, I've never wanted to taste a man's skin, until now.

"You are the sexiest man I have ever seen," I confess before giving in to temptation and trailing a line of kisses across his chest.

He pulls my dress over my head and tosses it somewhere behind him. His lips tease their way up my sensitive neck, and against my ear he whispers, "You are so beautiful."

We collapse onto the bed together.

Chapter Six

FRIDAY, DECEMBER 9, ALBURY, NSW
326 KM TO MELBOURNE, VIC

I wake up with a screaming headache. I groan, opening my eyes, which I regret immediately because the curtains are wide open and the sun is drilling into my brain painfully. As I lie there, trying to find the will to get up and pee, flashes from the night before hit me. The drinking, the laughing, getting naked, and then… nothing.

"Oh crap," I grumble. Did I get so drunk that I don't remember having sex with Liam? Impossible. Lifting the sheet covering my body, I see that I am, in fact, naked. "Double crap." I have never in my life gotten drunk and banged some random dude. Ever. That screams Lizzy, not me.

My phone rings on the side table. Speak of the devil, Lizzy's name pops up. I reach out, grab the phone, then pull the blankets over my head before I answer.

"Lizzy, everything is your fault."

"Well, good morning to you too, sunshine. You've blamed everything on me since I turned five, Kat. Some things are totally your fault."

"Not this. And you stole Mrs Hill's cat and let me take the blame."

"Oh my God! Stop blaming me for that. She locked the poor thing inside and never let it out. You wanted to save it just as much as I did."

"But I never would have stolen it!"

"Yeah, well, you've got no balls. Whereas I have giant lady balls."

"Ew, don't talk to me about your lady balls."

"You sound weird. Are you sick?"

"Hung-over. I drank way too much last night and at some point passed out naked," I state, preparing myself for the high-pitched backlash.

"What? You not only drank alcohol but woke up naked?"

"Yup, and it is everything I thought it would be. Stupid naked reality staring me in the face. I feel like an idiot, Lizzy."

"Sweet baby Jesus riding a unicorn! Did you drunk-fuck Liam? *Blake!*" she screams into the phone. "Liam banged my sister."

Their laughter is like tiny little knives stabbing behind my eyes. "Don't tell Blake! And I'm... not sure."

"What do you mean, you're not sure?"

"I remember being drunk and making out, clothes were taken off, and then… nothing. I woke up naked and alone."

I hear her mumbling something to Blake. "Blake is calling Liam to see what he remembers."

"God, this is so high school."

"Please, like you hooked up in high school."

"Fine, this is so you in high school."

She chuckles. "Yeah, it does sound familiar. Hang on a second," she says, followed by more murmuring in the background as she talks to Blake.

"Put me on speaker or I'm hanging up, Lizzy," I demand as I sit up in bed, clutching my pounding head and my rolling stomach. I need to get some food in my system ASAP or I'm going to puke. *Why did I have to drink so much?* A loud click signals that she's put me on speaker.

"Liam said you guys got seriously drunk, made out, and then right before you could do the deed, you passed out cold." She's laughing at me now.

Pathetic. Even when I try to be a badass, I fail miserably. "God, I'm such a mess."

"No, you're not! Stop being so hard on yourself."

"I met this amazing guy and all I do is bitch him out and then pass out naked. So embarrassing."

Blake's voice comes over the line. "Morning, Kat. Don't sweat it, honestly. Liam loves a girl with fire, and if you've bitched him out as you said, he probably deserved it. Honestly, it would make him respect you more. You're in good hands. Take a Panadol and drink a glass of water. You'll feel better soon."

"Thanks, Blake, really."

"No worries. See you in a few hours, love," he says, and then my sister is back.

"You okay?"

"Blake seems like a pretty awesome guy, Lizzy."

"I know." I can practically feel her smiling through the phone.

"Love you. See you later."

"Love you too, sista," she says before hanging up.

I shoot Crystal a quick text letting her know how my night went.

Me: Didn't get lucky ☹ I passed out naked.

Her response is quick.

Crystal: You're such an amateur.

I jump into the shower and try my best to scrub off a layer of skin, in hopes it'll cure my hangover. I need to find some food and something to tame this headache.

A knock sounds as I wrap a towel around myself, and I head over to open the door to Liam, who is looking sexy as hell.

"Good morning, beautiful," he says, walking past me, carrying coffee in one hand and a paper bag that smells amazing in the other. My heart leaps for joy at this sweet man's thoughtfulness.

"Thank you. I have a raging headache and am starved. You're a lifesaver," I say as I sneak into the bathroom to dress. I throw my clothes on and rejoin him within a minute.

"The new tyre is installed so we're all set to go. I thought I should let you sleep a bit longer. I brought you some Panadol. Figured you'd feel like shit after last night."

Settling on the bed, I groan. "Thank you. I'm so sorry about last night. That wasn't how I wanted the night to end. Believe me."

He beams at me and his shoulders start to shake with laughter. "Can't say I've ever had a girl pass out on me like that. After tucking you in, I went back to my room with a serious case of blue balls. How did you want it to end?" he asks, smiling.

Blushing, I say, "You wish I'd rocked your world."

"I really do," he says seriously. Leaning towards me, he places a kiss on my nose and then one on my lips; it's gentle and sweet and sets my heart racing.

"How far have we got until we reach Melbourne?"

"Should be there in just under four hours. You excited to see Lizzy? I mean, I know you came here to kick her arse, but are you a little excited?"

"God, I miss her so much it hurts. It's been almost six months. We've never been apart for this long. And now she wants to move here," I say, feeling the tears clog my throat and sting my eyes.

"You can always come visit," he offers, but I know that will never happen. The airfare alone would bankrupt me.

With a final bag check, I zip it up and lug it to Liam's car; it's time to check out and hit the road again. We stop to grab some snack foods for the drive before we leave Albury. Liam heads inside the store as I relax in his convertible, watching a paddleboat work its way up the river. It's such a beautiful day. Summer in December, so strange.

Funny, I was so terrified to come here, but it's such a beautiful country. It's not nearly as scary as I thought it would be.

A few birds flutter around in front of the car. One is sitting there watching me. My heart speeds up a bit, but I'm trying to relax. Every time I freak out, I look that much crazier, and Liam doesn't need to know how crazy I am… yet. I choose to ignore the feathered demon—that is, until it hops up and down on Liam's car. I can hear its little claws scratching the paint.

Deciding to be brave, I kneel up, waving my arms in the air. "Shoo! Fly away, you creepy-ass bird. Stop staring at me!" It squawks at me and flies away over my head. I sit proudly in my seat. "Not such a scaredy-cat now, am I?"

"Talking to yourself? Isn't that a little crazy, even for you?"

"I was chasing away a creepy bird, smartarse. I was super brave," I say, gloating.

"What kind of bird?"

"How the heck should I know? It was a black-and-white bird." A shiver runs through me. "I hate birds. I read that their feathers and poop dust can give you lung disease. Could you imagine willingly picking a pet that smothers you with tiny feathers for years until it kills you? People are so weird." Realising I have just gone off on a tangent, I close my eyes, sighing. *Rein in the crazy, Kat.* I open one eye to see Liam smiling at me. Not cringing or rolling his eyes like my last boyfriend.

"You are so fucking adorable. Sounds like a magpie. Watch out for those buggers. They can be really territorial."

"Yeah, right. Ooo… beware of the creepy Alfred Hitchcock birds. Let's get going before the bird comes back." I suddenly realise I'm dreading going home. I wish I could stay here with Liam a little longer. Damn Australia. First it entrances my hippy sister and now me. Maybe that's why so many people live here. It's not that they want to endure the wildlife trying to kill them; it's the men who lure them here!

"Hot Aussie men will get you every time," I accidently say out loud.

Liam laughs. "What was that?"

"You Aussie guys. You're what keeps all us girls here. You make up for all the spiders and demon birds."

"Don't forget snakes."

"Right, who could forget the ten-foot snakes that can eat a labradoodle."

He brushes his thumb over my cheekbone, then my lip. Sad longing shines in his eyes; the same look that I'm sure is mirrored in mine. Begging the universe for more time.

"Let's go," he says as he pulls onto the road.

After a few minutes, I decide to lay my cards on the table. "Walking away from you is going to break my heart. I know it's crazy. We barely know each other, but I'd be lying if I said leaving you wasn't going to hurt like hell. I really like you, Liam. I can't believe I finally find a decent guy and he lives in freaking Australia!" I curse the heavens.

He starts laughing. "I feel the same way, Kat. Everything will work out in the end." Then he stops in the middle of the road. Before I can question him, he kisses me deeply, stealing my thoughts and my heart. Leaning back in his seat, he winks at me and starts driving.

"So how is it you and Lizzy were raised in the same house but turned out so different?"

"Mom always said I was an old soul. That I wasn't born with the need to spin in circles until I puked like Lizzy. It was like I had already learned that lesson in a previous life. I don't think I've ever felt young and carefree. I'm a bit broken, I'm afraid."

"So, you're not a flighty flirt like Lizzy."

"Hey! Don't talk about Lizzy like that."

He holds his hands up in surrender as he backpedals. "Hey now, I mean that in the nicest way possible. I adore Lizzy and got a front-row seat to her and Blake falling in love."

I smile. "I keep forgetting you know her. So, she's lived across the hall from you the whole time? What was she like when she first got here? Did she ever talk about me?"

"Yeah, we were moving in on the same day as her. The moment she and Blake locked eyes, I swear I saw sparks. They've been inseparable since."

"And you didn't mind her stealing Blake away?"

"Nah, Lizzy is funny as hell and perfect for Blake. She told us all about her crazy sister, Kat," he says with a smirk.

"Shut up, she did not call me crazy!"

"Oh yes, she did. I believe she said you were crazy in the best possible ways and that you were her person, whatever that means."

I wave this off. "It's a girl thing." *Sigh.* "I miss her so much."

"A little longer, babe, and you'll see her."

"What about you? Where does your family live? Do you have any brothers and sisters?"

"Blake is the only family I have. He's my cousin. When my parents died in a car wreck when I was ten, my uncle, Blake's old man, took me in. He passed away a few years back, so now it's just us."

"Oh, Liam. I'm so sorry."

He rests his hand on my knee. "Thank you."

Chapter Seven

FRIDAY, DECEMBER 9, HUME FREEWAY, VIC
27 KM TO MELBOURNE, VIC

'Welcome to Melbourne,' the sign announces. Finding my sister means I'll leave Australia and Liam forever. My heart cracks at the thought. How can I rationalise these feelings for someone I just met? This is insane, even for me.

"Looks like we're here."

"Yup."

"When does your flight leave?"

"Three days. I have three days to get her to come to her senses and get her back to Sydney."

"What am I going to do without you?"

"Speed recklessly with little to no consequences?"

"So funny," he says, lifting my hand to his lips and placing a kiss on my palm.

We pull up in front of a large white Victorian home. "It's beautiful."

"Thanks."

"It's yours?"

"Blake's and mine, yeah. It was his old man's house. This is where we were raised."

"Whoa…."

"I know. We had no idea how to keep a house, but we can't bring ourselves to sell it. A couple friends rent out rooms full-time while we go between Sydney and Melbourne for uni."

The front door opens and Lizzy comes barrelling down the steps towards me, squealing. I manage to climb out of the car before I'm bear hugged by her.

"You're here! You're really here! And you're alive! I told you it wasn't scary."

"It was too!"

"A snake almost stole her vibrator." Liam chuckles.

Gasping, I smack him in the arm. "You shut it, mister. That was the meanest thing anyone has ever done to me."

"Sounds like a good story. Come on in," Blake says, laughing. He pulls me, with an attached Lizzy, in for a quick hug. "Nice to finally meet you, Kat."

"You too, Blake," I say, pulling away from the two of them and tucking myself into Liam's side.

"Oh, I see how it is." Blake smiles at Liam, who beams back.

"Damn Canadian girls. Crazy as hell, but they grow on you."

"Hey!" Lizzy and I say at the same time.

"You guys must be starving. Kat, help me make something and you can tell me all the dirty details about your trip," she says, leading me to the kitchen.

"I assure you there are no dirty details… unfortunately. So are you packed and ready to go back to Sydney? Our flight leaves Monday."

"Not this again. Kat, I love him. I can't just leave here and never see him again. It would rip my heart out."

"It wouldn't be goodbye forever, just for now. And if you mess with your visa, you could be banned for a year or more. That would be much worse."

"She's right, Liz," Blake says from the doorway. Walking over to her, he wraps an arm around her. "You have to go before your visa expires."

Tears start falling down her cheeks. "You… want me to go?"

"I want you to be my wife, but to do that, yes, you have to go home first."

"What did you just say?"

"Marry me, beautiful. I have a ticket and visa already set for next month. We say goodbye for now, but not forever."

I look at Liam, who is staring back at me. Blake is saying all the things I wish I could say to him. It's insane for me to have fallen for someone in a matter of days, but I have. Completely and hopelessly, and come Monday, I'll be a lonely wreck.

"Yes!" Lizzy shouts. Blake picks her up and swings her around in a circle. "I'm getting married!" she screams.

"Congratulations, Lizzy. I'm so happy for you." I hug her,

and we jump up and down like we did when we were little girls, while Blake and Liam do the man-hug, back-slap thing.

Our dinner turns into a celebration. We get happy drunk and the guys serenade us with their guitars. It's the best night of my life. A perfect night in Melbourne.

Eventually, we wind down. Lizzy is passed out in Blake's lap already. "I'm going to take her up to bed. Goodnight, guys."

"Night, Blake."

Liam stands in front of me with his hand out. Nervous butterflies flutter in my stomach as I place my hand in his. He leads me through the house to his room. Decorated simply in deep blues and greys, it's cosy.

"Let's pretend the future doesn't exist, just for one night. Just one night with nothing else but us."

"I miss you already," I whisper against his lips.

"Don't miss me yet. I'm right here," he says as he pulls his shirt over his head and repeats the motion with mine.

The sun comes up before we fall, exhausted and sated, into a blissful sleep wrapped in each other's arms.

Chapter Eight

SATURDAY, DECEMBER 10, MELBOURNE, VIC
13,192 KM FROM VANCOUVER, BC, CANADA

Morning breaks and I'm deliriously happy to wake up in Liam's arms. I sneak out of bed to take care of my morning routine before crawling back in next to him with fresh breath and an empty bladder. He must be a heavy sleeper; he doesn't stir once. I can't help but watch him sleep. He's a puzzle I can't work out. What is it about this man that wakes me up inside? I feel like my heart is beating for the first time, and I leave on Monday. How could I let myself fall so hard for someone I'll never see again? What a mess.

"I can hear you overthinking from here, babe," Liam says with his eyes still closed. He pulls me to his side, my head coming to rest on his chest. He starts playing with my hair while we lie in silence. So many thoughts spin around the room. If he feels half of what I do, we're in trouble.

I try to hold back the tears that clog my throat, but they won't be stopped. One slips down the tip of my nose and lands on Liam's chest. I hug him a little tighter. If I could freeze time it would be right now. Live in this moment for the rest of our lives, here in this room.

"Babe, come here," he says, pulling me closer. "Don't cry."

"Sorry. I'm a mess." I laugh, getting up and fussing over my clothes that were cast aside last night. He comes to my side, turning me to face him.

"Hey, we still have two days until you leave. Spend them with me. We can drive back to Sydney together and take our time. Let me show you *my* Australia. You'll love it."

"I think I already do. That's the problem," I confess.

He cups my cheeks, his thumbs brushing the tears that fall. Then he kisses my forehead before pulling me into a hug.

A knock on the door interrupts us. Lizzy pokes her head in, a big smile playing across her sweet face. "Morning! You guys want to go to Demazzi for lunch?"

"What's a Demazzi?"

"Only the best restaurant I've ever eaten at in my life," Lizzy says with an extremely straight face. She takes her food seriously, always has.

"Sounds good, Lizzy. We'll be right there," Liam answers, lifting my hand to his lips and placing a soft kiss on my palm before pulling me into his side.

We get ready and drive over to the restaurant, and damned

if Lizzy wasn't right. The burgers alone are enough of a reason to move to Melbourne.

At lunch, Liam says, "So I was thinking of taking Kat back to Sydney by myself, show her that Australia isn't all bad. If you guys don't mind heading back on your own."

"No, that's a great idea. We were hoping to stay here for another night anyway," Blake answers.

"Perfect," I say, smiling at Liam. Two days left. We'll have to make the most of it.

"If we leave now we could be there before midnight and spend your whole last day naked in bed," Liam whispers against my ear, causing a shiver to run through my body.

"I thought you wanted to show me your Australia?"

"Oh, I plan to," he says with a chuckle.

"Oh my lord, you're crazy."

"Don't call me crazy!" Liam says, mimicking my voice, which causes Lizzy to burst out laughing.

"Hey!" I fake offence.

"You do say that a lot. Way more than any sane person should," Lizzy butts in.

"So? Do you want to rush back so we can have some time to relax?" Liam asks.

"We can try. Look what happened last time. It took two days," I say, rolling my eyes.

"Whatever happens, I'll be happy to have you by my side as long as I can."

"Aww, that's so sweet! Blake, look, Liam is being all sweet." Lizzy beams at her new fiancé.

"I'd rather not. It makes me feel all weird and tingly

inside," Blake states, reaching out to Liam longingly.

He smacks Blake's hands away. "Piss off."

We all have a laugh and head home to get ready to go back out on the road to Sydney.

We make it back to Sydney in just under nine hours, with no accidents, injuries, or arrests. It's a bloody miracle. I almost wanted something to happen that would prolong my stay.

We happily lock ourselves in his apartment, and I spend the rest of the night imprinting every inch of Liam's body to memory.

Chapter Nine

SUNDAY, DECEMBER 11, SYDNEY, NSW
12,493 KM FROM VANCOUVER, BC, CANADA

I start my last twenty-four hours with Liam by doing tourist things around the city. Visiting the harbour, Bondi Beach, and enjoying an incredible lunch. It's a miracle we aren't arrested for indecent behaviour; is that a thing? We can't seem to keep our hands off each other. After lunch Liam finally gives up on the pretence of wanting to show me the city.

"Enough," Liam says against my ear, pressing his lips to that magical spot on my neck where my knees get weak. "Sydney has stolen enough of our time. Let's go home, Kat."

I smile at the pleading in his voice, happy to spend the rest of our time alone. "Are you sure you don't want to show me anything else?" I ask with a wicked smile.

"Oh, I've got something to show you, all right." He grabs his crotch.

I burst out laughing, causing a few people to look at me like I'm crazy. I don't care anymore.

"You are insane," I say before reaching up to kiss his sweet, soft lips. "Take me home, Liam. I need you."

Before I know what's happening, he has me upside down and swung over his shoulder, his glorious arse within easy grabbing reach.

I smack it as hard as I can. "Look at that fine arse."

"Oh, are we getting handsy in public now? Is that how you wanna play this?" he says, sliding his hand up to my arse, laughing.

"No!" I yell, trying to squirm out of his arms, which only makes him hold on tighter.

At his car, he slides me down his body so slowly, that I'm on fire by the time my toes touch the ground. Pressing me against the passenger door, he lays a kiss on me that I swear will still give me a shiver of desire when I'm a wrinkled old lady.

"Wow," I say, stunned. He opens my door for me before walking around to his side and climbing in.

"Keep your panties on until we get home, babe," he says with a sexy smile, driving us to his apartment. I decide to play with fire.

"Too late, I'm not wearing any," I say, then laugh at the expression on his face. He looks like he's battling with wanting to pull over right now and check, or get home as soon as possible.

Men. You say you aren't wearing panties and they lose their freaking minds!

***

In the back of my mind, through every moment of the day, a voice is screaming at me that I shouldn't walk away from him. But what can I do? Twelve thousand kilometres is one hell of a long-distance relationship. It would never work. I need to focus on enjoying the time we have left and mend my broken heart when I get home.

In the darkness of the night, I test out the words that have haunted my heart. I whisper them against his warm skin. "I'll never forget you."

Liam shifts under me, and I realise he's awake and staring at me.

"I... thought you were sleeping." I feel so awkward; I can't believe he heard me.

"I'll never let you forget me. You aren't getting rid of me that easily." He pulls me into his arms.

I cry, "I'm so stupid. I tried so hard to hold myself back, to protect myself from falling in love with you. I failed, so bad. Now I'll have to go home to my lonely life that will never be enough for me anymore. You broke me."

"I'm not trying to break you, Kat. I'm trying to make you understand that I refuse to say goodbye to you. You are not getting on that plane tomorrow and disappearing from my life. This is not goodbye. Do you understand?"

I nod. Silent tears fall down my cheeks as we snuggle back into bed, but I don't sleep. I can't. I stay awake all night wishing I could make him mine.

Chapter Ten

MONDAY DECEMBER 12, DEPARTURE DAY, SYDNEY, NSW
12,493 KM TO VANCOUVER, BC, CANADA

The alarm on my phone buzzes from somewhere beside me. I slide myself from under Liam's arm and search the pockets of the pants I wore yesterday. Once it's silenced, I stand there watching Liam sleep, trying to commit every detail of this beautiful man to memory. I'm leaving today. Tomorrow morning, I'll wake up alone in my apartment like nothing happened. Australia will be a distant memory. The very thought sends a rogue tear down my cheek. I adore this man. I run my hand over his scruffy chin, which scratched me so divinely last night. He moans and shifts before falling back to sleep.

I can't say goodbye to him. I want to remember him just like this. This one memory will sustain me for the rest of my life. My fling in Australia, when I was stupid enough to fall in love with a perfect stranger.

I meet Lizzy and Blake in the kitchen as I'm pulling my suitcase, ready to go.

"When did you guys get in last night?" I ask.

"Late, after one I think," Lizzy answers. She looks worse than I do this morning. Her eyes are red and puffy from crying. We're a hot mess. I pull her into a hug.

"Where's Liam? We need to be on the road in five minutes," Blake asks.

"I… I didn't wake him," I admit.

"Kat, no," Lizzy argues.

"I can't do it. I can't see him. It'll just break my heart all over again, Lizzy. Let me make a clean break. It'll be easier. Let's go."

We pack our stuff into the car and set out for the airport.

"This isn't right," Blake states bluntly. His posture is rigid. "This is gonna kill him."

"He'll be fine. He'll get over me." It kills me to admit that, but he will.

"No, he won't. He loves you," Blake insists.

"Don't be ridiculous. We just met."

"Why is it so ridiculous to believe he would fall in love with you when you obviously feel the same way?"

"I can't stay, and he can't leave. He lives here, and I live in freaking Canada. It's never going to work."

"You don't know that," Blake states. He's pissed at me.

Standing in the departure area, I'm trying so hard not to watch Blake and Lizzy making a scene, clinging to each other, whispering their tearful goodbyes. My throat is closing at the thought of taking a single breath without Liam by my side.

"I can't believe you tried to leave without saying goodbye to me," Liam says from behind me. I gasp and run into his arms.

"I'm so sorry. I just couldn't do it, Liam. You were sleeping so peacefully. It kills me to walk away from the best thing that's ever happened to me, but I can't stay."

"But you could come back," he offers.

"Ha! I barely survived this visit."

"But you did survive."

"With your help. I wouldn't have lasted a day without you."

"It's me who won't be able to survive a day without you busting my arse. Fuck, I'm going to miss you so much."

"How can I say goodbye to you?"

He pulls me firmly in his grasp. "This is not goodbye," he says against my hair.

The tears I've been trying to hold back burst from me in a sob against his strong chest as I cling to him, not wanting to let go.

"I love you, Liam. Call me crazy, but I love you."

"I love you too, crazy. Talk to you when you land."

Lizzy and I make it through immigration and board the plane in a mess of snot and tears, holding each other together. Once settled in our seats, I can't bear it any longer. "Damn you, Australia!" I yell, trying to fight off the tears.

The flight attendant comes to my side. "Is everything all right, ma'am?" Her eyes lock with mine and widen slightly. She remembers me from my flight in. "I see you survived," she says with a smile. "Have a pleasant flight, ma'am."

Loud sobbing echoes through the cabin. I look at Lizzy, who is a complete wreck. Mascara runs down her cheeks in deep lines and snot dangles from her pointy nose. My troubles are put away for a moment as my big sister gene kicks in. I may be heartbroken, leaving Liam, but it must be way worse for Lizzy, leaving her fiancé.

"Oh, honey. Come here," I say, pulling her close and letting her cry on my shoulder as I cry on hers, so glad I have her here. I'd be an even bigger mess without her with me. Together we can get through anything.

Chapter Eleven

JANUARY 12, VANCOUVER, BC, CANADA
12,493 KM FROM SYDNEY, NSW, AUSTRALIA

Lizzy demanded I come to the airport with her for Blake's arrival. He'll be here for a few months. They have a wedding to plan and all the paperwork that's required for my sister to move to Australia. I'm going to miss her so much, but I know Blake will take care of her. She's been a nervous wreck today, fidgeting with her dress and her make-up, making sure everything is perfect. I, on the other hand, am still in my sad little funk being away from Liam. True to his word, we've spoken almost every day since I left Australia. I'm more in love with him now than ever.

Lizzy nervously tucks her hair behind her ear, then untucks

it and smooths her hands over it again.

"You're beautiful, so stop fussing. He already agreed to marry you. A hair out of place isn't going to change his mind."

She looks over at me, sticking her tongue out. "Hush up, Kat. You're just mad that I'm getting laid tonight and you'll be alone in your apartment with BOB again."

"Shut your face, Elizabeth Grace."

"That totally rhymed," she says, giggling.

I point behind her to draw her attention to the line of people arriving as my phone starts ringing. Liam's name flashes across the screen, causing my heart to race. "Hey, babe."

"Hey, gorgeous. Blake land yet?"

"He should be, yeah. They're just unloading now."

"Good. How's Lizzy holding up?"

"A nervous wreck. She changed her outfit four times. She's been bouncing around like a freaking chihuahua on crack," I say, laughing.

"Shut up, ya ho! I'll have you know—*Blake*!" she yells, then takes off towards her love, who's just come into view. They crash into each other in a fit of tears and kissing. I turn my back to them before they get naked in the middle of the airport.

"He's here," I say quietly.

"How are you holding up?"

"Okay. I just... wish you were here." I try to keep the tears at bay but I can't help it. I miss him so much.

"As you wish" comes from behind me.

I spin around to find Liam standing in front of me. I launch myself at him, crying into his chest, "What are you doing here?

Am I dreaming?"

"I had to see you. And I couldn't let my only family get married on the other side of the world without me." He pats Blake's shoulder.

Lizzy pulls Liam into a hug. "I almost told her this morning. She was such a sullen little cow."

"Shut up! You're staying?"

"I told you it wasn't goodbye. I can stay for three months." He pulls me to the side. "Is this okay? We never really talked about this."

"Better than okay," I assure him, trying to wrap my head around the fact that he came all this way, for me.

"Did you miss me, my love?" he asks, brushing the tears off my cheeks with his thumbs.

"Like crazy," I say as we walk hand in hand through the airport with the promise of a lifetime of memories to be made.

The End

Finding Love Down Under

By S. Hart

Dedication

To new beginnings and finding love where you least expect it!

Chapter One

Dylan Phillips paused outside of the brick-faced building, looking up at the hanging sign that confirmed she had reached her destination. King's Pub. Not very original, but it would do for what she had in mind. Her Internet search had not identified it as one of the trendiest spots in the Surry Hills area, but the images were good and pretty spot on from what she could tell.

The wrought iron tables were at full capacity and many other patrons stood, huddled in groups as they talked and laughed. It would take her a while to get used to the seasons differing from home; if she were back in Georgia she would probably be wearing a sweet little summer dress instead of her light sweater and jeans. Luckily, her research was again spot on—though the opposite season she was used to in June, the mild winter weather seemed to be similar to what she was accustomed to in the South.

The questioning looks she received as she said "excuse me" and "thank you" while manoeuvring her way to the huge wooden bar did not go unnoticed. Dylan supposed that as unique as she found the Australian accent, hers was the one actually out of place.

She found a high-backed stool at the end of the bar and made herself at home, watching as the good-looking bartender made his rounds. He filled orders with precision, never distracted from the easy banter he carried on with females and males alike. Dylan grinned when she noticed a girl—yes, *a girl,* though she was probably twenty-one or twenty-two— batting her lashes and propping her abundant cleavage on the bar top. She guessed he was used to such displays, as he never missed a beat, filling her order and moving on to the next in line.

Glancing around the packed pub, Dylan wondered where his help was. She didn't have to wonder long, as a curvy brunette in skintight leather pants and matching vest sashayed up to him for a quick kiss. There was no other interaction as she dove right into work.

Dylan assessed the two, thinking that they made an appropriate couple though they looked nothing alike. After all, there was the old saying that opposites attract. He with his dirty-blond hair, tall, solid build, worn jeans and T-shirt next to her darker looks, shorter stature, and badass attire did paint a lovely picture. Perhaps they could become the muses for her writing.

Nah, Dylan silently corrected herself; she would be the

heroine in this story. She may have had an epic failure in her real-life love story, but on paper she was sure to have one hell of a happy ending.

"What'll ya have?"

Dylan stared back at the sexy bartender, who could most definitely be the muse for her hero. She had thought about what colour his eyes would be, but could never have imagined the startling blue that now seemed to be drinking her in.

She fought to suppress a giggle. He must have noticed because he asked, "Is something funny?"

Dylan shook her head. "No, I just thought of a place back home where I used to eat with my dad a lot." She and her father had gone to the Varsity before every football game they ever attended in Athens. She had loved the smell of fried foods and ice cream that flooded her senses when she stepped inside and the echo of "What'll ya have?" as patrons lined up to give their orders.

"Ah, a Yank. On holiday?"

"I'm not sure yet."

She was thankful he let her answer slide. Instead of asking what that meant, he said, "So, what can I get you to drink?"

"What's good?"

"We've got some good amber fluid on tap if you're a beer sort of girl."

Dylan nodded and smiled. "Sure, that'll work."

She studied him, taking note of every detail—how he moved, how his clothes fit him, the way his muscles flexed, *everything*—as he worked to pour her beer.

She thanked him as he set the full glass in front of her.

"May I start a tab?"

"Sure. Drinking with the flies, are you?" he asked before he requested her credit card.

Dylan swallowed the dark beer before shaking her head in response. "I'm sorry, I'm not sure what you're asking." In the South it would probably be a good question if you were trying to have a picnic on a hot summer day and couldn't manage to chase the flies away.

"Alone? Are you drinking alone tonight?"

***

"Oh, yeah. Sorry, I've never heard that phrase before."

Ian couldn't help but smile back at her. Her pale blush in response made him think she may be a little shy, but she was pretty outspoken with her thoughts and brave as hell to enter a pub on her own in a strange city.

He had noticed her when she sat down. He made it his business to keep an eye on his bar, the comings and goings of each customer. She was beautiful but not in an in-your-face, drop-dead-gorgeous sort of way. Her golden-brown hair fell in waves down her back; where it landed he didn't know, but was curious to find out. Her heart-shaped face was the perfect canvas for her full lips and sparkling hazel eyes. Although her lower half was blocked from his view, the baggy sweater could not hide the curves beneath.

And those dimples when she smiled. He had always had a weakness for dimples on a pretty girl.

He finished taking her info to put with her card as there had been more than one drunken customer over the years who left without theirs and resumed business, finding himself glancing her way often.

After her third, Ian noticed that Dylan became more talkative with the people around her, often throwing her head back to laugh at something someone said. He knew her name from her credit card and had been able to catch bits and pieces of her conversations: Dylan was from Atlanta, Georgia, visiting for an undetermined amount of time, and single.

One of the locals, David, had seemingly taken a quick liking to her and was trying to get a little too close for comfort.

Ian walked back over to check on her and asked, "Are you all right?"

Her smile lit up the room as she nodded. "Yes, very. Can I get another?" she asked, holding up her empty glass.

"Are you driving?"

Before Dylan could answer, David spoke up. "I can give her a ride."

"Rack off, Dave. You've got Buckley's."

When he started to protest, Ian cut him off. "I'm not asking. I'm telling you."

David slid off the stool next to Dylan and walked away without a backwards glance. He could feel her gaze on him.

"I can take care of myself," she said in a slightly slurred voice.

Ian didn't doubt she believed that, but he knew what a bloody pushy bastard David could be.

"I didn't say you couldn't. You're not the first sheila I've had to chase him off from."

When she didn't respond, Ian asked, "What? Never had a bloke take up for you?"

Dylan's expression suddenly changed. One second her eyes could have killed and the next they seemed empty and distant.

"I'd like to pay my tab now."

He wanted the vibrant woman from earlier to come back—the one he had watched laughing at the big piles of shit David had been talking. The woman who had told him she could take care of herself.

Something he had said had triggered this change. He couldn't imagine it had anything to do with not having anyone fight for her. She was gorgeous. And if the rest of her was as nice as the outside, there would likely have been more bloodshed for her than he could guess.

There was a story there; he knew it. There was always a story.

Chapter Two

Dylan was pissed. And tired. Suddenly she was exhausted. Maybe it was the long flight. Or drinking more than she had in a while. Perhaps it was her idiotic idea to quit her job and fly to the other side of the world to start over, or at least start the next chapter of her life. Well, until her tourist visa expired.

She had come to actually start the first chapter of her novel, the one she had always wanted to write. She had sat in front of her laptop, staring at the screen, and the only words that would come to mind were "What the hell am I doing here?"

She knew she would find that same question staring back at her when she booted her laptop back up. And she still didn't know the answer.

Dylan sloppily signed her name to the receipt for her tab, slammed the pen down on the bar, and turned to make her way out of the still-crowded pub. She stumbled but was caught in a pair of strong arms before she could make a complete and utter fool of herself.

When was the last time she had been stumbling drunk? Her thoughts were a little foggy, but she thought it might have been over four years back on her twenty-third birthday. It was the first birthday she had celebrated with Alex and the last time she had been this drunk.

How sad.

When had her life become so boring?

She allowed Ian to guide her through the crowd and out into the crisp night air before she attempted to slap his arm away.

"Easy now—I'll walk you home. Where are you staying?"

Dylan again tried to pull free of his support, but failed. "I am not telling you where I live. You could be a serial killer or rapist for all I know."

He chuckled in response. Dylan narrowed her eyes; one, hoping he would pick up what she was putting down, and two, because she was seeing double.

"Would a serial killer really waste his time being a gentleman? You're a pretty easy target right now."

"They say Ted Bundy was extremely charismatic."

"Yes, I've heard that. Now, where are you staying? I wouldn't be able to live with myself should an actual serial killer or rapist pick you up on your way home."

They made it only a few more steps before Dylan was bent over at the waist, throwing up. Right in the street. In the arms of a gorgeous man. Definitely not the beginning to her fairy-tale romance.

The irony was not lost on her even as she continued to expel the entire contents of her stomach. She would have fallen had he not held her upright with one arm while holding her hair back at the same time.

***

She wasn't the first drunken sheila he had held up while she spewed everywhere, and he reckoned she wouldn't be the last.

Ian knew he shouldn't be turned on by the spewing package in his arms, but the curve of her rounded arse pressing into his groin didn't help. And she smelled bloody fantastic. It wasn't hard for him to think of other opportunities that would allow him to bend her over and fist his hand in her hair.

He shook his head, attempting to clear the erotic thoughts from his not so gentlemanly mind.

Get your shit together before you crack a fat, Ian berated himself, holding back a laugh at the thought of her response should she feel his erection.

When Dylan finally stopped dry-heaving, Ian guided her to the footpath. He had watched for traffic as they stood in the middle of the street, but saw no reason to move her until necessary.

Even with pale, clammy skin she was stunning. He smiled down at her when she looked up at him with an embarrassed expression.

"I am so sorry about that. I haven't drunk that much in forever."

"No worries."

She shook her head. "Unfortunately all I do is worry, or so

Finding Love Down Under

I've been told."

More of the story, he suspected. Ian asked, "By who?"

"No one important."

He didn't like her defeated, sad tone but didn't press the issue. Instead he walked in silence, offering only his physical support until they stopped in front of an old Victorian townhouse. The outside wasn't much to look at, but Ian knew that most of the buildings had been renovated a few years back.

He let her pull out of his arms, as much as he wanted to resist, and watched as she climbed the stairs, holding on to the rail as if she might topple over at any moment. She fumbled with her keys, finally getting the right one in the hole before pushing the heavy wooden door open.

Ian planned to make sure she made it safely inside before turning back. It made him uneasy to think that he may never see her again.

Before closing the door, she paused. Leaning against it for support, she grinned at him and said, "Thank you for making sure I got home safe…."

When she trailed off, he supplied his name. "Ian."

"Ian," she repeated, and he had to admit he liked the sound of his name on her lips.

"You're welcome, Dylan Phillips."

He waited until he heard the locks click into place, then turned to walk the couple of blocks back to work.

Ian couldn't exactly say why, but he wanted to know more about the Southern Yank who may or may not be on holiday.

Chapter Three

Jasmine, or Jazz as he preferred to call her, was announcing last call when he walked back into the pub.

"Get her home all right?"

Ian didn't miss the knowing glance she gave him.

"Yep."

He didn't offer more, knowing she would needle him to the bloody end of time if she had the least idea that he was interested.

He chose to ignore her smile as he waited on a customer asking for one last beer.

In her typical sarcastic tone, Jazz proclaimed, "Your blood's worth bottling, Ian King."

"Yeah, yeah. Let's wrap up so we can get out of here at a decent hour tonight."

Jazz nodded and resumed chatting with a customer as she

spun a bottle before pouring.

"Oh," she said as if it were an afterthought, "your damsel in distress left her card. I put it in the drawer."

Ian refused to take the bait; he would not admit to his oldest friend that he was ecstatic to have a reason to call her.

***

Dylan closed her eyes as the warm water from the shower rained down on her. The heat of the water in direct contrast with the cool porcelain tub she lay stretched out in felt wonderful.

"I am an idiot," she mumbled under her breath.

Flashbacks of her bent over Ian the bartender's arm, spewing chunks all over the street, bombarded her.

What the hell had she been thinking?

A question she could answer: clearly, she had not been. Dylan had thought a couple of drinks would loosen her up, and she wanted to people-watch. Get some inspiration. Instead, she had gotten shit-faced and had set herself up for one hell of a hangover.

Damn it.

And what must Ian think of her? She was horrified by her behaviour. Alex would be beside himself, lecturing her on why she *should* be worried about what others would think of her.

What was it he always said?

Oh, yeah. "Dylan, once your looks are gone all you will have left will be your reputation."

She used to not worry about what her outfit looked like, her hair being styled in the latest fashion, what perfume would be the least offensive in the workplace—the list could go on and on—but Alex had changed all of that.

Appearances were very important to him. Not just how she dressed, but how they were viewed as a couple. Like her hair. No strand could be out of place, because his never was. And Lord forbid anyone thought they were having a lovers' spat.

Dylan shook her head. Her mother had cried when she'd told her she was quitting her job at the publishing company and cashing in her savings to travel to Australia. Her father had preached on 401Ks and having to start over in a competitive field. Truth be told, Dylan did love the world of publishing, but she wanted to be the one writing the novels that were being published, not the one reading through submissions.

But her content-with-life, don't-rock-the-boat parents couldn't understand that. Just like they couldn't understand why she'd been so lonely that she made up pretend brothers and sisters when she was growing up. Her parents would ask how could someone feel any such way with a room full of toys?

Dylan was a "describe the scene playing in her mind" kind of writer. She again closed her eyes and thought back on the night, narrating the unfortunate beginning to her newest story. But it really wasn't a story; more of a recap to her rather disappointing night.

Alone, in a country not her own, Dylan found herself at the local pub. Determined to leave the past behind her and begin the next chapter of her life, she went in search of everlasting love, instead finding only her blurred reflection in the bottom of an empty glass. Was it because the glass was frosted? No, it was because she had thoughtlessly opted to partake in one too many alcoholic beverages.

Ian, the unbelievably sexy bartender, had drunk her in as she gulped down the amber fluid he offered. There was a moment she had considered asking him back to her place. She would most likely never see him again, and it had been at least six months since her last sexual experience.

Experience? Each time with Alex had been just that; they'd never found their comfortable stride in bed even after three years. There were lots of awkward, fumbling motions and fake orgasms.

And as Dylan had not had much in the way of experience before Alex, she knew no different.

Of course, there were the book boyfriends who managed to soak her panties as they stroked their lovers to passionate cries. She had tried saying "oh, Alex" once, and nothing. He'd thought she was in need of more KY.

Dylan imagined that the gorgeous man who made serving beer seem so erotic would create a different sort of bedroom experience.

And then... and then... he had reminded her that no man had ever fought for her. Not even over her.

Suddenly she was standing in the middle of the past she was trying to escape.

She needed to flee, but she was physically unstable. Most likely mentally as well. Too many drinks had debilitated her ability to walk a straight line.

But Ian had come to her rescue. He had saved her from making an arse of herself in front of hundreds.

Such a gentleman, her grandmother would have said.

Yet her desire for a goodnight kiss was dashed when her body decided to purge itself of her liquid diet.

Nothing killed the libido like a bucket of fresh vomit.

Not the "once upon a time" beginning she had dreamed of during her flight overseas. In fact, it was more like her worst nightmare.

When the water had run cold, Dylan crawled out of the tub to dry herself off, brushed her tangled hair, and took two paracetamol before falling into bed.

Chapter Four

Dylan reached over to hit the snooze button on her phone, never lifting her face out of her pillow, but the ringing wouldn't stop. She finally lifted her leaden head and looked at the screen to find an unknown caller was attempting to reach her.

She hit Decline, as she wasn't in the mood to talk. She had just rolled to her other side when the phone started ringing again.

"Fuck," she half groaned, half croaked. She tried to swallow around cotton mouth, wishing for a glass of water but too lazy to get out of bed to get one.

She hit Decline again, hoping the bastard on the other end would take the hint and leave her in peace.

Dylan flopped over to her back and was staring at the ceiling when her phone started ringing for the third time.

"Why?" she asked the white speckled ceiling.

Grabbing her phone from the nightstand, she calmed herself, then said, "Hello?"

"Is this Dylan Phillips?"

"Sorry, wrong number—no men here." She had often been teased growing up for having a boy's name.

She thought she recognised the chuckle on the other end. Ian?

"So this isn't the female Dylan who visited King's last night?"

There was no doubt now. Certainty dawned on her as she recalled giving him her credit card and contact info when she opened her tab.

"Yes, sorry. I'm a little out of sorts this morning."

Another chuckle. "I can imagine, having been there a time or two myself."

"Yeah, about that—I'm really sorry. I hope I didn't puke on you or anything. And thanks for holding my hair and *me* while I did… you know."

"Like I told you last night, no worries."

"So, are you just calling to check on me? Part of King's hospitality package to check on patrons who drink too much?"

He actually laughed that time, the sound causing her to smile in response.

"No, we would have too many calls to make the next day. However, it is our duty to notify a person when she has left her credit card behind."

Dylan mentally slapped herself. What a dumbarse.

She sighed at her own stupidity. As if Ian, the sexy Aussie, would just call her.

"Thank you. I'll drop by later to pick it up. I will be the one wearing a mask with hopes no one will recognise me."

"I was actually thinking I could give it back to you when we meet for breakfast in an hour."

Had she agreed to a date last night? And who the hell wanted to date someone who threw up on them?

"I'm sorry. I don't remember us making any plans."

His voice was nonchalant. "We didn't, but there's this great little place just down the road from you."

The thought of eating something turned her stomach. "It's nice of you to invite me to breakfast, but I think I'll pass."

"Dingo's breakfast? I can't allow it. As someone who has suffered the same ailment and has some knowledge from a professional standpoint, I must advise against your decision." Even over the phone she could hear his attempt at humour.

"Who is Dingo? And what kind of breakfast is that?"

"Sorry. It's a saying for no breakfast."

"Oh. All I could think about was the *Seinfeld* episode when Elaine said"—in her best Australian accent—"'maybe the dingo ate your baby.'"

"I saw that one." He wasn't swayed by her significantly lacking attempt at humour to change the subject. "So what about breakfast?"

"Are you going to take no for an answer?"

His simple "no" in response made her giggle.

After agreeing to meet him, she hung up and awaited the text with the name of the café and the street it was on.

***

Ian was standing next to the entrance when she walked up. In the light of day she was even prettier than he'd recalled.

With her hair swept back into a messy ponytail, he noticed the light dusting of freckles across her slightly upturned nose and cheeks. Her outfit shouldn't rouse any sort of reaction from him, but the fitted tee, skinny jeans, and Uggs topped with one of those oversized cardigan things did.

She smiled up at him as he held the door open for her to enter. Those damn dimples again.

When she had slid into the booth across from him, Ian handed her card across the table.

"Thanks," she said as she waved it.

There was an awkward silence as she slid it into her pocket and glanced around.

Ian decided it was time for a proper introduction; this time he offered his empty hand to her. He watched as she reluctantly accepted and responded with a firm shake of her own.

"Dylan Phillips, I'm Ian King."

"Nice to meet you, Ian King." She paused for a thoughtful moment. "King? Any association to the pub?"

His pride and joy. Association was too mild a word.

"Too right. It's my place."

A look of surprise crossed her face. "Wow, you should really have bouncers or something to walk out the drunkards."

"Drunkards? Is it often you hit the turps then?"

Dylan laughed. "You mean like a binge? I've read that phrase in a historical romance before."

"I'll have to take your word on the historical romance, but yeah."

She was shaking her head, but was interrupted by the waitress before she could answer. He figured on having to ask again once they had placed their orders and the waitress left, but Dylan picked back up where she had left off.

"No, I don't drink very often at all. As I am sure you could tell."

He thanked the waitress for his coffee, then asked, "So what brought you to my pub last night?"

Dylan sat spinning her juice glass between her hands. "I needed an escape from my escape."

***

Taking in Ian's puzzled expression, Dylan couldn't explain why she wanted to open up to him. Maybe it was because their acquaintance would be short-lived?

All she knew was that she felt very comfortable with him. It was like they were old friends, the kind you can go months, even years without seeing and when you get together it's as if no time has passed at all.

"What were you needing to escape?"

"Which time?" she mumbled before thinking better of it. Before he could ask, she said, "I came here to start a new career. Or I should say try my hand at a new career. I was feeling a little overwhelmed with my decision and searched local pubs in the area."

Dylan was expecting him to make some corny joke or

pickup line about her walking into his bar, but instead he asked, "Tell me about your career change?"

"I was working for a publishing company in Atlanta, mainly weeding through submissions. It was a great job, especially because I love to read, but it wasn't my dream job. I want to write."

She waited for the laughter that she was used to. That sarcastic, "what the hell are you talking about" laugh that often came with the "you're batshit crazy" look. The one Alex had given her when she first tried to discuss the topic with him.

"You came to Australia to give it a go? Why here?"

She assumed he was asking why she came all this way to test her talent. "Well, it was between Ireland and Australia. I've always wanted to travel to both places, and I have to admit the men are pretty inspirational for writing purposes, so I flipped a coin."

"You have a thing for Crocodile Dundee, eh?"

"Though I must admit that Paul Hogan is an attractive man, I would lean more towards Chris Hemsworth."

He waited for the waitress to set their food on the table before asking the next question.

"No romantic inspiration back home?"

Dylan felt the pangs of discomfort and regret that typically followed thoughts of Alex trying to take root, but she decided what the hell. She had nothing to lose there. Nothing to lose with Ian. "Nope, not anymore."

"Is that part of what you were trying to escape by coming here?"

Dylan's mind went blank but she could feel herself nodding.

"Want to talk about it? I've been told that a bartender is the next best thing to a counsellor."

"I suppose that could be true. On one hand, people have paid a fortune to get themselves inebriated before losing control of their mouths in a bar, whereas on the other, they give a fortune to lie on a couch and answer 'how did that make you feel' questions."

"Either way, I'm a good listener."

Dylan took a bite of her toast and chewed, watching him across the table. He sat patiently, no pressure, just a sexy grin that she wanted to kiss off his face.

She felt the heat rise to her cheeks and turned her focus to drinking her juice instead.

After a pregnant pause, she reconsidered and answered, "Alex and I were together for almost three years. I thought we would get married and have a family, but…."

"But?" he prompted, seeming genuinely interested.

"Alex decided to have an affair with his secretary."

He sucked in a breath and grimaced. "Ouch. Let me guess—a blonde with long legs and huge breasts?"

Dylan smiled. "Close. A blond with long legs, but no breasts. At all."

She wanted to laugh at his confusion. "Trey is his secretary's name. Apparently he helped Alex come out of the proverbial closet."

Ian didn't say "oh" but his expression did.

"Yep. I used to joke that if he ever cheated on me I hoped

she was younger and hotter so there would be a good excuse, while secretly thinking I would prefer she be hideous so everyone would be like 'what the hell is he thinking,' but having your man leave you for another man? Not a good feeling."

"So, you two didn't split on good terms?"

"I was furious at him for cheating on me. Period. But for following his heart, no. I wish I had followed mine sooner. I loved Alex, still do, but I was never in love with him. It was just comfortable. Sort of like when a guy has a beard for so long and gets used to it, then is scared to shave it because he doesn't know how he'll look without it. Honestly, when I think about it, Alex was like that bitchy girlfriend always nagging about what's for dinner, what you should or shouldn't wear. I thought he wanted the perfect woman, when actually he didn't. He wanted the perfect man, just like me."

His expression appeared a little sceptical at the thought she would have let being screwed over go so easily, so Dylan added, "But before I took the high road and wished him well, I did use his fear of jack-o'-lanterns against him."

Ian smiled. "Jack-o'-lanterns?"

"Yep. He hates them, has been terrified of them since he was a child. I cut the backs of several of his favourite shirts to look like a jack-o'-lantern face." In response to his laugh she said, "It was very gratifying in the moment, but then I felt really guilty and I don't carry that burden well, so I had some new shirts sent to him with an apology note."

Ian seemed to find the last bit even funnier. Finally he regained his calm.

"You don't have to answer if you don't want," he said, raising his hands, "but how did you not know he was gay?"

Dylan half laughed. "Good question," she answered, pointing her fork at him. "The signs were there, but I ignored them. And I made it easy for him to as well, until Trey entered his life.

"Anyway, enough about me. The girl at the bar. Is she your girlfriend?" Dylan had noticed he wasn't wearing a wedding band.

"Jasmine?" Dylan shrugged, and Ian said, "No, Jazz and I are just friends. We grew up together. She's actually dating a doctor. They've been together a couple of years now, planning to get married this summer."

"Sorry, it really isn't any of my business. I just thought… well, when I saw her kiss you, I thought maybe y'all were together."

Ian laughed. "She'd get a kick out of that. Bobby probably wouldn't, but she would."

Dylan smiled, realizing that Ian had a way of making her feel like she too knew Jazz and Bobby. "So, did you guys grow up around here?"

Ian shook his head, "Nah, we grew up in the country. I never wanted to be a jackaroo so after uni I stayed in the city. Jazz followed."

By the time she finished eating, Dylan felt much better. She was even more comfortable with Ian after they talked about their favourite musicians, movies, books, even the differences in weather.

Chapter Five

Dylan stood in front of the mirror checking herself out. She wasn't counting or anything, but this was like date number seven with Ian. Sure, they were just having pizza at her place, but she still wanted to look nice without looking like she was trying to look nice.

She felt like she couldn't breathe in the fitted sweater she had picked before her shower. She pulled it over her head and tossed it in the pile with the other discarded clothes she had tried.

Groaning, Dylan slid her jeans off and pulled on a pair of black leggings to go with her oversized sweater and ankle boots.

She was just about to fourth-guess that outfit when she heard the knock at her door.

Dylan continued to be surprised by the way her stomach

flipped when she saw Ian. She felt like a teenager again, waiting up for his calls at night, and found chatting on the phone to be one of her favourite pastimes.

They were becoming more and more comfortable with one another after a month of friendship.

Dylan held the door open, allowing Ian to step inside. He offered her one of his sultry smiles before walking into the kitchen with the pizzas.

"So, how was business tonight?"

Ian took a beer from the bag he had carried in as well and turned to lean against the counter. "Good. We were rushed off our feet, actually. I'm not sure what sort of company I will be tonight—sorry."

Dylan waved him off and took a beer for herself before putting the rest away.

"Are you hungry?" she asked.

"Not right now. Maybe later."

Dylan followed Ian into the small living room. She had no choice but to sit next to him on the couch, as the only other furnishings in the room were a coffee table and TV above the fireplace.

She curled her legs beneath her and watched as he closed his eyes and let his head drop back. Dylan had really been trying to ignore her feelings for Ian. She wasn't even sure if what they were doing constituted dating or not. She had been working on mustering up the courage to ask, but wasn't sure this was the right time.

***

Ian could feel her watching him. He loved it. He liked the way his skin tingled from just the thought of what her touch would feel like. He was trying to be patient, but it was becoming harder and harder to resist.

Hell, he hadn't even kissed her yet.

"What's on your mind?"

"Excuse me?" she asked, sounding shocked by his question.

"I don't have to have my eyes open to know you're worrying over something."

He listened as she drank and then fought back a groan at the sound of the bottle popping free of her mouth. His stomach tightened as he thought about her full lips wrapped around his dick

He opened his eyes to let go of the image.

Damn, but she was beautiful. Ian was sure she would tell him to rack off if she knew what he was thinking every time he was around her. No matter how hard he tried, he couldn't stop thinking about stripping her bare, feasting on her body, and then driving into her until he was able to work her out of his system.

He'd be rooted if he got a taste of her and then she left. The troubling part was that Ian wasn't so sure he could work her out of his system.

Dylan bit her bottom lip, leaving a dent, then smiled as if she were embarrassed by what she was about to say. "I probably should have asked this sooner, but I've been so happy to have a friend here that I didn't want to step on your toes…."

Ian rose to be closer to her. "Out with it already."

"Are you with anyone? In a romantic way?" He could tell she was having a difficult time with the question, but she didn't break eye contact with him.

Ian shook his head and smiled as he took Dylan's hand. He watched as he rubbed his thumb across her knuckles, then looked her in the eye. "Dylan, I'm not that type. I wouldn't spend so much time with you if there was someone else."

He had been, for a long time and still could be, but something felt different with her.

"I didn't mean to imply you would. I just wanted to be sure."

Ian finished his beer before setting it on the table in front of them.

"There was a time when I didn't consider someone else's feelings as I should have, and when I lost her I realised I should have been honest with myself and her to have truly given it a fair go. I don't like to make the same mistake twice."

"What happened?"

"The better question is what didn't happen. I worked late, always put the bar first. Instead of making sure she knew there was no reason to be insecure, it annoyed the bloody hell out of me that she constantly thought I was cheating. I wasn't, but instead of making sure she knew that, I just let her believe whatever she wanted to."

"If you don't mind me asking, what finally ended it?"

He couldn't mask the pain that always followed the guilt when he talked about Sophie. "Another good question. Unfortunately I'll never know the answer."

Seeing the confusion etched on her face, Ian saved her from having to ask another question.

"We had a fight, another one. As I was going out the door Sophie yelled that she wouldn't be there when I got back. I didn't think much of it—she had said the same thing the week before. But then I got a call that she had been in a car accident. I remember the feeling I had when I found out she didn't survive and the feeling when I left that night, but I can't remember what we were arguing about. It had become a daily thing...."

Ian zoned out for a bit, lost in the past, but when he focused back on Dylan, his present—maybe his future—he paused. Even with tears streaking down her face she was breathtaking. But even more than her beauty, he understood that she was crying for him, not herself. Ian had known this conversation would come about at some point if they continued to spend time together; it had in the past with other women, but it had never ceased to amaze him when the woman seemed more upset at the fact that he had perhaps loved someone else.

Ian gently wiped the tears from Dylan's face, then traced her lips before leaning in for their first kiss.

Chapter Six

Dylan would have been shocked had she not suspected what type of man Ian actually was. In another time and place, with someone else, she would have figured this was when he would put the moves on her. After breaking her heart with his memory, he would have offered to heal it… in the bedroom. But she didn't believe that of Ian.

Ian's hands never left her face and neck. The kiss made her feel things she never had before, which made her more emotional.

She gazed at him through watery eyes when he pulled back.

"I'm sorry, Dylan. That probably wasn't the best time to kiss you."

Dylan then took his hand, for the first time realising she had dropped her empty bottle during their kiss.

"Don't apologise. It was an emotional moment for both of us." Dylan paused, searching for the right words but not finding them. So she asked anyway, needing to know for some unexplainable reason. "You loved her?"

Ian nodded. "Yeah, I did, though I couldn't be bothered to tell her as often as I should have, and I damn well didn't show her as often as I should have."

When she didn't speak, Ian added, "I'm sorry for putting you in such a mood. It wasn't what I had planned when I came over here tonight."

She shook her head. "No, I mean, I do feel sad for you, but it's more. I don't know how to put it into words, which is funny since that's not usually my problem. Hearing you talk about Sophie makes me sad for me too. Alex is still alive, but it still shouldn't have been so easy to get over him. Don't you agree?"

"I don't know what to say. Love affects us all differently, I think."

"But how can I write about love when I haven't experienced it? How can I write about sex that is filled with desire and passion when I've never known it to be that way? I've never even really felt the pain of losing anyone."

***

Ian wanted to tell her that he would be more than happy to give her a taste of the desire he had for her, but he didn't want another of their firsts to follow that conversation.

"Listen to me. Your relationship with Alex was different.

That's okay. You can build from that too."

"How did you build from losing Sophie?"

"I take time for myself now and spend it with the people I want to. Used to be I would have never left Jazz in charge of closing up, but I didn't think twice tonight. I wanted to see you. I want to spend every minute I can with you."

A few years back Ian would have never considered pouring his heart out that way. He would have harassed his friends about shit like that leading to them being tied to a missus.

Ian didn't understand the pull he had to Dylan, but he knew she needed honesty. And he wanted to give it to her, along with so much more.

He started to fidget when he realised they had been sitting, staring at one another.

"Want another stubby?" he asked as he stood and started walking towards the kitchen.

"Sure." It was a simple answer, but there was a question in her tone, not because of the beer—she was actually starting to adjust to some of the terminology, but because of his mood.

He handed her a bottle of beer before sitting back down, then asked, "Anything in particular you want to watch tonight?"

Chapter Seven

She felt the awkwardness of the situation as it cloaked them, but the raw emotion from their kiss still clawed at her. She wanted passion and fire. And she wanted it with him.

Dylan wasn't sure where Ian's mind had gone—perhaps he was thinking about Sophie or his bar. But she wanted his mind on her. His hands and mouth on her.

Dylan had never actually come on to a guy before. It had just sort of happened.

She shrugged in response to his question and sipped her beer while she pondered question after question and how she should answer.

Would she be any good at seduction?

Would she go to hell for seducing a man who'd just poured his heart out about his lost love?

Should she play it sweet and demure or go straight for the

gut with something like "I want to watch your throbbing penis slide in and out of me."

Dylan choked on her beer at the thought. She coughed out a "thank you" as Ian patted her back.

She definitely couldn't say that.

"You all right?"

Dylan blinked back the pools in her eyes and smiled at the concerned look on Ian's face. He was such a gentleman. She was willing to bet he would be just as much in bed too. Truth be told, Dylan dreamed about a "ladies first" man.

"Yeah, I'm fine."

"So, do you want to watch a movie, or would you rather call it a night?"

It was now or never.

***

Ian didn't want to leave, but the mood had shifted. He wanted to tell Dylan that he was ready to move on, that he wanted to move on with her, but reckoned she would think him off his rocker.

What man went around talking about that shit? She would think he was trying to get her in the sack.

"No, I don't want to call it a night."

He cursed himself for the instant flood of relief he felt.

"Well, what do you want to do?"

Ian's blood felt like it was starting to boil as he watched a light blush spread across Dylan's cheeks. She bit her lower lip and glanced down.

He rubbed his thumb across her lip, instantly going hard when he felt the moisture there.

Something sparked between them.

His voice was hoarser than normal when he spoke. "Talk to me, Dylan."

A fist to the gut wouldn't have had as strong an impact as the lust in her eyes when she looked up at him.

"I want you, Ian. I just—"

He didn't let her finish her sentence; instead he took her mouth with his, letting all of his want flood into her.

He couldn't think of anything but her; he was consumed. The way she felt, her smell, the sounds she made as he deepened the kiss and finally allowed his hands to roam her body.

Dylan's moan turned to a surprised squeak when he pulled her onto his lap. He pushed against her until she gasped.

"Bloody hell, I want you so bad I'm afraid I'll hurt you."

Dylan shook her head. "I want all of it, all of you."

And he gave her all of it.

Chapter Eight

Dylan sat before her computer and smiled at the screen. Her writing had been going well, but the scene she'd dreaded had arrived. Her smile was because she no longer dreaded that moment. There would be no awkwardness or need for inappropriate wit to mask the fact that she had no idea what she was talking about.

No, now she would write from experience. Dylan giggled at the thought that most of her story so far had been written from experience, and she was loving it. Every word. Every scene. For the first time in a long time, she was excited about her life and looked forward to what the next day held.

Dylan closed her eyes and was swept back to the night before. To the moments that followed her real-life hero sweeping her off her feet and carrying her to her bedroom where she experienced passion as never before.

The sensitive skin beneath Isabella's ear pebbled as Jack muttered his desire against her neck. Her stomach twisted in the best way possible at the sound of his accent. She loved it. And she loved him, though she couldn't bring herself to admit it out loud just yet.

It was too soon, wasn't it?

"Oh, God," she moaned as his warm breath and wet kisses made a trail from her neck down the column of her tilted throat to her bare chest. There was no time to ponder questions. All she knew was that this moment with Jack was right.

She needed him and did not resist saying it out loud. He chuckled against her skin in response but did not speed up his torture as he slid farther down her body, igniting flames wherever his lips touched.

Isabella gasped when he settled between her spread legs. She had only experienced this once, and the panic at the memory made her want to push him away. Subconsciously, she attempted to close her legs, but Jack wasn't having it. He pushed her thighs apart until she lay before him, completely exposed.

The knot in her stomach slowly untied as he began to place hot, wet, open-mouthed kisses to her core. She relaxed more as he sucked and flicked his tongue, each attentive movement drawing her closer to the edge.

Isabella moaned his name as she jumped, her body cresting and falling until it felt heavy and sated. Weakly, she pushed at him to stop, but he refused until she found her release once more.

Jack kissed the inside of her thigh before kissing his way back up her body to take her mouth. She never opened her eyes. She couldn't. Not from embarrassment or because she didn't want to find a blank expression staring back at her, but because she was so drained in the best possible way.

She could taste herself on his lips and tongue and suddenly realised why the hottest romance authors included this in their stories.

She anxiously watched as Jack tore the condom package with his teeth and rolled it on before he teased her with the head of his cock, rubbing it against her sensitive nub, causing her to moan and arch into him.

Finally. Finally, he entered.

Jack groaned, empowering her, encouraging her to meet his thrusts.

"Fuck, Isabella. I knew you would feel like heaven."

Neither spoke coherent words after that; their speech slurred with pleasure and interrupted by moans of ecstasy.

She was close again. So close her body had started to shake.

Jack thrust harder and faster.

"Fuck, let go."

Instinctively she knew he wasn't talking about the grip her legs had around his waist or a directive to himself to release her arms that he held above her head.

Isabella allowed the feeling to completely overtake her and cried out a moment later.

"Ah, fuck," Jack groaned as he followed.

He rested his forehead against hers as he attempted to hold his full weight off her, but Isabella wanted to feel him completely against her. No, needed to feel him. She reached up and pulled him to her, kissing him slowly as she purred her appreciation.

Again, Dylan realised she was smiling at the screen. Words could not describe the way he had made her feel, but she hoped her readers would feel a little of the heat.

Dylan took a sip of water, then resumed typing. She was nearing the end of her chapter when her cell phone rang. She wanted to ignore it but glanced over to see Alex's picture on the screen.

She groaned before answering, but knew he wouldn't call unless it was for something important.

Chapter Nine

Ian had been trying to call her for hours. He knew she often turned her phone on silent when working, but she had to check the bloody thing occasionally. His gut told him something was off.

Ian left Jazz in charge of the pub and walked the short distance to Dylan's townhouse. An older man came out as he approached.

"G'day," the man said when he saw Ian. "Can I help ya?"

"Um, I was just dropping in to visit Dylan, the lady staying here."

The older man smiled. "Yeah, I know her name, but she isn't here."

"I'm sorry, are you a friend of hers?"

"Landlord. Or was. Not sure that she's coming back."

Ian felt his heart drop until it hit his stomach. "What do

you mean?"

"She's gone. Got a call from some bloke named Alex and booked a flight home."

Ian mumbled, "Ta," as he turned and walked away.

He was physically sick, choking back his confusion, anger, and anxiety. He was pissed off that she'd taken off without saying a word.

He was a nong to think that she would feel the same way he did after one night together.

But what the hell did she have to go back to? Had Alex promised her security? Did she think he couldn't give her that?

***

Ian couldn't concentrate; he kept forgetting orders and spilled more than one drink. He was consumed by unanswered questions. Was she running to Alex, or was she running from him? Was there a difference?

He jerked when he felt a hand on his back but relaxed when he looked down into the face of his best friend. Her typical life-loving expression was gone and had been replaced with concern.

He was confused when he noticed Jazz's fiancé standing behind her, pouring whisky.

"Come on," she prompted as she took his hand and pulled him to the supply room. "What is going on with you, Ian? You're moving like a bloody zombie out there and don't look much better."

Ian shook his head as he ran his hands down the side of his face. "I've gone as mad as a cut snake."

"What are you talking about?"

He started to pace. "Dylan. She's gone. I went to check on her and she's gone without a bloody word. Just up and fucking left. Back to America. Back to Alex."

"Go."

Ian froze, staring at Jazz. "Didn't you hear what I said? She's gone."

"I heard you, but more, I see you. Go after her. She obviously took your heart with her."

Ian knew this side of Jazz—the romantic, mushy side she often covered with leather and fake tattoos.

His defeat spoke for him. "It's over. It was a fling. Why the hell am I so torn up over it?"

"Because it wasn't a fling. You've had more than your fair share of those, and you know the difference. You'll regret it if you don't go after her. Even if she turns you away, you'll leave knowing you tried."

Something was building inside of Ian—hope that maybe Jazz was right.

"I don't know where the hell she lives."

A mischievous smile spread across Jazz's face. "Lucky for you, I do."

"How?"

"I may have looked up her address for billing purposes, just in case."

Ian laughed. "But what about the pub?"

"Bobby has some time off. He's not as fast or charming

with the ladies, but he can manage."

Ian inhaled deeply and nodded, letting her convince him before he lost his nerve.

"Okay, okay…." He started to leave, then paused and turned back to his oldest friend. "I love you, Jazz."

The tears in her eyes didn't go unnoticed, but he didn't call attention to it as she waved him off. "Yeah, yeah, I know. I love you too. Now go before Bobby gets suspicious, or more likely spills a drink on someone."

Chapter Ten

She should have called Ian before she left, but she was in such a hurry she forgot to charge her dying phone, and it was too late by the time her cab arrived. She was lucky that she didn't have to wait for a flight, but unfortunately it meant she didn't have time to call Ian before she boarded.

What would he think? Would he care? Maybe she would be back before he realised she was gone? Dylan shook her head at the ridiculous thought. Of course he would realise she was gone; they had spent almost every night together before they'd slept together.

Oh God, what if he thinks I'm running because we slept together?

Her greatest fear was that he wouldn't care. That he would carve another notch in his belt before moving on to the next woman.

No, Ian didn't strike her as that type. But wasn't she deluding herself in thinking he could be as invested as she was after such a short time?

She had tried to call him several times since her arrival but hadn't been able to reach him. She had even tried the bar, but some guy answered and said he wasn't there.

It had been almost three days since she had left, though it felt like only hours. Everything had happened in a blur. The flight, the hospital, the battle to manage an early release for Alex. The list just went on and on.

Dylan was staring down into her empty wine glass when Trey interrupted her thoughts. He held out the bottle of red as an offering, which she gladly accepted. After pouring himself a glass, he took the seat across from her.

Dylan admitted for the first time that Trey suited the apartment much better than she ever had. Truth be told, she had no decorating style—it had all been arranged with Alex's tastes in mind.

"Thank you," she said, before taking a long sip.

"I'm the one who should be thanking you, Dylan." Trey shook his head as he wiped an escaped tear away. "I would have lost him if you hadn't got here when you did."

Dylan reached across to take Trey's hand. There had been a time when she wanted to beat the shit out of him, but that time had passed. She knew now that she had never been in love with Alex, and she was happy that someone was.

"Alex is strong. He'll recover and you two will have a long, happy life ahead of you."

Trey nodded and chuckled. "You know his mother still

prefers you."

Dylan smiled as she leaned back. "Well, of course. I'm the woman scorned and you're the home-wrecking bitch."

At that Trey tossed his head back and laughed. "To Alex," he said as he raised his glass in the air.

"To Alex," Dylan responded before drinking. "I really do wish the two of you the best. And we'll get all the legal designation of another paperwork changed before I leave."

A muffled groan came from the direction of the bedroom and Trey was instantly on his feet, moving. "Sounds like our patient needs us."

Dylan shook her head, feeling no guilt or remorse. "Nope, just you."

She laid her head back against the couch that felt like hers, but not. The home that was once hers felt foreign now. Trey wasn't out of place in it, she was. In fact, she felt out of place in the city she loved now.

Dylan had just closed her eyes, hoping for a few minutes of rest, when the intercom buzzed.

"Damn it," she mumbled as she rose to find out who it was.

"Yes?" she asked.

"Dylan?"

She recognised his voice immediately. Her heart began to race.

"Ian?"

She knew her voice sounded panicked, but she couldn't help it. What was he doing in Atlanta?

"Dylan, I need to talk to you. Can you come down?"

"Yeah, sure…. Just a minute."

Dylan looked down at the old T-shirt and sweats she was wearing and cursed. "Oh shit."

"What's the matter? Who's here?"

Dylan turned to find Trey standing in the kitchen, holding an empty water glass.

"Ian."

"*Ian*, Ian? Your Aussie lover?"

"What?" she asked, confused. She had never said anything about them being lovers.

"Come on, every time you talk about Australia his name is mentioned."

"Oh God. Look at me—I'm a total mess."

Trey nodded in agreement. "You're right. Run and change into one of those cute dresses in the closet and spritz a little perfume on. Your hair looks fine." He made a shooing motion when she didn't move. "Hurry."

***

Dylan ran her fingers through her long hair as she walked to the door, glancing briefly in the mirror as she passed. The dress was simple, but pretty. Her face was flushed from the quick change and combination of nervousness and excitement coursing through her body.

She found Ian pacing back and forth. He stopped when he saw her, apparently speechless.

"What are you doing here, Ian?"

He took a step towards her, then paused.

"I went to see you, but your landlord said you had left."

"I should have called. I didn't mean to worry you. But my phone died while I was packing, and I had to make my flight arrangements online. I wasn't thinking straight after Trey's call."

Ian interrupted her. "Trey's call. I thought you came back to Alex."

"I did. Well, not back to Alex, but back for Alex. He was in a car accident and needed surgery. I was down as the person to sign for him, and his mother was out of the country with her newest fiancé and Trey couldn't reach her. The doctors wouldn't let Trey, so I came home. He was stable, but he has some other health issues that could have changed that at any time, so—"

"So you didn't come back to be with him?"

Dylan looked at him, questioning. She suddenly realised that Ian thought she had left him to come back to Alex, and the thought was hilarious. She attempted to contain her laughter in the face of his stoic expression.

"No, Ian. I just needed to get here to sign for him. This isn't my home anymore. It's theirs. I was planning to come back as soon as we signed all the necessary paperwork."

Ian stepped closer to where she stood on the stoop, putting him almost eye level with her.

Dylan pressed her face into his hand when he placed it on her cheek. She stood, watching him as he traced the curve of her jaw and then her lips. It felt like he was examining her for any changes.

"I thought you had left." His unspoken words were there. He thought she had left *him*. The thought that she had made him feel any pain was like a knife to the gut.

"I'm so sorry, Ian. I—" She fell quiet, but it was almost as if he sensed what she wanted to say.

"Say it, Dylan."

She looked him in the eye and smiled. "I love you, Ian King."

He released a held breath and returned her smile. "I love you too."

Dylan bit down on her bottom lip to restrain a giggle. "You do?"

"Hell yes. Why else do you think I came after you?"

"I had hoped. I just never thought it would take me going all the way to Australia to find love."

"Dylan, I can't stay here."

She nodded. She already knew that and had come to the same conclusion for herself.

"I know. Neither can I."

She felt light-headed after Ian had kissed her breathless.

"Let's hurry up and go home."

"Absolutely," Dylan agreed. "I've got a happily ever after I need to write."

Her knees went weak at the sexy grin he gave her. "And I've got a lot of inspiration for you."

The End

About the Publisher

Hot Tree Publishing opened its doors in 2015 with an aspiration to bring quality fiction to the world of readers. With the initial focus on romance and a wide spread of romance sub-genres, we envision opening up to alternative genres in the near future.

Firmly seated in the industry as a leading editing provider to independent authors and small publishing houses, Hot Tree Publishing is the sister company to Hot Tree Editing, founded in 2012. Having established in-house editing and promotions, plus having a well-respected market presence, Hot Tree Publishing endeavours to be a leader in bringing quality stories to the world of readers.

Interested in discovering more amazing reads brought to you by Hot Tree Publishing or perhaps you're interested in submitting a manuscript and joining the HTPubs family? Either way, head over to the website for information:

WWW.HOTTREEPUBLISHING.COM